Roald Dahl's
Book of Ghost Stories

Roald Dahl's
Book of Ghost Stories

Farrar · Straus · Giroux

NEW YORK

For James Kelly

Acknowledgments

L. P. Hartley, *W.S.* copyright 1954 by L. P. Hartley; © renewed 1973 by Hamish Hamilton Ltd., the Executors of the Estate of the late L. P. Hartley. Reprinted by kind permission of Hamish Hamilton Ltd., Executors of the Estate of the late L. P. Hartley. / Jonas Lie, *Elias and the Draug* copyright 1902 by Gyldendal Norsk, Oslo. / A. M. Burrage, *Playmates* copyright 1927 by A. M. Burrage. Reprinted by kind permission of the author. / A. M. Burrage (Ex Private X), *The Sweeper* copyright 1931 by A. M. Burrage. Reprinted by kind permission of the author. / Rosemary Timperley, *Christmas Meeting* copyright 1952 by Rosemary Timperley. Reprinted by kind permission of the author. / Rosemary Timperley, *Harry* copyright 1955 by Rosemary Timperley. Reprinted by kind permission of the author. / Robert Aickman, *Ringing the Changes* copyright © 1964 by Robert Aickman. Reprinted by kind permission of the Executors of the Estate of the late Robert Aickman. / Mary Treadgold, *The Telephone* copyright 1955 by Mary Treadgold. Reprinted by kind permission of David Higham Associates Ltd. / Edith Wharton, *Afterward* copyright 1902, 1910 by The Century Co.; copyright renewed 1937, 1938 by D. Appleton-Century Co., Inc. Reprinted by kind permission of William R. Tyler and Watkins Loomis Agency Inc. / E. F. Benson, *In the Tube* copyright 1923 by E. F. Benson. Reprinted by kind permission of the Executors of the Estate of the Reverend K.S.P. McDowall. / Cynthia Asquith, *The Corner Shop* copyright 1951 by Lady Cynthia Asquith. Reprinted by permission of the Hutchinson Publishing Group.

Contents

Roald Dahl's
Book of Ghost Stories

ROALD DAHL

Introduction

My wise and venerable old friend Alfred Knopf, the American publisher, had a half-brother called Edwin. Edwin was a film producer in Hollywood, and a long time ago, back in 1958, I went to him with the idea that we should do a television series together of nothing but ghost stories. I pointed out that no one had done this before. I said there existed a whole world of ghost stories to choose from and that it wouldn't be difficult to come up with a stunning batch of tales. All one needed for a series like this was twenty-four stories.

Eddie Knopf thought it over. He talked with his associates and everyone agreed that it was a splendid idea. Emlyn Williams was approached and he agreed to be the introducer of each episode. My own primary task was to search out the twenty-four super ghost stories. I was also to write the screenplay for the first one (the pilot) and for several others.

On the face of it, my job didn't appear too onerous. In the second half of the last century and in the early part of this one, ghost stories were very much the fashion. Dickens had written one. J. M. Barrie had done several. So had Bulwer-Lytton and D. K. Broster and George Eliot and Anatole France and Mrs Gaskell and Théophile Gautier and L. P. Hartley and Nathaniel Hawthorne and Thomas Hardy and Washington Irving and Henry James and Walter de la Mare and Maugham and Maupassant and Poe and Sir Walter Scott and Mark Twain and H. G. Wells and Elizabeth

Bowen. Even Oscar Wilde had written one called *The Canterville Ghost*. Great names all of these. I looked forward very much to making my selections.

One of the first things I did was to call on Lady Cynthia Asquith who was an acknowledged expert on ghost stories and had published several anthologies. She was old and frail and she was in bed when she received me. But she was as bright as ever and gave me lots of good advice about how to start the great search.

After a tremendous amount of scuttling around, including several visits to the British Museum Library, I managed to collect just about every ghost story that had ever been written. My house was filled with books and piles of old magazines, both bought and borrowed. Then I began to read.

I got a bit of a shock. The first batch of fifty or so stories I read were so bad it was difficult to finish them. They were trivial, poorly written and not in the least spooky. Spookiness is, after all, the real purpose of the ghost story. It should give you the creeps and disturb your thoughts. The stories I was reading did none of this. Some of the worst ones were written by the most famous writers. I read on. I couldn't believe how bad they were. Nevertheless, I carefully recorded every single story I read in a notebook and I gave each one of them marks. Most of them got nought out of ten.

Then suddenly a bright star flashed across the murky sky. I had found a good one. The end of it gave me the shivers. It was called *Harry* by Rosemary Timperley. That bucked me up and I went on with my labours.

I read another hundred or so bad ones. Then I found a second good one. It was *The Open Door* by Mrs Oliphant.

After I had read altogether some three hundred published stories, I had succeeded in discovering seven good ones. That was not many, but it was anyway a beginning. The seven, including the two just mentioned by Rosemary Timperley and Mrs Oliphant, were *The Telephone* by Mary Treadgold, *Afterward* by Edith Wharton, *Spinsters Rest* by Clemence Dane and *The Four-Fifteen Express* by Amelia B. Edwards.

Hang on a second, I thought. What was going on here? Every single one of these stories was written by a woman! What an extraordinary thing. I began to wonder whether the really good ghost story belonged solely to the female. Was she perhaps more sensitive in that small delicate area than the male? It was beginning to look like it.

With a feeling that I was perhaps making a rather remarkable literary discovery, I ploughed on. And by golly, if the next good one wasn't also by a woman! It was Cynthia Asquith's *God Grante That She Lie Stille*. I got rather excited.

But alas, the next excellent one was by a man. It was *Playmates* by A. M. Burrage. And what a good one it was. After that, there followed a whole group of men, L. P. Hartley, Dickens, E. F. Benson, John Collier and the rest. The men were catching up.

At the end of this marathon reading session, I counted that I had read seven hundred and forty-nine ghost stories. I was completely dazed by reading so much rubbish, but as I staggered away from the piles of books and magazines, I had the satisfaction of knowing that I had found twenty-four good ones and another ten possibles for Eddie Knopf's television series.

The male ghost story writers did eventually catch up with the females, but only just. Out of my best twenty-four (there is not room to include all of them in this book), the final score was thirteen to the men and eleven to the women. These figures were intriguing and I'll tell you why. Many people have been fascinated and perplexed by the failure of women to reach the top rank in two of the three major creative arts, music and painting. With writing it is different. Ever since the Brontës and Jane Austen got them going, there have been plenty of fine women novelists around. But this is not true of music or of painting and sculpture. In the whole of history there has never been a woman musical composer anywhere near the top rank. There hasn't really been one in painting or sculpture either. The greatest woman painter was probably Popova, followed by two other Russians, Goncharova and Exter. There was also Mary Cassatt, Barbara Hepworth and possibly Georgia O'Keeffe. But none of them could hold a candle to the huge mass of great male names in painting, from Dürer to Picasso.

But to go back to women as writers. For about a hundred and thirty years they have been producing good novels, even some great ones. But they don't seem to be able to write plays or top-rate short stories. I don't think a woman has ever written a classic play. And as for short stories – no, not really. By this I mean great short stories. The greatest twenty-five short stories ever written (if it were possible to agree on which they were) might conceivably include one by Katherine Mansfield, one by Willa Cather and one by Shirley Jackson. But that would be all. The score would be twenty-two to three in favour of the men.

And yet – and here is the interesting thing – ghost stories, at least the kind I am talking about – *are* short stories. And in that particular and very special category the women run the men very close indeed, a lot closer even than in the novel, with the score at thirteen to the men and eleven to the women. But it is the women who have written some of the very best ones.

So perhaps there is something after all in the theory that women have an unusual flair for writing about the supernatural. Who can forget Shirley Jackson's marvellous story, *The Lottery*? Admittedly it isn't a ghost story. But it deals with the same sort of eerie and unfathomable events and does it in a manner I have never seen matched by any male short story writer.

I have no doubts at all where women stand when it comes to one of the most important facets of all creative literature. I mean of course children's books. You may scream all you like when you read that statement, and I do not say it because I sometimes write children's books myself. I say it because I am convinced that they *are* one of the most important. All other forms of fiction are written purely to divert and entertain the adult mind. Children's books must also divert and entertain, but they do something else at the same time. They actually teach a child the habit of reading. They teach him to be literate, they teach him vocabulary and nowadays they teach him that there can be better ways of passing the time than watching television.

The manner in which children's books are virtually ignored by literary magazines, by Sunday newspaper reviewers and by the so-called literary establishment in general is scandalous. Biographies are given the most attention of all, then adult novels, then poetry. Children's books are only noticed every now and again. And yet — now listen carefully please — and yet, let any of these high-blown authors or critics attempt to *write* a children's book, I mean a fine children's book that children will fall in love with and which will endure through the years, and he will almost certainly fail.

I am fairly sure that it is more difficult to write a fine and enduring children's book than a fine and enduring novel. My reason for making this contentious statement is as follows. How many adult novels are written every year that will still be read widely twenty years later? Probably about half a dozen. How many children's books are written every year that will still be read widely and avidly twenty years later? Possibly only one.

You may argue that the big writers do not bother even to try to write children's books. You would be wrong. Most of them *have* tried. Quite a long time ago, a New York publisher called Crowell Collier had what they thought was a brilliant idea. They decided to invite all the most celebrated writers in the English speaking world to write a children's story. They would tempt them with a high fee. They would then combine all the results in one volume and they'd have a classic on their hands.

The invitations went out, and because of the high fee and the relative shortness of the task, all the writers accepted. These were big names, mind you, famous novelists, so-called giants of the literary world. I won't mention who they were but you would know them all.

The stories came in. I saw each one of them. Only one writer, Robert Graves, had any conception of how to write for children. The rest of the stories were guaranteed to anaesthetize in two minutes flat any unfortunate child who got hold of them. They were unpublishable. The project was abandoned and the publishers lost a good deal of money.

When it comes to writing classic children's books, women

triumph over the men. They are pretty good at novels, they are better still at ghost stories, but they are best of all at children's books. You have Frances Hodgson Burnett's *The Secret Garden*. You have Beatrix Potter. You have P. L. Travers's *Mary Poppins* and Dodie Smith's *One Hundred and One Dalmatians*. You have Astrid Lindgrin's *Pippi Longstocking*, E. Nesbit's *The Railway Children*, Mary Norton's *The Borrowers* and quite a few more. Now these are classics, and by that I mean that at least half of all the children between the ages six and ten in the United States, the United Kingdom, Europe and Japan will have read them. That is many millions. I venture to say it is several millions more than the number of adults alive today who have read, let us say, a fine Graham Greene novel or a Nabokov.

The writer of a classic children's book can go into any school or any home where there are children in any of the countries I have mentioned and he or she will be known and welcomed. I don't mean middle-class homes only, which is where the good novels are read. I mean *any* home. None of the entrenched literary establishments of London, New York or Paris realize the power of a children's book once children have fallen in love with it. Or if they do, they don't want to admit it. Generation after generation of children continue to read a classic children's book over and over again and school teachers keep it always in their classrooms.

I have wandered away from ghost stories. I apologize for this, but I have wanted for a long time to have my little say about children's books and especially to pay tribute to the part that women writers have played in creating the classic library.

But to go back to Eddie Knopf and the great television ghost series. By now the series had been officially christened 'Ghost Time'. My twenty-four choices were sent off to California and were read with immense enthusiasm. It looked, so thought the moguls out there, as if we had a winner on our hands. All we had to do now was to make the films. We couldn't go wrong. The big boys figured that a series of chilling ghost stories flashed on to the television screens from coast to coast in the winter evenings when it was pitch dark outside would give the entire nation the creeps. No one would dare to go to bed and turn out the light afterwards. Old ladies living alone would be found dead from fright the next morning. Strong Texans would quiver in their high leather boots and fire their six-shooters at the screen to silence it for ever. Children watching the show would be afraid of the dark for the rest of their lives. Psychiatrists would double their business. The Church would protest. And everyone would watch our show every week. It was a heady prospect.

The first step was to make the pilot film. The pilot is important in any series. It has to be good. This is the film that is shown to the network bosses, the advertising agencies and to the advertisers themselves, and after looking at it they either turn thumbs up or thumbs down on putting up the millions that are required to make the whole series. The pilot indicates the flavour and quality of the series and gives a fair idea of what the other twenty-three episodes will be like.

So a really good strong story was essential for the pilot. Out of my twenty-four, the men in California selected *The Hanging of Alfred Wadham* by E. F. Benson. It *was* a good story, and it would dramatize nicely.

I wrote the screenplay. The film was shot at Elstree Studios with a first-rate director and top actors, though I've forgotten who they were. Emlyn Williams spoke a splendid introduction and a good introductory theme tune was chosen. When all was ready, our great pilot film (it *was* awfully good) was flown to America and then it was shown to the powerful men who make the mighty decisions.

It was a disaster. The film itself was all right. But we had made a terrible mistake. We had chosen the one story that no American television network would dare to show. It dealt, you see, with Roman Catholicism, and the whole plot of the story revolves around the fact that a priest must never, under any circumstances, reveal to others what he has learnt during confession. Alfred Wadham is convicted of murder and is about to be hanged. He protests his innocence but no one believes him. Then, on the evening before the hanging is to take place, another man goes to the prison priest and confesses that it was he and not poor Alfred Wadham who committed the murder. The priest begs him to own up. He refuses. He also reminds the priest very forcibly that he cannot break the secrecy rule of the confessional. The priest, bound by his religious vows, is therefore unable to save the wrong man from being hanged. After the hanging, the ghost of Alfred Wadham does some horrid things to the wretched priest.

You can see it's a good story. But the sight of it on the television screen would be guaranteed to inflame the hearts of millions of Catholics across the United States. The advertising men and the television bosses who saw the pilot were apoplectic. They threw it out and refused to have anything more to do with our splendid ghost series venture. I have still not quite got over the shock of that rejection and that is probably why I have not included *Alfred Wadham* in this collection.

So I was left, in the end, with nothing but a very complete knowledge of the ghost stories of the world. I still have all my notes, three large notebooks full of them. So now, some twenty-five years later, it seems a good idea to put the good ones together in a book.

Good ghost stories, like good children's books, are damnably difficult to write. I am a short story writer myself, and although I have been doing it for forty-five years and have always longed to write just one decent ghost story, I have never succeeded in bringing it off. Heaven knows, I have tried. Once I thought I had done it. It was with a story that is now called *The Landlady*. But when it was finished and I examined it carefully, I knew it wasn't good enough. I hadn't brought it off. I simply hadn't got the secret. So finally I altered the ending and made it into a non-ghost story.

The best ghost stories don't have ghosts in them. At least you don't see the ghost. Instead you see only the result of his actions. Occasionally you can *feel* it brushing past you, or you are made aware of its presence by subtle means. For example, the temperature in a room always drops dramatically when a ghost is around. This was scientifically proved by Harry Price in his interesting book *The Most Haunted House in England*. If a story does permit a ghost to be seen, then he doesn't look like one. He looks like an ordinary person.

To me, one of the most compelling of all the stories in the book you are now holding was written by a Norwegian, Jonas Lie. It really is a cruel and wonderful tale, though it suffers a good deal in the translation. Jonas Lie, who died in 1908, is a national hero in Norway although he is very little known beyond those shores. I happen to have a fine painting of him by Heyerdal in my living-room. He is wearing a wide-brimmed black hat and a black cloak, and wherever I sit, he is glaring at me through steel-rimmed spectacles with a terrible icy stare. He looks more than anything else like an undertaker who knows he's going to get you in the end. But he was a splendid writer and I am certain you will be disturbed by this story of his called *Elias and the Draug*. I hope you will be equally disturbed by all the other stories in this book. They were written with precisely that end in mind.

I think I should mention that since 1958 when I originally did my research into ghost stories, I have continued to read as many new ones as I could lay my hands on. I may have missed one or two, but nothing I have seen that has been published since then has come anywhere near the standard of the select group in this book.

L. P. HARTLEY

W.S.

The first postcard came from Forfar.

I thought you might like a picture of Forfar, it began. *You have always been so interested in Scotland, and that is one reason why I am interested in you. I have enjoyed all your books, but do you really get to grips with people? I doubt it. Try to think of this as a handshake from your devoted admirer,*   W.S.

Like other novelists, Walter Streeter was used to getting communications from strangers. Generally they were friendly but sometimes they were critical. In either case he always answered them, for he was conscientious. But answering them took up the time and energy he needed for his writing, so that he was rather relieved that W.S. had given no address. The photograph of Forfar was uninteresting and he tore it up. His anonymous correspondent's criticism, however, lingered in his mind. Did he really fail to come to grips with his characters? Perhaps he did. He was aware that in most cases they were either projections of his own personality, or, in different forms, the antitheses of it. The Me and the Not Me. Perhaps W.S. had spotted this. Not for the first time Walter made a vow to be more objective.

About ten days later arrived another postcard, this time from Berwick-on-Tweed. *What do you think of Berwick-on-Tweed?* it said. *Like you, it's on the Border. I hope this doesn't*

sound rude. I don't mean that you are a border-line case!
You know how much I admire your stories. Some people call
them other-worldly. I think you should plump for one world or
the other. Another warm handshake from   W.S.

Walter Streeter pondered over this and began to wonder
about the sender. Was his correspondent a man or a woman?
It looked like a man's handwriting – commercial, un-
selfconscious, and the criticism was like a man's. On the
other hand, it was like a woman to probe – to want to make
him feel at the same time flattered and unsure of himself. He
felt the faint stirrings of curiosity but soon dismissed them;
he was not a man to experiment with acquaintances. Still, it
was odd to think of this unknown person speculating about
him, sizing him up. Other-worldly, indeed! He re-read the
last two chapters he had written. Perhaps they didn't have
their feet firm on the ground. Perhaps he was too ready to
escape, as other novelists were nowadays, into an ambiguous
world, a world where the conscious mind did not have things
too much its own way. But did that matter? He threw the
picture of Berwick-on-Tweed into his November fire and
tried to write; but the words came haltingly, as though
contending with an extra-strong barrier of self-criticism.
And as the days passed, he became uncomfortably aware of
self-division, as though someone had taken hold of his
personality and was pulling it apart. His work was no longer
homogeneous; there were two strains in it, unreconciled and
opposing, and it went much slower as he tried to resolve the
discord. Never mind, he thought: perhaps I was getting into
a groove. These difficulties may be growing pains; I may
have tapped a new source of supply. If only I could correlate
the two and make their conflict fruitful, as many artists have!

The third postcard showed a picture of York Minster. *I*
know you are interested in cathedrals, it said. *I'm sure this*
isn't a sign of megalomania in your case, but smaller
churches are sometimes more rewarding. I'm seeing a good
many churches on my way south. Are you busy writing or are
you looking around for ideas? Another hearty handshake from
your friend,   W.S.

It was true that Walter Streeter was interested in
cathedrals. Lincoln Cathedral had been the subject of one of

his youthful fantasies and he had written about it in a travel book. And it was also true that he admired mere size and was inclined to undervalue parish churches. But how could W.S. have known that? And was it really a sign of megalomania? And who was W.S., anyhow?

For the first time it struck him that the initials were his own. No, not for the first time. He had noticed it before, but they were such commonplace initials; they were Gilbert's, they were Maugham's, they were Shakespeare's – a common possession. Anyone might have them. Yet now it seemed to him an odd coincidence; and the idea came into his mind – suppose I have been writing postcards to myself? People did such things, especially people with split personalities. Not that he was one of them, of course. And yet there was this unexplained development – the dichotomy in his writing, which had now extended from his thought to his style, making one paragraph languorous with semi-colons and subordinate clauses, and another sharp and incisive with main verbs and full-stops.

He looked at the handwriting again. It had seemed the perfection of ordinariness – anybody's hand – so ordinary as perhaps to be disguised. Now he fancied he saw in it resemblances to his own. He was just going to pitch the postcard in the fire when suddenly he decided not to. I'll show it to somebody, he thought.

His friend said, 'My dear fellow, it's all quite plain. The woman's a lunatic. I'm sure it's a woman. She has probably fallen in love with you and wants to make you interested in her. I should pay no attention whatsoever. People in the public eye are always getting letters from lunatics. If they worry you, destroy them without reading them. That sort of person is often a little psychic, and if she senses that she's getting a rise out of you, she'll go on.'

For a moment Walter Streeter felt reassured. A woman, a little mouse-like creature, who had somehow taken a fancy to him! What was there to feel uneasy about in that? Then his subconscious mind, searching for something to torment him with, and assuming the authority of logic, said: Supposing those postcards are a lunatic's, and you are writing them to yourself; doesn't it follow that you must be a lunatic too?

He tried to put the thought away from him; he tried to destroy the postcard as he had the others. But something in him wanted to preserve it. It had become a piece of him, he felt. Yielding to an irresistible compulsion, which he dreaded, he found himself putting it behind the clock on the chimney-piece. He couldn't see it, but he knew that it was there.

He now had to admit to himself that the postcard business had become a leading factor in his life. It had created a new area of thoughts and feelings and they were most unhelpful. His being was strung up in expectation of the next postcard.

Yet when it came it took him as the others had, completely by surprise. He could not bring himself to look at the picture. *I am coming nearer*, the postcard said; *I have got as near as Coventry. Have you ever been sent to Coventry? I have, in fact you sent me. It isn't a pleasant experience, I can tell you. Perhaps we shall come to grips after all. I advised you to come to grips with your characters, didn't I? Have I given you any new ideas? If I have, you ought to thank me, for they are what novelists want, I understand. I have been re-reading your novels, living in them, I might say. Je vous serre la main. As always.* W.S.

A wave of panic surged up in Walter Streeter. How was it that he had never noticed, all this time, the most significant fact about the postcards – that each one came from a place geographically closer to him than the last? *I am coming nearer.* Had his mind, unconsciously self-protective, worn blinkers? If it had, he wished he could put them back. He took an atlas and idly traced W.S.'s itinerary. An interval of eighty miles or so seemed to separate the stopping-places. Walter lived in a large West Country town about that distance from Coventry.

Should he show the postcards to an alienist? But what could an alienist tell him? He would not know, what Walter wanted to know, whether he had anything to fear from W.S.

Better go to the police. The police were used to dealing with poison-pens. If they laughed at him, so much the better.

They did not laugh, however. They said they thought the

postcards were a hoax and that W.S. would never show up in the flesh. Then they asked if there was anyone who had a grudge against him. 'No one that I know of,' Walter said. They, too, took the view that the writer was probably a woman. They told him not to worry but to let them know if further postcards came.

A little comforted, Walter went home. The talk with the police had done him good. He thought it over. It was quite true what he had told them – that he had no enemies. He was not a man of strong personal feelings; such feelings as he had went into his books. In his books he had drawn some pretty nasty characters. Not of recent years, however. Of recent years he had felt a reluctance to draw a very bad man or woman: he thought it morally irresponsible and artistically unconvincing, too. There was good in everyone: Iagos were a myth. Latterly – but he had to admit that it was several weeks since he laid pen to paper, so much had this ridiculous business of the postcards weighed upon his mind – if he had to draw a really wicked person he represented him as a Communist or a Nazi – someone who had deliberately put off his human characteristics. But in the past, when he was younger and more inclined to see things as black or white, he had let himself go once or twice. He did not remember his old books very well but there was a character in one, *The Outcast*, into whom he had really got his knife. He had written about him with extreme vindictiveness, just as if he was a real person whom he was trying to show up. He had experienced a curious pleasure in attributing every kind of wickedness to this man. He never gave him the benefit of the doubt. He never felt a twinge of pity for him, even when he paid the penalty for his misdeeds on the gallows. He had so worked himself up that the idea of this dark creature, creeping about brimful of malevolence, had almost frightened him.

Odd that he couldn't remember the man's name. He took the book down from the shelf and turned the pages – even now they affected him uncomfortably. Yes, here it was, William . . . William . . . he would have to look back to find the surname. William Stainsforth.

His own initials.

He did not think the coincidence meant anything, but it coloured his mind and weakened its resistance to his obsession. So uneasy was he that when the next postcard came, it came as a relief.

Does this remind you of anything? he read, and involuntarily turned the postcard over. He saw a picture of a gaol – Gloucester gaol. He stared at it as if it could tell him something, then with an effort went on reading. *I am quite close now. My movements, as you may have guessed, are not quite under my control, but all being well, I look forward to seeing you some time this weekend. Then we can really come to grips. I wonder if you'll recognize me! It won't be the first time you have given me hospitality. Ti stringo la mano. As always.*   W.S.

Walter took the postcard straight to the police station, and asked if he could have police protection over the weekend. The officer in charge smiled at him and said he was quite sure it was a hoax; but he would tell someone to keep an eye on the place.

'You still have no idea who it could be?' he asked.

Walter shook his head.

It was Tuesday; Walter Streeter had plenty of time to think about the weekend. At first he felt he would not be able to live through the interval but, strange to say, his confidence increased instead of waning. He set himself to work as though he could work, and presently he found he could – differently from before, and, he thought, better. It was as though the nervous strain he had been living under had, like an acid, dissolved a layer of non-conductive thought that came between him and his subject: he was nearer to it now, and instead of responding only too readily to his stage directions, his characters gave themselves wholeheartedly to all the tests he put them to. So passed the days, and the dawn of Friday seemed like any other day until something jerked him out of his self-induced trance, and suddenly he asked himself, 'When does a weekend begin?'

A long weekend begins on Friday. At that his panic returned. He went to the street door and looked out. It was a suburban, unfrequented street of detached Regency houses

like his own. They had tall square gateposts, some crowned
with semi-circular iron brackets holding lanterns. Most of
these were out of repair: only two or three were ever lit. A car
went slowly down the street; some people crossed it:
everything was normal.

Several times that day he went to look and saw nothing
unusual, and when Saturday came, bringing no postcard, his
panic had almost subsided. He nearly rang up the police to
tell them not to bother to send anyone after all.

But they were as good as their word: they did send
someone. Between tea and dinner, the time when weekend
guests most commonly arrive, Walter went to the door and
there, between two unlit gateposts, he saw a policeman
standing – the first policeman he had ever seen in Charlotte
Street. At the sight, and the relief it brought him, he realized
how anxious he had been. Now he felt safer than he had ever
felt in his life, and also a little ashamed at having given extra
trouble to a hard-worked body of men. Should he go and
speak to his unknown guardian, offer him a cup of tea or a
drink? It would be nice to hear him laugh at Walter's fancies.
But no – somehow he felt his security the greater when its
source was impersonal and anonymous. 'P.C. Smith' was
somehow less impressive than 'police protection'.

Several times from an upper window (he didn't like to
open the door and stare) he made sure that his guardian was
still there; and once, for added proof, he asked his
housekeeper to verify the strange phenomenon. Disappoint-
ingly, she came back saying she had seen no policeman; but
she was not very good at seeing things, and when Walter
went a few minutes later, he saw him plain enough. The man
must walk about, of course; perhaps he had been taking a
stroll when Mrs Kendal looked.

It was contrary to his routine to work after dinner but tonight
he did – he felt so much in the vein. Indeed, a sort of
exaltation possessed him; the words ran off his pen; it would
be foolish to check the creative impulse for the sake of a little
extra sleep. On, on. They were right who said the small
hours were the time to work. When his housekeeper came in
to say good night, he scarcely raised his eyes.

In the warm, snug little room the silence purred around him like a kettle. He did not even hear the door-bell till it had been ringing for some time.

A visitor at this hour?

His knees trembling, he went to the door, scarcely knowing what he expected to find; so what was his relief, on opening it, to see the doorway filled by the tall figure of a policeman. Without waiting for the man to speak, 'Come in, come in, my dear fellow,' he exclaimed. He held his hand out, but the policeman did not take it. 'You must have been very cold standing out there. I didn't know that it was snowing, though,' he added, seeing the snowflakes on the policeman's cape and helmet. 'Come in and warm your-self.'

'Thanks,' said the policeman. 'I don't mind if I do.'

Walter knew enough of the phrases used by men of the policeman's stamp not to mistake this for a grudging acceptance. 'This way,' he prattled on. 'I was writing in my study. By Jove, it *is* cold, I'll turn the gas on more. Now won't you take your traps off, and make yourself at home?'

'I can't stay long,' the policeman said, 'I've got a job to do, as *you* know.'

'Oh, yes,' said Walter, 'such a silly job, a sinecure.' He stopped, wondering if the policeman would know what a sinecure was. 'I suppose you know what it's about – the postcards?'

The policeman nodded.

'But nothing can happen to me as long as you are here,' said Walter. 'I shall be as safe . . . as safe as houses. Stay as long as you can, and have a drink.'

'I never drink on duty,' said the policeman. Still in his cape and helmet, he looked round. 'So this is where you work?' he said.

'Yes, I was writing when you rang.'

'Some poor devil's for it, I expect,' the policeman said.

'Oh, why?' Walter was hurt by his unfriendly tone, and noticed how hard his gooseberry eyes were.

'I'll tell you in a minute,' said the policeman, and then the telephone bell rang. Walter excused himself and hurried from the room.

'This is the police station,' said a voice. 'Is that Mr Streeter?'

Walter said it was.

'Well, Mr Streeter, how is everything at your place? All right, I hope? I'll tell you why I ask. I'm sorry to say we quite forgot about that little job we were going to do for you. Bad co-ordination, I'm afraid.'

'But,' said Walter, 'you did send someone.'

'No, Mr Streeter, I'm afraid we didn't.'

'But there's a policeman here, here in this very house.'

There was a pause, then his interlocutor said, in a less casual voice:

'He can't be one of our chaps. Did you see his number by any chance?'

'No.'

After another pause the voice said:

'Would you like us to send somebody now?'

'Yes, p–please.'

'All right then, we'll be with you in a jiffy.'

Walter put back the receiver. What now? he asked himself. Should he barricade the door? Should he run out into the street? Should he try to rouse his housekeeper? A policeman of any sort was something to be reckoned with: but a *rogue* policeman! A law-keeper turned law-breaker, roaming about loose, savaging people! How long would it take the real police to come? What was a jiffy in terms of minutes? While he was debating, the door opened and his guest came in.

'No room's private when the street door's once passed,' he said. 'Had you forgotten I was a policeman?'

'Was?' said Walter, edging away from him. 'You *are* a policeman.'

'I have been other things as well,' the policeman said. 'Thief, pimp, blackmailer, not to mention murderer. *You* should know.'

The policeman, if such he was, seemed to be moving towards him and Walter suddenly became alive to the importance of small distances – the space between the sideboard and the table, and between one chair and another.

'I don't know what you mean,' he said. 'Why do you speak like that? I've never done you any harm. I've never set eyes on you before.'

'Oh, haven't you?' the man said. 'But you've thought about me, and' – his voice rose – 'you've written about me. You got some fun out of me, didn't you? Now I'm going to get some fun out of you. You made me just as nasty as you could. Wasn't that doing me harm? You didn't think what it would feel like to be me, did you? You didn't put yourself in my place, did you? You hadn't any pity for me, had you? Well, I'm not going to have any pity for you.'

'But I tell you,' cried Walter, clutching the table's edge, 'I don't know you!'

'And now you say you don't know me! You did all that to me and then forgot me.' His voice became a whine, charged with self-pity. 'You forgot William Stainsforth.'

'William Stainsforth!'

'Yes. I was your scapegoat, wasn't I? You unloaded all your self-dislike on me. You felt pretty good while you were writing about me. Now, as one W.S. to another, what shall I do, if I behave in character?'

'I – I don't know,' muttered Walter.

'You don't know?' Stainsforth sneered. 'You ought to know, you fathered me. What would William Stainsforth do if he met his old dad in a quiet place, his kind old dad who made him swing?'

Walter could only stare at him.

'You know what he'd do as well as I,' said Stainsforth. Then his face changed and he said abruptly, 'No you don't, because you never really understood me. I'm not so black as you painted me.' He paused and a flame of hope flickered in Walter's breast. 'You never gave me a chance, did you? Well, I'm going to give you one. That shows you never understood me, doesn't it?'

Walter nodded.

'And there's another thing you have forgotten.'

'What is that?'

'I was a kid once,' the ex-policeman said.

Walter said nothing.

'You admit that?' said William Stainsforth grimly. 'Well, if you can tell me of one virtue you ever credited me with – just one kind thought – just one redeeming feature – '

'Yes?' said Walter, trembling.

'Well, then I'll let you off.'

'And if I can't?' whispered Walter.

'Well, then, that's just too bad. We'll have to come to grips and you know what that means. You took off one of my arms but I've still got the other. "Stainsforth of the iron arm", you called me.'

Walter began to pant.

'I'll give you two minutes to remember,' Stainsforth said.

They both looked at the clock. At first the stealthy movement of the hand paralysed Walter's thought. He stared at William Stainsforth's face, his cruel, crafty face, which seemed to be always in shadow, as if it was something the light could not touch. Desperately he searched his memory for the one fact that would save him; but his memory, clenched like a fist, would give up nothing. 'I must invent something,' he thought, and suddenly his mind relaxed and he saw, printed on it like a photograph, the last page of the book. Then, with the speed and magic of a dream, each page appeared before him in perfect clarity until the first was reached, and he realized with overwhelming force that what he looked for was not there. In all that evil there was not one hint of good. And he felt, compulsively and with a kind of exultation, that unless he testified to this, the cause of goodness everywhere would be betrayed.

'There's nothing to be said for you!' he shouted. 'Of all your dirty tricks this is the dirtiest! You want me to whitewash you, do you? Why, the very snowflakes on you are turning black! How dare you ask me for a character? I've given you one already! God forbid that I should ever say a good word for you! I'd rather die!'

Stainsforth's one arm shot out. 'Then die!' he said.

The police found Walter Streeter slumped across the dining table. His body was still warm, but he was dead. It was easy to tell how he died, for not only had his mauled, limp hand been shaken, but his throat too. He had been strangled. Of his assailant there was no trace. And how he came to have snowflakes on him remained a mystery, for no snow was reported from any district on the day he died.

ROSEMARY TIMPERLEY

Harry

Such ordinary things make me afraid. Sunshine. Sharp shadows on grass. White roses. Children with red hair. And the name – Harry. Such an ordinary name.

Yet the first time Christine mentioned the name, I felt a premonition of fear.

She was five years old, due to start school in three months' time. It was a hot, beautiful day and she was playing alone in the garden, as she often did. I saw her lying on her stomach in the grass, picking daisies and making daisy-chains with laborious pleasure. The sun burned on her pale red hair and made her skin look very white. Her big blue eyes were wide with concentration.

Suddenly she looked towards the bush of white roses, which cast its shadow over the grass, and smiled.

'Yes, I'm Christine,' she said. She rose and walked slowly towards the bush, her little plump legs defenceless and endearing beneath the too short blue cotton skirt. She was growing fast.

'With my mummy and daddy,' she said clearly. Then, after a pause, 'Oh, but they *are* my mummy and daddy.'

She was in the shadow of the bush now. It was as if she'd walked out of the world of light into darkness. Uneasy, without quite knowing why, I called her:

'Chris, what are you doing?'

'Nothing.' The voice sounded too far away.

'Come indoors now. It's too hot for you out there.'

'Not too hot.'

'Come indoors, Chris.'

She said: 'I must go in now. Goodbye,' then walked slowly towards the house.

'Chris, who were you talking to?'

'Harry,' she said.

'Who's Harry?'

'Harry.'

I couldn't get anything else out of her, so I just gave her some cake and milk and read to her until bedtime. As she listened, she stared out at the garden. Once she smiled and waved. It was a relief finally to tuck her up in bed and feel she was safe.

When Jim, my husband, came home I told him about the mysterious 'Harry'. He laughed.

'Oh, she's started that lark, has she?'

'What do you mean, Jim?'

'It's not so very rare for only children to have an imaginary companion. Some kids talk to their dolls. Chris has never been keen on her dolls. She hasn't any brothers or sisters. She hasn't any friends her own age. So she imagines someone.'

'But why has she picked that particular name?'

He shrugged. 'You know how kids pick things up. I don't know what you're worrying about, honestly I don't.'

'Nor do I really. It's just that I feel extra responsible for her. More so than if I were her real mother.'

'I know, but she's all right. Chris is fine. She's a pretty, healthy, intelligent little girl. A credit to you.'

'And to you.'

'In fact, we're thoroughly nice parents!'

'And so modest!'

We laughed together and he kissed me. I felt consoled. Until next morning.

Again the sun shone brilliantly on the small, bright lawn and white roses. Christine was sitting on the grass, cross-legged, staring towards the rose bush, smiling.

'Hello,' she said. 'I hoped you'd come . . . Because I like you. How old are you? . . . I'm only five and a piece . . . I'm *not* a baby! I'm going to school soon and I shall have a new

dress. A green one. Do you go to school? . . . What do you do
then?' She was silent for a while, nodding, listening,
absorbed.

I felt myself going cold as I stood there in the kitchen.
'Don't be silly. Lots of children have an imaginary
companion,' I told myself desperately. 'Just carry on as if
nothing were happening. Don't listen. Don't be a fool.'

But I called Chris in earlier than usual for her mid-
morning milk.

'Your milk's ready, Chris. Come along.'

'In a minute.' This was a strange reply. Usually she rushed
in eagerly for her milk and the special sandwich cream
biscuits, over which she was a little gourmande.

'Come now, darling,' I said.

'Can Harry come too?'

'No!' The cry burst from me harshly, surprising me.

'Goodbye, Harry. I'm sorry you can't come in but I've got
to have my milk,' Chris said, then ran towards the house.

'Why can't Harry have some milk too?' she challenged me.

'Who *is* Harry, darling?'

'Harry's my brother.'

'But Chris, you haven't got a brother. Daddy and mummy
have only got one child, one little girl, that's you. Harry can't
be your brother.'

'Harry's my brother. He says so.' She bent over the glass of
milk and emerged with a smeary top lip. Then she grabbed at
the biscuits. At least 'Harry' hadn't spoilt her appetite!

After she'd had her milk, I said, 'We'll go shopping now,
Chris. You'd like to come to the shops with me, wouldn't
you?'

'I want to stay with Harry.'

'Well you can't. You're coming with me.'

'Can Harry come too?'

'No.'

My hands were trembling as I put on my hat and gloves. It
was chilly in the house nowadays, as if there were a cold
shadow over it in spite of the sun outside. Chris came with
me meekly enough, but as we walked down the street, she
turned and waved.

I didn't mention any of this to Jim that night. I knew he'd

only scoff as he'd done before. But when Christine's 'Harry' fantasy went on day after day, it got more and more on my nerves. I came to hate and dread those long summer days. I longed for grey skies and rain. I longed for the white roses to wither and die. I trembled when I heard Christine's voice prattling away in the garden. She talked quite unrestrainedly to 'Harry' now.

One Sunday, when Jim heard her at it, he said:

'I'll say one thing for imaginary companions, they help a child on with her talking. Chris is talking much more freely than she used to.'

'With an accent,' I blurted out.

'An accent?'

'A slight cockney accent.'

'My dearest, every London child gets a slight cockney accent. It'll be much worse when she goes to school and meets lots of other kids.'

'We don't talk cockney. Where does she get it from? Who can she be getting it from except Ha . . .' I couldn't say the name.

'The baker, the milkman, the dustman, the coalman, the window cleaner – want any more?'

'I suppose not.' I laughed ruefully. Jim made me feel foolish.

'Anyway,' said Jim, '*I* haven't noticed any cockney in her voice.'

'There isn't when she talks to us. It's only when she's talking to – to him.'

'To Harry. You know, I'm getting quite attached to young Harry. Wouldn't it be fun if one day we looked out and saw him?'

'Don't!' I cried. 'Don't say that! It's my nightmare. My waking nightmare. Oh, Jim, I can't bear it much longer.'

He looked astonished. 'This Harry business is really getting you down, isn't it?'

'Of course it is! Day in, day out, I hear nothing but "Harry this," "Harry that," "Harry says," "Harry thinks," "Can Harry have some?", "Can Harry come too?" – it's all right for you out at the office all day, but I have to live with it: I'm – I'm afraid of it, Jim. It's so queer.'

'Do you know what I think you should do to put your mind at rest?'

'What?'

'Take Chris along to see old Dr Webster tomorrow. Let him have a little talk with her.'

'Do you think she's ill – in her mind?'

'Good heavens, no! But when we come across something that's a bit beyond us, it's as well to take professional advice.'

Next day I took Chris to see Dr Webster. I left her in the waiting-room while I told him briefly about Harry. He nodded sympathetically, then said:

'It's a fairly unusual case, Mrs James, but by no means unique. I've had several cases of children's imaginary companions becoming so real to them that the parents got the jitters. I expect she's rather a lonely little girl, isn't she?'

'She doesn't know any other children. We're new to the neighbourhood, you see. But that will be put right when she starts school.'

'And I think you'll find that when she goes to school and meets other children, these fantasies will disappear. You see, every child needs company of her own age, and if she doesn't get it, she invents it. Older people who are lonely talk to themselves. That doesn't mean that they're crazy, just that they need to talk to someone. A child is more practical. Seems silly to talk to oneself, she thinks, so she invents someone to talk to. I honestly don't think you've anything to worry about.'

'That's what my husband says.'

'I'm sure he does. Still, I'll have a chat with Christine as you've brought her. Leave us alone together.'

I went to the waiting-room to fetch Chris. She was at the window. She said: 'Harry's waiting.'

'Where, Chris?' I said quietly, wanting suddenly to see with her eyes.

'There. By the rose bush.'

The doctor had a bush of white roses in his garden.

'There's no one there,' I said. Chris gave me a glance of unchildlike scorn. 'Dr Webster wants to see you now, darling,' I said shakily. 'You remember him, don't you? He gave you sweets when you were getting better from chicken pox.'

'Yes,' she said and went willingly enough to the doctor's surgery. I waited restlessly. Faintly I heard their voices through the wall, heard the doctor's chuckle, Christine's high peal of laughter. She was talking away to the doctor in a way she didn't talk to me.

When they came out, he said: 'Nothing wrong with her whatever. She's just an imaginative little monkey. A word of advice, Mrs James. Let her talk about Harry. Let her become accustomed to confiding in you. I gather you've shown some disapproval of this "brother" of hers so she doesn't talk much to you about him. He makes wooden toys, doesn't he, Chris?'

'Yes, Harry makes wooden toys.'

'And he can read and write, can't he?'

'And swim and climb trees and paint pictures. Harry can do everything. He's a wonderful brother.' Her little face flushed with adoration.

The doctor patted me on the shoulder and said: 'Harry sounds a very nice brother for her. He's even got red hair like you, Chris, hasn't he?'

'Harry's got red hair,' said Chris proudly, 'Redder than my hair. And he's nearly as tall as daddy only thinner. He's as tall as you, mummy. He's fourteen. He says he's tall for his age. What *is* tall for his age?'

'Mummy will tell you about that as you walk home,' said Dr Webster. 'Now, goodbye, Mrs James. Don't worry. Just let her prattle. Goodbye, Chris. Give my love to Harry.'

'He's there,' said Chris, pointing to the doctor's garden. 'He's been waiting for me.'

Dr Webster laughed. 'They're incorrigible, aren't they?' he said. 'I knew one poor mother whose children invented a whole tribe of imaginary natives whose rituals and taboos ruled the household. Perhaps you're lucky, Mrs James!'

I tried to feel comforted by all this, but I wasn't. I hoped sincerely that when Chris started school this wretched Harry business would finish.

Chris ran ahead of me. She looked up as if at someone beside her. For a brief, dreadful second, I saw a shadow on

the pavement alongside her own – a long, thin shadow – like
a boy's shadow. Then it was gone. I ran to catch her up and
held her hand tightly all the way home. Even in the
comparative security of the house – the house so strangely
cold in this hot weather – I never let her out of my sight. On
the face of it she behaved no differently towards me, but in
reality she was drifting away. The child in my house was
becoming a stranger.

For the first time since Jim and I had adopted Chris, I
wondered seriously: Who is she? Where does she come from?
Who were her real parents? Who is this little loved stranger
I've taken as a daughter? Who *is* Christine?

Another week passed. It was Harry, Harry all the time.
The day before she was to start school, Chris said:

'Not going to school.'

'You're going to school tomorrow, Chris. You're looking
forward to it. You know you are. There'll be lots of other
little girls and boys.'

'Harry says he can't come too.'

'You won't want Harry at school. He'll – ' I tried hard to
follow the doctor's advice and appear to believe in
Harry – 'He'll be too old. He'd feel silly among little boys
and girls, a great lad of fourteen.'

'I won't go to school without Harry. I want to be with
Harry.' She began to weep, loudly, painfully.

'Chris, stop this nonsense! Stop it!' I struck her sharply on
the arm. Her crying ceased immediately. She stared at me,
her blue eyes wide open and frighteningly cold. She gave me
an adult stare that made me tremble. Then she said:

'You don't love me. Harry loves me. Harry wants me. He
says I can go with him.'

'I will not hear any more of this!' I shouted, hating the
anger in my voice, hating myself for being angry at all with a
little girl – *my* little girl – mine –

I went down on one knee and held out my arms.

'Chris, darling, come here.'

She came, slowly. 'I love you,' I said. 'I love you, Chris,
and I'm real. School is real. Go to school to please me.'

'Harry will go away if I do.'

'You'll have other friends.'

'I want Harry.' Again the tears, wet against my shoulder now. I held her closely.

'You're tired, baby. Come to bed.'

She slept with the tear stains still on her face.

It was still daylight. I went to the window to draw her curtains. Golden shadows and long strips of sunshine in the garden. Then, again like a dream, the long thin clear-cut shadow of a boy near the white roses. Like a mad woman I opened the window and shouted:

'Harry! Harry!'

I thought I saw a glimmer of red among the roses, like close red curls on a boy's head. Then there was nothing.

When I told Jim about Christine's emotional outburst he said: 'Poor little kid. It's always a nervy business, starting school. She'll be all right once she gets there. You'll be hearing less about Harry too, as time goes on.'

'Harry doesn't want her to go to school.'

'Hey! You sound as if you believe in Harry yourself!'

'Sometimes I do.'

'Believing in evil spirits in your old age?' he teased me. But his eyes were concerned. He thought I was going 'round the bend' and small blame to him!

'I don't think Harry's evil,' I said. 'He's just a boy. A boy who doesn't exist, except for Christine. And who *is* Christine?'

'None of that!' said Jim sharply. 'When we adopted Chris we decided she was to be our own child. No probing into the past. No wondering and worrying. No mysteries. Chris is as much ours as if she'd been born of our flesh. Who is Christine indeed! She's our daughter – and just you remember that!'

'Yes, Jim, you're right. Of course you're right.'

He'd been so fierce about it that I didn't tell him what I planned to do the next day while Chris was at school.

Next morning Chris was silent and sulky. Jim joked with her and tried to cheer her, but all she would do was look out of the window and say: 'Harry's gone.'

'You won't need Harry now. You're going to school,' said Jim.

Chris gave him that look of grown-up contempt she'd given me sometimes.

She and I didn't speak as I took her to school. I was almost in tears. Although I was glad for her to start school, I felt a sense of loss at parting with her. I suppose every mother feels that when she takes her ewe-lamb to school for the first time. It's the end of babyhood for the child, the beginning of life in reality, life with its cruelty, its strangeness, its barbarity. I kissed her goodbye at the gate and said:

'You'll be having dinner at school with the other children, Chris, and I'll call for you when school is over, at three o'clock.'

'Yes, mummy.' She held my hand tightly. Other nervous little children were arriving with equally nervous parents. A pleasant young teacher with fair hair and a white linen dress appeared at the gate. She gathered the new children towards her and led them away. She gave me a sympathetic smile as she passed and said: 'We'll take good care of her.'

I felt quite light-hearted as I walked away, knowing that Chris was safe and I didn't have to worry.

Now I started on my secret mission. I took a bus to town and went to the big, gaunt building I hadn't visited for over five years. Then, Jim and I had gone together. The top floor of the building belonged to the Greythorne Adoption Society. I climbed the four flights and knocked on the familiar door with its scratched paint. A secretary whose face I didn't know let me in.

'May I see Miss Cleaver? My name is Mrs James.'

'Have you an appointment?'

'No, but it's very important.'

'I'll see.' The girl went out and returned a second later. 'Miss Cleaver will see you, Mrs James.'

Miss Cleaver, a tall, thin, grey haired woman with a charming smile, a plain, kindly face and a very wrinkled brow, rose to meet me. 'Mrs James. How nice to see you again. How's Christine?'

'She's very well. Miss Cleaver, I'd better get straight to the point. I know you don't normally divulge the origin of a child to its adopters and vice versa, but I must know who Christine is.'

'Sorry, Mrs James,' she began, 'our rules . . .'

'Please let me tell you the whole story, then you'll see I'm not just suffering from vulgar curiosity.'

I told her about Harry.

When I'd finished, she said: 'It's very queer. Very queer indeed. Mrs James, I'm going to break my rule for once. I'm going to tell you in strict confidence where Christine came from.

'She was born in a very poor part of London. There were four in the family, father, mother, son and Christine herself.'

'Son?'

'Yes. He was fourteen when – when it happened.'

'When what happened?'

'Let me start at the beginning. The parents hadn't really wanted Christine. The family lived in one room at the top of an old house which should have been condemned by the Sanitary Inspector in my opinion. It was difficult enough when there were only three of them, but with a baby as well life became a nightmare. The mother was a neurotic creature, slatternly, unhappy, too fat. After she'd had the baby she took no interest in it. The brother, however, adored the little girl from the start. He got into trouble for cutting school so he could look after her.

'The father had a steady job in a warehouse, not much money, but enough to keep them alive. Then he was sick for several weeks and lost his job. He was laid up in that messy room, ill, worrying, nagged by his wife, irked by the baby's crying and his son's eternal fussing over the child – I got all these details from neighbours afterwards, by the way. I was also told that he'd had a particularly bad time in the war and had been in a nerve hospital for several months before he was fit to come home at all after his demob. Suddenly it all proved too much for him.

'One morning, in the small hours, a woman in the ground floor room saw something fall past her window and heard a thud on the ground. She went out to look. The son of the family was there on the ground. Christine was in his arms. The boy's neck was broken. He was dead. Christine was blue in the face but still breathing faintly.

'The woman woke the household, sent for the police and the doctor, then they went to the top room. They had to break down the door, which was locked and sealed inside. An overpowering smell of gas greeted them, in spite of the open window.

'They found husband and wife dead in bed and a note from the husband saying:

"I can't go on. I am going to kill them all.
It's the only way."

'The police concluded that he'd sealed up door and windows and turned on the gas when his family were asleep, then lain beside his wife until he drifted into unconsciousness, and death. But the son must have wakened. Perhaps he struggled with the door but couldn't open it. He'd be too weak to shout. All he could do was pluck away the seals from the window, open it, and fling himself out, holding his adored little sister tightly in his arms.

'Why Christine herself wasn't gassed is rather a mystery. Perhaps her head was right under the bedclothes, pressed against her brother's chest – they always slept together. Anyway, the child was taken to hospital, then to the home where you and Mr James first saw her . . . and a lucky day that was for little Christine!'

'So her brother saved her life and died himself?' I said.

'Yes. He was a very brave young man.'

'Perhaps he thought not so much of saving her as of keeping her with him. Oh dear! That sounds ungenerous. I didn't mean to be. Miss Cleaver, what was his name?'

'I'll have to look that up for you.' She referred to one of her many files and said at last: 'The family's name was Jones and the fourteen-year-old brother was called "Harold".'

'And did he have red hair?' I murmured.

'That I don't know, Mrs James.'

'But it's Harry. The boy was Harry. What does it mean? I can't understand it.'

'It's not easy, but I think perhaps deep in her unconscious mind Christine has always remembered Harry, the companion of her babyhood. We don't think of children as having much memory, but there must be images of the past tucked away somewhere in their little heads. Christine doesn't *invent* this Harry. She *remembers* him. So clearly that she's almost brought him to life again. I know it sounds far-fetched, but the whole story is so odd that I can't think of any other explanation.'

'May I have the address of the house where they lived?'

She was reluctant to give me this information, but I persuaded her and set out at last to find No. 13 Canver Row, where the man Jones had tried to kill himself and his whole family and almost succeeded.

The house seemed deserted. It was filthy and derelict. But one thing made me stare and stare. There was a tiny garden. A scatter of bright uneven grass splashed the bald brown patches of earth. But the little garden had one strange glory that none of the other houses in the poor sad street possessed – a bush of white roses. They bloomed gloriously. Their scent was overpowering.

I stood by the bush and stared up at the top window.

A voice startled me: 'What are you doing here?'

It was an old woman, peering from the ground floor window.

'I thought the house was empty,' I said.

'Should be. Been condemned. But they can't get me out. Nowhere else to go. Won't go. The others went quickly enough after it happened. No one else wants to come. They say the place is haunted. So it is. But what's the fuss about? Life and death. They're very close. You get to know that when you're old. Alive or dead. What's the difference?'

She looked at me with yellowish, bloodshot eyes and said: 'I saw him fall past my window. That's where he fell. Among the roses. He still comes back. I see him. He won't go away until he gets her.'

'Who – who are you talking about?'

'Harry Jones. Nice boy he was. Red hair. Very thin. Too determined though. Always got his own way. Loved Christine too much I thought. Died among the roses. Used to sit down here with her for hours, by the roses. Then died there. Or do people die? The church ought to give us an answer, but it doesn't. Not one you can believe. Go away, will you? This place isn't for you. It's for the dead who aren't dead, and the living who aren't alive. Am I alive or dead? You tell me. I don't know.'

The crazy eyes staring at me beneath the matted white fringe of hair frightened me. Mad people are terrifying. One can pity them, but one is still afraid. I murmured:

'I'll go now. Goodbye,' and tried to hurry across the hard hot pavements although my legs felt heavy and half-paralysed, as in a nightmare.

The sun blazed down on my head, but I was hardly aware of it. I lost all sense of time or place as I stumbled on.

Then I heard something that chilled my blood.

A clock struck three.

At three o'clock I was supposed to be at the school gates, waiting for Christine.

Where was I now? How near the school? What bus should I take?

I made frantic inquiries of passers-by, who looked at me fearfully, as I had looked at the old woman. They must have thought I was crazy.

At last I caught the right bus and, sick with dust, petrol fumes and fear, reached the school. I ran across the hot, empty playground. In a classroom, the young teacher in white was gathering her books together.

'I've come for Christine James. I'm her mother. I'm so sorry I'm late. Where is she?' I gasped.

'Christine James?' The girl frowned, then said brightly: 'Oh, yes, I remember, the pretty little red-haired girl. That's all right, Mrs James. Her brother called for her. How alike they are, aren't they? And so devoted. It's rather sweet to see a boy of that age so fond of his baby sister. Has your husband got red hair, like the two children?'

'What did – her brother – say?' I asked faintly.

'He didn't say anything. When I spoke to him, he just smiled. They'll be home by now, I should think. I say, do you feel all right?'

'Yes, thank you. I must go home.'

I ran all the way home through the burning streets.

'Chris! Christine, where are you? Chris! Chris!' Sometimes even now I hear my own voice of the past screaming through the cold house. 'Christine! Chris! Where are you? Answer me! Chrrriiiiiss!' Then: 'Harry! Don't take her away! Come back! Harry! Harry!'

Demented, I rushed out into the garden. The sun struck me like a hot blade. The roses glared whitely. The air was so still I seemed to stand in timelessness, placelessness. For a moment, I seemed very near to Christine, although I couldn't see her. Then the roses danced before my eyes and turned red. The world turned red. Blood red. Wet red. I fell through redness to blackness to nothingness – to almost death.

For weeks I was in bed with sunstroke which turned to brain fever. During that time Jim and the police searched for Christine in vain. The futile search continued for months. The papers were full of the strange disappearance of the red-haired child. The teacher described the 'brother' who had called for her. There were newspaper stories of kidnapping, baby-snatching, child-murders.

Then the sensation died down. Just another unsolved mystery in police files.

And only two people knew what had happened. An old crazed woman living in a derelict house, and myself.

Years have passed. But I walk in fear.

Such ordinary things make me afraid. Sunshine. Sharp shadows on grass. White roses. Children with red hair. And the name – Harry. Such an ordinary name!

CYNTHIA ASQUITH

The Corner Shop

Peter Wood's executors found their task a very easy one. He had left his affairs in perfect order. The only surprise yielded by his methodical writing-table was a sealed envelope on which was written: 'Not wishing to be bothered by well-meaning Research Societies, I have never shown the enclosed to anyone, but after my death all are welcome to read what, to the best of my knowledge, is a true story.'

The manuscript which bore a date three years previous to the death of the writer was as follows.

'I have long wished to record an experience of my youth. I won't attempt any explanation. I draw no conclusions. I merely narrate certain events.

'One foggy evening, at the end of a day of enforced idleness in my chambers – I had just been called to the Bar – I was rather dejectedly walking back to my lodgings when my attention was drawn to the brightly lit window of a shop. Seeing the word "Antiques" on its sign-board, and remembering that I owed a wedding present to a lover of bric-à-brac, I grasped the handle of the green door. Opening with one of those cheerful jingle-jangle bells, it admitted me into large rambling premises, thickly crowded with all the traditional treasure and trash of a curiosity shop. Suits of armour, warming-pans, cracked, misted mirrors, church vestments, spinning-wheels, brass kettles, chandeliers, gongs, chess-men – furniture of every size and every period. Despite all the clutter, there was none of the dusty gloom one associates with such collections. Far from being dingy, the room was brightly lit and a crackling fire leapt up the chimney. In fact, the atmosphere was so warm and cheerful that after the cold dank fog outside it struck me as most agreeable.

'At my entrance, a young woman and a girl – by their resemblance obviously sisters – rose from armchairs. Bright, bustling, gaily dressed, they were curiously unlike the type of people who usually preside over such wares. A flower or a cake-shop would have seemed a far more appropriate setting. Inwardly awarding them high marks for keeping the place so clean, I wished the sisters good evening. Their smiling faces and easy manners made a very pleasant impression on me; but though they were most obliging in showing me all their treasures and displayed considerable knowledge as well as appreciation, they seemed wholly indifferent as to whether or not I made any purchase.

'I found a small piece of Sheffield plate very moderately priced and decided that this was the very present for my friend. Explaining that I was without sufficient cash, I asked the elder sister if she would take a cheque.

' "Certainly," she answered, briskly producing pen and ink. "Will you please make it out to the 'Corner Curio Shop'?"

'It was with conscious reluctance that I left the cheerful precincts and plunged back into the saffron fog.

' "Good evening, sir. Always pleased to see you at any time," rang out the elder sister's pleasant voice, a voice so engaging that I left almost with a sense of having made a friend.

'I suppose it must have been a week later that, as I walked home one bitter cold evening – fine powdery snow brushing against my face, a cutting wind lashing down the streets – I remembered the welcoming warmth of the cheerful Corner Shop, and decided to revisit it. I found myself to be in the very street, and there – yes! – there was the very corner.

'It was with a sense of disappointment out of all proportion to the event, that I found the shop wore that baffling, shut-eyed appearance, and read the uncompromising word CLOSED.

'An icy gust of wind whistled round the corner; my wet trousers flapped dismally against my chapped ankles. Longing for the warmth and glow within, I felt annoyingly thwarted. Rather childishly – for I was certain the door was locked – I grasped the handle and shook it. To my surprise it turned in my hand, but not in answer to its pressure. The door was opened from within, and I found myself looking into the dimly-lit countenance of a very old and extremely frail-looking little man.

' "Please to come in, sir," said a gentle, rather tremulous voice, and feeble footsteps shuffled away ahead of me.

'It is impossible to describe the altered aspect of the place. I supposed the electric light had fused, for the darkness of the large room was thinned only by two guttering candles, and in their wavering light, dark shapes of furniture, formerly brightly lit, now loomed towering and mysterious, casting weird, almost menacing shadows. The fire was out. Only one faintly glowing ember told that any had lately been alive. Other evidence there was none, for the grim cold of the atmosphere was such as I had never experienced. The phrase "it struck chill" is laughably inadequate. In retrospect the street seemed almost agreeable. At least its biting cold there had been bracing. One way and another the atmosphere of the shop was now as gloomy as it had been bright before. I felt a strong impulse to leave at once, but the surrounding darkness thinned, and I saw the old man busily lighting candles here and there.

' "Anything I can show you, sir?" he quavered, approaching, taper in hand. I now saw him comparatively distinctly. His appearance made an indescribable impression on me. As I stared, Rembrandt flitted through my mind. Who else could have given any idea of the weird shadows on that ravaged face? Tired is a word we use lightly. Never before had I known what it might mean. Such ineffable, patient weariness! Deep sunk in his withered face, the eyes seemed as extinct as the fire. And the wan frailty of the small tremulous bent frame!

'The words "dust and ashes, dust and ashes," strayed through my brain.

'On my first visit, I had, you may remember, been

surprised by the uncharacteristic cleanliness of the place. The queer fancy now struck me that this old man was like an accumulation of all the dust one might have expected to find distributed over such premises. In truth, he looked scarcely more solid than a mere conglomeration of dust and cobwebs that might be dispersed at a breath or a touch.

'What a fantastic old creature to be employed by those well-to-do looking girls! He must, I thought, be some old retainer kept on out of charity.

' "Anything I can show you, sir?" repeated the old man. His voice had little more body than the tearing of a cobweb; but there was a curious, almost pleading insistence in it, and his eyes were fixed on me in a wan yet devouring stare. I wanted to leave, yes at once. The mere proximity of the poor old man distressed me – made me feel wretchedly dispirited; none the less, involuntarily murmuring, "Thank you, I'll look round," I found myself following his frail form, and absentmindedly inspecting various objects temporarily illuminated by his trembling taper.

'The chill silence broken only by the tired shuffle of his carpet slippers got on my nerves.

' "Very cold night," I hazarded.

' "Cold, is it? Cold? Yes, I daresay it is cold." In his grey voice was the apathy of utter indifference.

'For how many years, I wondered, had this poor old fellow been "incapable of his own distress"?

' "Been at this job long?" I asked, dully contemplating a four-poster bed.

' "A long, long, long time." The answer came softly as a sigh, and as he spoke, time seemed no longer a matter of days, weeks, months, years, but a weariness that stretched immeasurably. Suddenly I began to resent the old man's exhaustion and melancholy, the contagion of which so unaccountably weighed down my own spirits.

' "How long, O Lord, how long?" I said as jauntily as I could manage, adding with odious jocularity, "Old age pension about due, what?"

'No response.

'In silence he drifted across the other side of the room.

' "Quaint piece, this," said my guide, picking up a

grotesque little frog that lay on a shelf amongst various other odds and ends. It seemed to be made of some substance similar to jade – soapstone I guessed. Struck by its oddity, I took the frog from the old man's hand. It was strangely cold.

' "Rather fun," I said. "How much?"

' "Half a crown, sir," whispered the old man, glancing up at my face. Again his voice was scarcely more audible than the slithering of dust, but there was a queer gleam in his eyes. Was it eagerness? Could it be?

' "Only half a crown? Is that all? I'll have it," said I. "Don't bother to pack up old Anthony Rowley. I'll put him in my pocket."

'As I gave the old man the coin, I inadvertently touched his hand. I could scarcely suppress a start. I have said the frog struck cold, but, compared to that desiccated skin, its substance was tepid! I can't describe the chill of that second's contact. Poor old fellow! thought I, he isn't fit to be about – not in this lonely place. I wonder those kind-looking girls allow such an old wreck to struggle on.

' "Good night," I said.

' "Good night, sir. Thank you, sir," quavered the feeble old voice. He shut the door behind me.

'Turning my head as I breasted the driving snow, I saw his form, scarcely more solid than a shadow, dimly outlined against the candlelight. His face was pressed against the big glass pane, and as I walked away I pictured his exhausted patient eyes peering after me.

'Somehow I was unable to dismiss the thought of that old, old man. Long, long after I was in bed and courting sleep I saw that ravaged face with its maze of wrinkles, those great eyes like lifeless planets, staring, staring at me, and in their steady gaze there seemed something that beseeched. Yes, I was strangely perturbed by that old man.

'Even after I achieved sleep, my dreams were full of him. Haunted, I suppose by a sense of his infinite tiredness, I was trying to force him to rest – to compel him to lie down. But no sooner did I succeed in laying out his frail form on the four-poster bed I had seen in the shop – only now it seemed more like a grave than a bed, and the brocade coverlet had turned into sods of turf – than he would slip from my grasp, and totteringly resume his rambles round and round the shop. On and on I chased him, down endless avenues of weird furniture, but still he eluded me.

'Now the dim shop seemed to stretch on and on unendingly – to merge into an infinity of sunless, airless space until at length, exhausted, breathless, I myself collapsed and sank into the four-poster grave.

'The very next morning an urgent summons took me out of London, and in the anxiety of the ensuing week the episode of the Corner Shop was banished from my mind. As soon as my father was pronounced out of danger, I returned to my dreary lodgings. Dejectedly engaged in adding up my wretched bills and wondering where on earth to find the money to pay my next quarter's rent, I was agreeably surprised by a visit from an old schoolfellow, at that time practically the only friend I had in London. He was employed by one of the best known firms of Fine Art Dealers and Auctioneers.

'After some minutes' conversation, he rose in search of a light. My back was turned to him. I heard the sharp scratch of a match, followed by propitiatory noises to his pipe. Suddenly they were broken off by an exclamation.

' "Good God, man!" he shouted. "Where did you get this?"

'Turning my head, I saw he had snatched up my purchase of the other night, the funny little frog, whose presence on my mantelpiece I had all but forgotten.

'Closely scrutinizing it through a magnifying glass, he held it under the gas-jet, his hands shaking with excitement.

' "Where *did* you get this?" he repeated. "Have you any idea what it is?"

'Briefly I told him that, rather than leave a shop empty-handed I had bought the frog for a half a crown.

' "*Half a crown!* My dear fellow, I can't swear to it, but I believe you've had one of those amazing pieces of luck one hears of. Unless I'm very much mistaken, this is a piece of jade of the Hsia Dynasty. If so, it's practically unique."

'These words conveyed little to my ignorance.

' "Do you mean it's worth money?"

' "Worth money? Phew!" he ejaculated. "Look here. Will you leave this business to me? Let me have the thing for my firm to handle. They'll do the best they can by you. I shall be able to get it into Thursday's sale."

'Certain that I could implicitly trust my friend, I agreed. Reverently enwrapping the frog in cottonwool, he hurried off.

'Friday morning I had the shock of my life. Shock does not necessarily imply bad news.

'I assure you that for some seconds after opening the one envelope lying on my dingy breakfast-tray, the room spun round and round. The envelope contained an account from Messrs Spunk, Fine Art Dealers and Auctioneers: "To sale of Hsia jade, £2,000, less 10 per cent commission, £1,800," and there, neatly folded, made out to Peter Wood, was Messrs Spunk's cheque for eighteen hundred pounds! For some time I was completely bewildered. My friend's words had raised hopes – hopes that my chance purchase might facilitate the payment of next quarter's rent – might possibly even provide for a whole year's rent – but that so large a sum was involved had never so much as crossed my mind. Could it be true, or was it some hideous joke? Surely, in the trite phrase, it was much, much too good to be true! It wasn't the sort of thing that happened to oneself.

'Still feeling physically dizzy, I rang up my friend. His voice and the heartiness of his congratulations convinced me of the truth of my astounding good fortune. It was neither joke, nor dream. I, Peter Wood, whose bank account was at present twenty pounds overdrawn, who, but for shares amounting to one hundred and fifty pounds, possessed no securities whatever, now held in my hand a piece of paper convertible into eighteen hundred golden sovereigns! I sat down to think, to try to realize, to readjust. From my jumble of plans, problems and emotions, one fact emerged crystal clear. Obviously I could not take advantage of that nice girl's ignorance, nor of her poor old caretaker's incompetence – whichever was to blame. No, I couldn't accept this amazing gift from fate, merely because, by a sheer fluke, I had bought a treasure for half a crown.

'Clearly I must give back at least half the sum to my unconscious benefactors. Otherwise I should feel I had robbed them almost as if, like a thief in the night, I had broken into their shop. I remembered their pleasant, open countenances. What fun to astonish them with my wonderful news! I felt a strong impulse to rush to the shop, but having for once a case in court, was obliged to go to the Temple. Endorsing Messrs Spunk's cheque, I addressed it to my bankers, and filled in one of my own for £900 made out to the Corner Curio Shop.

'It was late before I was free to leave the Law Courts, and, when I arrived at the shop I was disappointed, but not surprised to read the notice CLOSED. Even supposing the old caretaker to be on duty, there was no particular point in seeing him. My business was with his mistress. Deciding to postpone my visit to the following day, I was just on the point of hurrying home when exactly as though I were expected, the door opened. There on the threshold stood the old man peering out into the darkness.

' "Anything I can do for you, sir?"

'His voice was even queerer than before. I now realized that I had dreaded re-encountering him, yet I found myself irresistibly compelled to enter. The atmosphere was as grimly cold as on my last visit. I felt myself actually shiver. Several candles, obviously only just lit, were burning. By their glimmer I saw the old man's questioning gaze intently fixed on me. What a face! I had not exaggerated its weirdness. Never had I seen anyone so singular, so striking. No wonder I had dreamt of him. How I wished he had not opened the door!

' "Anything I can show you tonight, sir?" His voice trembled.

' "No thanks. I've come about that thing you sold me the other day. I find it's of great value. Please tell your mistress that I'll pay her a proper price for it tomorrow."

'As I spoke there spread over the old man's face the most wonderful smile. I use the word *smile* for lack of a better word, but how to convey the beauty of the indefinable expression that transfigured that time-worn face? Tender triumph; gentle joy; rapturous reverence. What mystery did

I witness? It was like iron frost yielding to sunshine – the thawing of grief in the dawn-radiance of some unsurmisable redemption. For the first time in my life I had some inkling of the word "beatitude".

'I can't describe the impression made on me. The moment, as it were, brimmed over. Time ceased. I became conscious of infinite things.

'The silence was now broken by the gathering-itself-together sound of an old clock about to strike. I turned my head towards one of those wonderful, intricate pieces of mediaeval workmanship – a Nuremburg grandfather clock. From the recess beneath its exquisitely painted face, quaint figures emerged, and while one struck a bell, others demurely stepped through the mazes of a minuet. My attention was riveted by the pretty spectacle. Not till the last sounds had trembled into silence did I turn my head.

'I found myself alone.

'The old man had vanished. Surprised that he should leave me, I looked all round the large room. Oddly enough, the fire, which I had supposed dead, had flared into unexpected life, and now cast a cheerful glow; but neither fire nor candlelight revealed any trace of the old caretaker.

' "Hullo? Hullo?" I called interrogatively.

'No answer. No sound save the loud ticking of clocks and the crackle of the fire. I walked all round the big room. I even looked into the great four-poster bed of my dreams. Then I saw that there was a smaller adjoining room. Snatching up a candle, I hastened to explore this. At its far end I discovered a winding staircase leading up to a little gallery. The old man must have withdrawn into some upstairs lair. I would follow him. I groped my way to the foot of the stairs, and began to climb, but the steps creaked under my feet; I was conscious of crumbling woodwork. There was an icy draught; my candle went out. Cobwebs brushed against my face. To go any further was most uninviting. I desisted.

'After all, what did it matter? Let the old man hide himself!

'I had given my message. Best be gone. But the main room to which I had returned was now quite warm and cheerful. What had ever made me think it sinister? It was with a distinct sense of regret that I left the shop. I felt baulked. I longed to see that radiant face again. Strange old man! How could I ever have fancied that I feared him?

'The next Saturday I was free to go straight to the shop. All the way there my mind was agreeably occupied anticipating the welcome the grateful sisters were sure to give me. As the jingle-jangle of the bell announced my opening of the door, the two girls, who were busily dusting their goods, turned to see who came at so unusually early an hour. Recognizing me, to my surprise they bowed amiably but quite casually, as though to a mere acquaintance.

'With such a fairy-tale bond between us, I had expected a very different kind of greeting. I supposed that they had not yet heard the news, and when I told them I had brought the cheque, I saw that my surmise was right. They looked quite blank.

' "Cheque?"

' "Yes, for the frog I bought the other day."

' "Frog? What frog? I only remember your buying a piece of Sheffield plate."

'So they knew nothing, not even of my second visit to their shop! By degrees I told them the whole story. They were overcome with astonishment. The elder sister seemed quite dazed.

' "But I *can't* understand it! I can't understand it!" she repeated. "Holmes, the old caretaker, isn't even supposed to admit anyone in our absence – far less to sell things. He merely comes to take charge on the evenings we leave early, and is only supposed to stay till the night policeman comes on duty. I can't believe he let you in and never told us he'd sold you something. It's too extraordinary! What time was it?"

' "Round about six, I should think."

' "He generally leaves at half past five," said the girl. "But I suppose the policeman must have been late."

' "It was later when I came yesterday."

' "Did you come again?" she asked.

'Briefly I told her of my visit and the message I had left with the caretaker.

' "What an extraordinary thing!" she exclaimed. "I can't

begin to understand it. But we shall soon hear his explanation. I expect him at any moment now. He comes in every morning to sweep the floors."

'At the prospect of meeting the remarkable old man again I felt a thrill of excitement. How would he look by daylight? Should I see him smile again?

' "Very old, isn't he?" I hazarded.

' "Old? Yes, I suppose he is getting on, but it's a very easy job. He's a good, honest fellow. I can't imagine his doing anything on the sly. I'm afraid we've been rather slack in our cataloguing lately. I wonder if he does sell odds and ends for himself? Oh no, I can't believe it! By the way, can you remember whereabouts this frog was?"

'I pointed to the shelf from which the caretaker had produced the piece of jade.

' "Oh, from that odd lot I bought the other day for next to nothing. I haven't sorted or priced any of the things yet. I can't remember any frog. What an incredible thing to happen!"

'At this moment the telephone rang. She lifted the receiver.

' "Hullo? Hullo? Yes, Miss Wilson speaking. Yes, Mrs Holmes, what is it?"

'A few seconds' startled pause, and then, "Dead? *Dead?* But how? Why? Oh, I *am* sorry!"

'After a few more words she replaced the receiver and turned to us, her eyes full of tears.

' "Oh, Bessie," she said to her sister. "Poor old Holmes is dead. When he got home yesterday he complained of pain, and he died in the middle of the night – heart failure. No one had any idea there was anything the matter with him. Oh, poor Mrs Holmes! What will she do? We must go to her at once!"

'Both girls were so much upset that I thought it best to leave.

'The singular old man had made so haunting an impression upon me that I was deeply moved to hear of his sudden death. How strange that, except for his wife, I should have been the very last person to speak with him. No doubt pain had seized him in my very presence. That was why he had left so abruptly and without a word. Had death already brushed against his consciousness? That lovely, inexplicable smile? Was that the beginning of the peace that passes all understanding?

'Next day I told Miss Wilson and her sister all the details of the fabulous sale of the frog, and presented my cheque. Here I met with unexpected opposition. The sisters showed great unwillingness to accept the money. It was, they said, all mine. Besides they had no need of it.

' "You see," explained Miss Wilson, "my father had a flair for this business amounting to a sort of genius. He made quite a large fortune. When he became too old to carry on the shop, we kept it open, partly out of sentiment, partly for the sake of occupation. But we don't need to make any profit."

'At last I prevailed upon them to accept the money, if only to spend it on the various charities in which they were interested. It was a relief to my mind when the matter was settled.

'The extraordinary incident of the jade frog made a bond between us, and in the course of our amicable arguments we became very friendly. I fell into the way of dropping in on them quite often, and soon began quite to rely on their sympathetic companionship.

'I never forgot the impression made on me by the old man, and often questioned the sisters about their poor caretaker, but they had nothing of any interest to tell me. They merely described him as an "old dear" who had been in their father's service for years and years. No further light was thrown on his sale of the frog. Naturally, they did not like to question his widow.

'One evening while I was having tea in the inner room with the elder sister, I picked up a photograph album. Turning its pages, I came on a remarkably fine likeness of the old man. There, before my eyes was that strange, striking countenance; but evidently this photograph had been taken many years before I saw him. The face was fuller and had not yet acquired the frail, infinitely wearied look I remembered. But what magnificent eyes! There certainly was something extraordinarily impressive about the man.

' "What a splendid photograph of poor old Holmes!" I said.

' "Photograph of Holmes? I'd no idea there was one. Let's see."

'As I handed her the open book, her young sister, Bessie, looked in through the open door.

' "I'm off to the movies now," she called out. "Father's just rung up to say he'll be round in a few minutes to have a look at that Sheraton sideboard."

' "All right, Bessie, I'll be here, and very glad to have father's opinion," said Miss Wilson, taking the album from my hand.

' "I can't see any photograph of old Holmes," she said.

'I pointed to the top of the page.

' "That?" she exclaimed. "Why, that's my dear father!"

' "Your *father*!" I gasped.

' "Yes, I can't imagine any two people more unlike. It must have been very dark when you saw Holmes!"

' "Yes, yes; it *was* very dark," I said quickly – just to gain time to think, for I felt bewildered. No degree of darkness could possibly explain any such mistake. I had no moment's doubt as to the identity of the man I had taken for the caretaker with the one whose photograph I held in my hand. But what an amazing, inexplicable thing!

'Her *father*? Why on earth should he have been in the shop unknown to his daughters? For what possible motive had he concealed his sale of the frog? And when he heard of its value, why had he left the girls under the impression that it was Holmes, the dead caretaker, who had sold it?

'Had he been ashamed to confess his own inadvertence? Or was it possible that the girls had never told him the astonishing sequel to the sale? Did they perhaps not want him to know of their sudden acquisition? Into what strange family intrigue had I stumbled? But, whoever it was who had been so secretive, it was none of my business. I didn't want to give anyone away. No, I must hold my tongue.

'The younger sister had said the father was just coming. Would he recognize me as his customer? If so, it might be rather embarrassing.

' "It's a splendid face," I said shyly.

' "*Isn't* it?" she said with pleased eagerness. "So clever and strong, don't you think? I remember when that photograph was taken. It was just before he got religion." The girl spoke as if she referred to some distressing illness.

' "Did he suddenly become very religious?"

' "Yes," she said reluctantly. "Poor father! He made friends with a priest, and became so changed. He was never the same again."

'From the break in the girl's voice, I guessed she thought her father's reason had been affected. Perhaps this explained the whole affair? On the two occasions when I had seen him, was he wandering in mind as well as body?

' "Did his religion make him unhappy?" I ventured to ask, for I was most anxious for more light on the strange being before I met him again.

' "Yes, dreadfully." The girl's eyes were full of tears. "You see . . . it was . . . " She hesitated, but after a glance at me went on, "There's really no reason why I shouldn't tell you. I've come to look on you as a real friend. My poor father began to think he had done something very wrong. He couldn't quiet his conscience. You remember me telling you of his extraordinary flair? Well, his fortune had really been founded on three marvellous strokes of business. You see, he had exactly the same sort of luck you had here the other day – that's why I decided to tell you. It seems such an odd coincidence."

'She paused.

' "Please go on," I urged.

' "Well, on three separate occasions he bought for a few shillings, objects that were of immense value. Only unlike you – he *did* know what he was about. The profit made on their sale was no surprise to him. Unlike you, he did not then see any obligation to make it up to the ignorant people who had thrown away fortunes. After all, most dealers wouldn't, would they?" she asked defensively. "Well, father grew richer and richer . . . Years later, he met this priest, and then he seemed to go sort of – er – morbid. He began to think that our wealth had been founded on what was really no better than theft. He reproached himself bitterly for having taken advantage of those three men's ignorance. Unhappily in each case he succeeded in discovering what had ultimately happened to those he called his 'victims'. Most unfortunately, all three customers had died destitute. This discovery made him incurably miserable. Two of these men had died without leaving any children, so, as no relations could be found, my father was unable to make amends.

' "The son of the third he traced to America: but there he, too, had died leaving no family. So poor father could find no means of making reparation. That was what he longed for – to make reparation. His failure preyed and preyed on him, until his poor dear mind became quite unhinged. As religion gained stronger and stronger hold on him, he took a queer sort of notion into his head – a regular obsession. 'The next best thing to doing a good deed yourself,' he would say, '*is to provide someone else with the opportunity* – to give him his cue. In our sins Christ is crucified afresh. Because I sinned against Him thrice, I must somehow be the cause of three correspondingly good actions that will counter-balance my own sins. In no other way can I atone for my crimes against Christ, for crimes they were.'

' "In vain we argued with him, assuring him he had done only as nearly all other men would have done. It was no use. 'Other men must judge for themselves. I have done what I know to be wrong,' he would moan. He grew more and more fixed in his idea of – er – expiation. It became positive religious mania!

' "Determined to find three human beings who, by their good actions, would, as it were, *cancel* out the pain caused to Divinity by what he called his 'three crimes', he busied himself in finding insignificant-looking works of art which he would offer for a few shillings.

' "Poor old father! Never shall I forget his joy when one day a man brought back a vase he had bought for five shillings and then discovered to be worth six hundred pounds: 'I think you must have made a mistake,' the man said. Just as you did, bless you!

' "Five years later a similar thing occurred, and he was, oh, so radiant. Two of humanity's crimes cancelled out – two-thirds of his expiation achieved!

' "Then followed years and years of weary disappointment. 'I shall never rest. I can't. No, never, never, until I find the third,' he used to say."

'Here the girl began to weep. Hiding her face behind her hands, she murmured, "Oh, if only *you* had come sooner!"

'I heard the jingle-jangle of the bell.

' "How he must have suffered!" I said. "I'm so glad I had the luck to be the third. Is he satisfied now?"

'Her hands dropped from her face; she stared at me.

'I heard footsteps approach.

' "I'm so glad I'm going to meet him again," I said.

' "Meet him?" she echoed in amazement as the footsteps neared.

' "Yes, I may stay and see your father, mayn't I? I heard your sister say he would soon be here."

' "Oh, now I understand!" she exclaimed. "You mean *Bessie's* father! But Bessie and I are only step-sisters. *My* poor father died years and years ago." '

E. F. BENSON

In the Tube

'It's a convention,' said Anthony Carling cheerfully, 'and not
a very convincing one. Time, indeed! There's no such thing
as Time really; it has no actual existence. Time is nothing
more than an infinitesimal point in eternity, just as space is
an infinitesimal point in infinity. At the most, Time is a sort
of tunnel through which we are accustomed to believe that
we are travelling. There's a roar in our ears and a darkness in
our eyes which makes it seem real to us. But before we came
into the tunnel we existed for ever in an infinite sunlight, and
after we have got through it we shall exist in an infinite
sunlight again. So why should we bother ourselves about the
confusion and noise and darkness which only encompass us
for a moment?'

For a firm-rooted believer in such immeasurable ideas as
these, which he punctuated with brisk application of the
poker to the brave sparkle and glow of the fire, Anthony has a
very pleasant appreciation of the measurable and the finite,
and nobody with whom I have acquaintance has so keen a
zest for life and its enjoyments as he. He had given us this
evening an admirable dinner, had passed round a port
beyond praise, and had illuminated the jolly hours with the
light of his infectious optimism. Now the small company had
melted away, and I was left with him over the fire in his
study. Outside the tattoo of wind-driven sleet was audible on
the window-panes, over-scoring now and again the flap of the
flames on the open hearth, and the thought of the chilly

blasts and the snow-covered pavement in Brompton Square, across which, to skidding taxicabs, the last of his other guests had scurried, made my position, resident here till tomorrow morning, the more delicately delightful. Above all there was this stimulating and suggestive companion, who, whether he talked of the great abstractions which were so intensely real and practical to him, or of the very remarkable experiences which he had encountered among these conventions of time and space, was equally fascinating to the listener.

'I adore life,' he said. 'I find it the most entrancing plaything. It's a delightful game, and, as you know very well, the only conceivable way to play a game is to treat it extremely seriously. If you say to yourself, "It's only a game," you cease to take the slightest interest in it. You have to know that it's only a game, and behave as if it was the one object of existence. I should like it to go on for many years yet. But all the time one has to be living on the true plane as well, which is eternity and infinity. If you come to think of it, the one thing which the human mind cannot grasp is the finite, not the infinite, the temporary, not the eternal.'

'That sounds rather paradoxical,' said I.

'Only because you've made a habit of thinking about things that seem bounded and limited. Look it in the face for a minute. Try to imagine finite Time and Space, and you find you can't. Go back a million years, and multiply that million of years by another million, and you find that you can't conceive of a beginning. What happened before that beginning? Another beginning and another beginning? And before that? Look at it like that, and you find that the only solution comprehensible to you is the existence of an eternity, something that never began and will never end. It's the same about space. Project yourself to the farthest star, and what comes beyond that? Emptiness? Go on through the emptiness, and you can't imagine it being finite and having an end. It must needs go on for ever: that's the only thing you can understand. There's no such thing as before or after, or beginning or end, and what a comfort that is! I should fidget myself to death if there wasn't the huge soft cushion of eternity to lean one's head against. Some people say – I believe I've heard you say it yourself – that the idea of eternity is so tiring; you feel that you want to stop. But that's because you are thinking of eternity in terms of Time, and mumbling in your brain, "And after that, and after that?" Don't you grasp the idea that in eternity there isn't any "after", any more than there is any "before"? It's all one. Eternity isn't a quantity: it's a quality.'

Sometimes, when Anthony talks in this manner, I seem to get a glimpse of that which to his mind is so transparently clear and solidly real, at other times (not having a brain that readily envisages abstractions) I feel as though he was pushing me over a precipice, and my intellectual faculties grasp wildly at anything tangible or comprehensible. This was the case now, and I hastily interrupted.

'But there is a "before" and "after",' I said. 'A few hours ago you gave us an admirable dinner, and after that – yes, after – we played bridge. And now you are going to explain things a little more clearly to me, and after that I shall go to bed – '

He laughed.

'You shall do exactly as you like,' he said, 'and you shan't be a slave to Time either tonight or tomorrow morning. We won't even mention an hour for breakfast, but you shall have it in eternity whenever you awake. And as I see it is not midnight yet, we'll slip the bonds of Time, and talk quite infinitely. I will stop the clock, if that will assist you in getting rid of your illusion, and then I'll tell you a story, which to my mind, shows how unreal so-called realities are; or, at any rate, how fallacious are our senses as judges of what is real and what is not.'

'Something occult, something spookish?' I asked, pricking up my ears, for Anthony has the strangest clairvoyances and visions of things unseen by the normal eye.

'I suppose you might call some of it occult,' he said, 'though there's a certain amount of rather grim reality mixed up in it.'

'Go on; excellent mixture,' said I.

He threw a fresh log on the fire.

'It's a longish story,' he said. 'You may stop me as soon as you've had enough. But there will come a point for which I claim your consideration. You, who cling to your "before" and "after", has it ever occurred to you how difficult it is to say *when* an incident takes place? Say that a man commits some crime of violence, can we not, with a good deal of truth, say that he really commits that crime when he definitely plans and determines upon it, dwelling on it with gusto? The actual commission of it, I think we can reasonably argue, is the mere material sequel of his resolve: he is guilty of it when he makes that determination. When, therefore, in the term of "before" and "after", does the crime truly take place? There is also in my story a further point for your consideration. For it seems certain that the spirit of a man, after the death of his body, is obliged to re-enact such a crime, with a view, I suppose we may guess, to his remorse and his eventual redemption. Those who have second sight have seen such re-enactments. Perhaps he may have done his deed blindly in this life; but then his spirit re-commits it with its spiritual eyes open, and able to comprehend its enormity. So, shall we view the man's original determination and the material commission of his crime only as preludes to the real commission of it, when with eyes unsealed he does it and repents of it? . . . That all sounds very obscure when I speak in the abstract, but I think you will see what I mean, if you follow my tale. Comfortable? Got everything you want? Here goes then.'

He leaned back in his chair, concentrating his mind, and then spoke:

'The story that I am about to tell you,' he said, 'had its beginning a month ago, when you were away in Switzerland. It reached its conclusion, so I imagine, last night. I do not, at any rate, expect to experience any more of it. Well, a month ago I was returning late on a very wet night from dining out. There was not a taxi to be had, and I hurried through the pouring rain to the tube station at Piccadilly Circus, and thought myself very lucky to catch the last train in this direction. The carriage into which I stepped was quite empty except for one other passenger, who sat next the door immediately opposite to me. I had never, to my knowledge, seen him before, but I found my attention vividly fixed on him, as if he somehow concerned me. He was a man of middle age, in dress-clothes, and his face wore an expression

of intense thought, as if in his mind he was pondering some
very significant matter, and his hand which was resting on
his knee clenched and unclenched itself. Suddenly he looked
up and stared me in the face, and I saw there suspicion and
fear, as if I had surprised him in some secret deed.

'At that moment we stopped at Dover Street, and the
conductor threw open the doors, announced the station and
added, "Change here for Hyde Park Corner and Gloucester
Road." That was all right for me since it meant that the train
would stop at Brompton Road, which was my destination. It
was all right apparently, too, for my companion, for he
certainly did not get out, and after a moment's stop, during
which no one else got in, we went on. I saw him, I must
insist, after the doors were closed and the train had started.
But when I looked again, as we rattled on, I saw that there
was no one there. I was quite alone in the carriage.

'Now you may think that I had had one of those swift
momentary dreams which flash in and out of the mind in the
space of a second, but I did not believe it was so myself, for I
felt that I had experienced some sort of premonition or
clairvoyant vision. A man, the semblance of whom, astral
body or whatever you may choose to call it, I had just seen,
would sometime sit in that seat opposite to me, pondering
and planning.'

'But why?' I asked. 'Why should it have been the astral
body of a living man which you thought you had seen? Why
not the ghost of a dead one?'

'Because of my own sensations. The sight of the spirit of
someone dead, which has occurred to me two or three times
in my life, has always been accompanied by a physical
shrinking and fear, and by the sensation of cold and of
loneliness. I believed, at any rate, that I had seen a phantom
of the living, and that impression was confirmed, I might say
proved, the next day. For I met the man himself. And the
next night, as you shall hear, I met the phantom again. We
will take them in order.

'I was lunching, then, the next day with my neighbour
Mrs Stanley: there was a small party, and when I arrived we
waited but for the final guest. He entered while I was talking
to some friend, and presently at my elbow I heard Mrs

Stanley's voice –

' "Let me introduce you to Sir Henry Payle," she said.

'I turned and saw my *vis-à-vis* of the night before. It was quite unmistakably he, and as we shook hands he looked at me I thought with vague and puzzled recognition.

' "Haven't we met before, Mr Carling?" he said. "I seem to recollect – "

'For the moment I forgot the strange manner of his disappearance from the carriage, and thought that it had been the man himself whom I had seen last night.

' "Surely, and not so long ago," I said. "For we sat opposite each other in the last tube-train from Piccadilly Circus yesterday night."

'He still looked at me, frowning, puzzled, and shook his head.

' "That can hardly be," he said. "I only came up from the country this morning."

'Now this interested me profoundly, for the astral body, we are told, abides in some half-conscious region of the mind or spirit, and has recollections of what has happened to it, which it can convey only very vaguely and dimly to the conscious mind. All lunch-time I could see his eyes again and again directed to me with the same puzzled and perplexed air, and as I was taking my departure he came up to me.

' "I shall recollect some day," he said, "where we met before, and I hope we may meet again. Was it not – ?" – and he stopped. "No: it has gone from me," he added.'

The log that Anthony had thrown on the fire was burning bravely now, and its high-flickering flame lit up his face.

'Now, I don't know whether you believe in coincidences as chance things,' he said, 'but if you do, get rid of the notion. Or if you can't at once, call it a coincidence that that very night I again caught the last train on the tube going westwards. This time, so far from my being a solitary passenger, there was a considerable crowd waiting at Dover Street, where I entered, and just as the noise of the approaching train began to reverberate in the tunnel I caught sight of Sir Henry Payle standing near the opening from which the train would presently emerge, apart from the rest of the crowd. And I thought to myself how odd it was that I should have seen the phantom of him at this very hour last night and the man himself now, and I began walking towards him with the idea of saying, "Anyhow, it is in the tube that we meet tonight." . . . And then a terrible and awful thing happened. Just as the train emerged from the tunnel he jumped down on to the line in front of it, and the train swept along over him up the platform.

'For a moment I was stricken with horror at the sight, and I remember covering my eyes against the dreadful tragedy. But then I perceived that, though it had taken place in full sight of those who were waiting, no one seemed to have seen it except myself. The driver, looking out from his window, had not applied his brakes, there was no jolt from the advancing train, no scream, no cry, and the rest of the passengers began boarding the train with perfect nonchalance. I must have staggered, for I felt sick and faint with what I had seen, and some kindly soul put his arm round me and supported me into the train. He was a doctor, he told me, and asked if I was in pain, or what ailed me. I told him what I thought I had seen and he assured me that no such accident had taken place.

'It was clear then to my own mind that I had seen the second act, so to speak, in this psychical drama, and I pondered next morning over the problem as to what I should do. Already I had glanced at the morning paper, which, as I knew would be the case, contained no mention whatever of what I had seen. The thing had certainly not happened, but I knew in myself that it would happen. The flimsy veil of Time had been withdrawn from my eyes, and I had seen into what you would call the future. In terms of Time of course it was the future, but from my point of view the thing was just as much in the past as it was in the future. It existed, and waited only for its material fulfilment. The more I thought about it, the more I saw that I could do nothing.'

I interrupted his narrative.

'You did nothing?' I exclaimed. 'Surely you might have taken some step in order to try to avert the tragedy.'

He shook his head.

'What step precisely?' he said. 'Was I to go to Sir Henry and tell him that once more I had seen him in the tube in the act of committing suicide? Look at it like this. Either what I had seen was pure illusion, pure imagination, in which case it had no existence or significance at all, or it was actual and real, and essentially it had happened. Or take it, though not very logically, somewhere between the two. Say that the idea of suicide, for some cause of which I knew nothing, had occurred to him or would occur. Should I not, if that was the case, be doing a very dangerous thing, by making such a suggestion to him? Might not the fact of my telling him what I had seen put the idea into his mind, or, if it was already there, confirm it and strengthen it? "It's a ticklish matter to play with souls," as Browning says.'

'But it seems so inhuman not to interfere in any way,' said I, 'not to make any attempt.'

'What interference?' asked he. 'What attempt?'

The human instinct in me still seemed to cry aloud at the thought of doing nothing to avert such a tragedy, but it seemed to be beating itself against something austere and inexorable. And cudgel my brain as I would, I could not combat the sense of what he had said. I had no answer for him, and he went on.

'You must recollect, too,' he said, 'that I believed then and believe now that the thing had happened. The cause of it, whatever that was, had begun to work, and the effect, in this material sphere, was inevitable. That is what I alluded to when, at the beginning of my story, I asked you to consider how difficult it was to say when an action took place. You still hold that this particular action, this suicide of Sir Henry, had not yet taken place, because he had not yet thrown himself under the advancing train. To me that seems a materialistic view. I hold that in all but the endorsement of it, so to speak, it had taken place. I fancy that Sir Henry, for instance, now free from the material dusks, knows that himself.'

Exactly as he spoke there swept through the warm lit room a current of ice-cold air, ruffling my hair as it passed me, and making the wood flames on the hearth to dwindle and flare. I looked round to see if the door at my back had opened, but nothing stirred there, and over the closed window the curtains were fully drawn. As it reached Anthony, he sat up quickly in his chair and directed his glance this way and that about the room.

'Did you feel that?' he asked.

'Yes: a sudden draught,' I said. 'Ice-cold.'

'Anything else?' he asked. 'Any other sensation?'

I paused before I answered, for at the moment there occurred to me Anthony's differentiation of the effects produced on the beholder by a phantasm of the living and the apparition of the dead. It was the latter which accurately described my sensation now, a certain physical shrinking, a fear, a feeling of desolation. But yet I had seen nothing. 'I felt rather creepy,' I said.

As I spoke I drew my chair rather closer to the fire, and sent a swift and, I confess, a somewhat apprehensive scrutiny round the walls of the brightly lit room. I noticed at the same time that Anthony was peering across to the chimney-piece, on which, just below a sconce holding two electric lights, stood the clock which at the beginning of our talk he had offered to stop. The hands I noticed pointed to twenty-five minutes to one.

'But you saw nothing?' he asked.

'Nothing whatever,' I said. 'Why should I? What was there to see? Or did you – '

'I don't think so,' he said.

Somehow this answer got on my nerves, for the queer feeling which had accompanied that cold current of air had not left me. If anything it had become more acute.

'But surely you know whether you saw anything or not?' I said.

'One can't always be certain,' said he. 'I say that I don't think I saw anything. But I'm not sure, either, whether the story I am telling you was quite concluded last night. I think there may be a further incident. If you prefer it, I will leave the rest of it, as far as I know it, unfinished till tomorrow morning, and you can go off to bed now.'

His complete calmness and tranquillity reassured me.

'But why should I do that?' I asked.

Again he looked round on the bright walls.

'Well, I think something entered the room just now,' he said, 'and it may develop. If you don't like the notion, you had better go. Of course there's nothing to be alarmed at;

whatever it is, it can't hurt us. But it is close on the hour when on two successive nights I saw what I have already told you, and an apparition usually occurs at the same time. Why that is so, I cannot say, but certainly it looks as if a spirit that is earth-bound is still subject to certain conventions, the conventions of time for instance. I think that personally I shall see something before long, but most likely you won't. You're not such a sufferer as I from these – these delusions – '

I was frightened and knew it, but I was also intensely interested, and some perverse pride wriggled within me at his last words. Why, so I asked myself, shouldn't I see whatever was to be seen? . . .

'I don't want to go in the least,' I said. 'I want to hear the rest of your story.'

'Where was I, then? Ah, yes: you were wondering why I didn't do something after I saw the train move up to the platform, and I said that there was nothing to be done. If you think it over, I fancy you will agree with me . . . A couple of days passed, and on the third morning I saw in the paper that there had come fulfilment to my vision. Sir Henry Payle, who had been waiting on the platform of Dover Street Station for the last train to South Kensington, had thrown himself in front of it as it came into the station. The train had been pulled up in a couple of yards, but a wheel had passed over his chest, crushing it in and instantly killing him.

'An inquest was held, and there emerged at it one of those dark stories which, on occasions like these, sometimes fall like a midnight shadow across a life that the world perhaps had thought prosperous. He had long been on bad terms with his wife, from whom he had lived apart, and it appeared that not long before this he had fallen desperately in love with another woman. The night before his suicide he had appeared very late at his wife's house, and had a long and angry scene with her in which he entreated her to divorce him, threatening otherwise to make her life a hell to her. She refused, and in an ungovernable fit of passion he attempted to strangle her. There was a struggle, and the noise of it caused her manservant to come up, who succeeded in overmastering him. Lady Payle threatened to proceed against him for assault with the intention to murder her. With this hanging over his head, the next night, as I have already told you, he committed suicide.'

He glanced at the clock again, and I saw that the hands now pointed to ten minutes to one. The fire was beginning to burn low and the room surely was growing strangely cold.

'That's not quite all,' said Anthony, again looking around. 'Are you sure you wouldn't prefer to hear it tomorrow?'

The mixture of shame and pride and curiosity again prevailed.

'No: tell me the rest of it at once,' I said.

Before speaking, he peered suddenly at some point behind my chair, shading his eyes. I followed his glance, and knew what he meant by saying that sometimes one could not be sure whether one saw something or not. But was that an outlined shadow that intervened between me and the wall? It was difficult to focus; I did not know whether it was near the wall or near my chair. It seemed to clear away, anyhow, as I looked more closely at it.

'You see nothing?' asked Anthony.

'No: I don't think so,' said I. 'And you?'

'I think I do,' he said, and his eyes followed something which was invisible to mine. They came to rest between him and the chimney-piece. Looking steadily there, he spoke again.

'All this happened some weeks ago,' he said, 'when you were out in Switzerland, and since then, up till last night, I saw nothing further. But all the time I was expecting something further. I felt that, as far as I was concerned, it was not all over yet, and last night, with the intention of assisting any communication to come through to me from – from beyond, I went into the Dover Street tube station at a few minutes before one o'clock, the hour at which both the assault and the suicide had taken place. The platform when I arrived on it was absolutely empty, or appeared to be so, but presently, just as I began to hear the roar of the approaching train, I saw there was the figure of a man standing some twenty yards from me, looking into the tunnel. He had not come down with me in the lift, and the moment before he had not been there. He began moving towards me, and then I saw who it was, and I felt a stir of wind icy-cold coming towards me as he approached. It was not the draught that heralds the approach of a train, for it came from the opposite direction. He came close up to me, and I saw there was recognition in his eyes. He raised his face towards me and I saw his lips move, but, perhaps in the increasing noise from the tunnel, I heard nothing come from them. He put out his hand, as if entreating me to do something, and with a cowardice for which I cannot forgive myself, I shrank from him, for I knew, by the sign that I have told you, that this was one from the dead, and my flesh quaked before him, drowning for the moment all pity and all desire to help him, if that was possible. Certainly he had something which he wanted of me, but I recoiled from him. And by now the train was emerging from the tunnel, and next moment, with a dreadful gesture of despair, he threw himself in front of it.'

As he finished speaking he got up quickly from his chair, still looking fixedly in front of him. I saw his pupils dilate, and his mouth worked.

'It is coming,' he said. 'I am to be given a chance of atoning for my cowardice. There is nothing to be afraid of: I must remember that myself . . .'

As he spoke there came from the panelling above the chimney-piece one loud shattering crack, and the cold wind again circled about my head. I found myself shrinking back in my chair with my hands held in front of me as instinctively I screened myself against something which I knew was there but which I could not see. Every sense told me that there was a presence in the room other than mine and Anthony's, and the horror of it was that I could not see it. Any vision, however terrible, would, I felt, be more tolerable than this clear certain knowledge that close to me was this invisible thing. And yet what horror might not be disclosed of the face of the dead and the crushed chest . . . But all I could see, as I shuddered in this cold wind, was the familiar walls of the room, and Anthony standing in front of me stiff and firm, making, as I knew, a call on his courage. His eyes were focused on something quite close to him, and some semblance of a smile quivered on his mouth. And then he spoke again.

'Yes, I know you,' he said. 'And you want something of me. Tell me, then, what it is.'

There was absolute silence, but what was silence to my ears could not have been so to his, for once or twice he nodded, and once he said, 'Yes: I see. I will do it.' And with the knowledge that, even as there was someone here whom I could not see, so there was speech going on which I could not hear, this terror of the dead and of the unknown rose in me with the sense of powerlessness to move that accompanies nightmare. I could not stir, I could not speak. I could only strain my ears for the inaudible and my eyes for the unseen, while the cold wind from the very valley of the shadow of death streamed over me. It was not that the presence of death itself was terrible; it was that from its tranquillity and serene keeping there had been driven some unquiet soul unable to rest in peace for whatever ultimate awakening rouses the countless generations of those who have passed away, driven, no less, from whatever activities are theirs, back into the material world from which it should have been delivered. Never, until the gulf between the living and the dead was thus bridged, had it seemed so immense and so unnatural. It is possible that the dead may have communication with the living, and it was not that exactly that so terrified me, for such communication, as we know it, comes voluntarily from them. But here was something icy-cold and crime-laden, that was chased back from the peace that would not pacify it.

And then, most horrible of all, there came a change in these unseen conditions. Anthony was silent now, and from looking straight and fixedly in front of him, he began to glance sideways to where I sat and back again, and with that I felt that the unseen presence had turned its attention from him to me. And now, too, gradually and by awful degrees I began to see . . .

There came an outline of shadow across the chimney-piece and the panels above it. It took shape: it fashioned itself into the outline of a man. Within the shape of the shadow details began to form themselves, and I saw wavering in the air, like something concealed by haze, the semblance of a face, stricken and tragic, and burdened with such a weight of woe

as no human face had ever worn. Next, the shoulders
outlined themselves, and a stain livid and red spread out
below them, and suddenly the vision leaped into clearness.
There he stood, the chest crushed in and drowned in the red
stain, from which broken ribs, like the bones of a wrecked
ship, protruded. The mournful, terrible eyes were fixed on
me, and it was from them, so I knew, that the bitter wind
proceeded . . .

Then, quick as the switching off of a lamp, the spectre
vanished, and the bitter wind was still, and opposite to me
stood Anthony, in a quiet, bright-lit room. There was no
sense of an unseen presence any more; he and I were then
alone, with an interrupted conversation still dangling
between us in the warm air. I came round to that, as one
comes round after an anaesthetic. It all swam into sight
again, unreal at first, and gradually assuming the texture of
actuality.

'You were talking to somebody, not to me,' I said. 'Who
was it? What was it?'

He passed the back of his hand over his forehead, which
glistened in the light.

'A soul in hell,' he said.

Now it is hard ever to recall mere physical sensations,
when they have passed. If you have been cold and are
warmed, it is difficult to remember what cold was like: if you
have been hot and have got cool, it is difficult to realize what
the oppression of heat really meant. Just so, with the passing
of that presence, I found myself unable to recapture the
sense of the terror with which, a few moments ago only, it
had invaded and inspired me.

'A soul in hell?' I said. 'What are you talking about?'

He moved about the room for a minute or so, and then
came and sat on the arm of my chair.

'I don't know what you saw,' he said, 'or what you felt, but
there has never in all my life happened to me anything more
real than what these last few minutes have brought. I have
talked to a soul in the hell of remorse, which is the only
possible hell. He knew, from what happened last night, that
he could perhaps establish communication through me with
the world he had quitted, and he sought me and found me. I

am charged with a mission to a woman I have never seen, a message from the contrite . . . You can guess who it is . . . '

He got up with a sudden briskness.

'Let's verify it anyhow,' he said. 'He gave me the street and the number. Ah, there's the telephone book! Would it be a coincidence merely if I found that at No. 20 in Chasemore Street, South Kensington, there lived a Lady Payle?'

He turned over the leaves of the bulky volume.

'Yes, that's right,' he said.

ROSEMARY TIMPERLEY

Christmas Meeting

I have never spent Christmas alone before.

It gives me an uncanny feeling, sitting alone in my 'furnished room', with my head full of ghosts, and the room full of voices of the past. It's a drowning feeling – all the Christmases of the past coming back in a mad jumble: the childish Christmas, with a house full of relations, a tree in the window, sixpences in the pudding, and the delicious, crinkly stocking in the dark morning; the adolescent Christmas, with mother and father, the war and the bitter cold, and the letters from abroad; the first really grown-up Christmas, with a lover – the snow and the enchantment, red wine and kisses, and the walk in the dark before midnight, with the grounds so white, and the stars diamond bright in a black sky – so many Christmases through the years.

And, now, the first Christmas alone.

But not quite loneliness. A feeling of companionship with all the other people who are spending Christmas alone – millions of them – past and present. A feeling that, if I close my eyes, there will be no past or future, only an endless present which *is* time, because it is all we ever have.

Yes, however cynical you are, however irreligious, it makes you fell queer to be alone at Christmas time.

So I'm absurdly relieved when the young man walks in. There's nothing romantic about it – I'm a woman of nearly fifty, a spinster schoolma'am with grim, dark hair, and myopic eyes that once were beautiful, and he's a kid of twenty, rather unconventionally dressed with a flowing, wine-coloured tie and black velvet jacket, and brown curls which could do with a taste of the barber's scissors. The effeminacy of his dress is belied by his features – narrow, piercing, blue eyes, and arrogant, jutting nose and chin. Not that he looks strong. The skin is fine-drawn over the prominent features, and he is very white.

He bursts in without knocking, then pauses, says: 'I'm so sorry. I thought this was my room.' He begins to go out, then hesitates and says: 'Are you alone?'

'Yes.'

'It's – queer, being alone at Christmas, isn't it? May I stay and talk?'

'I'd be glad if you would.'

He comes right in, and sits down by the fire.

'I hope you don't think I came in here on purpose. I really did think it was my room,' he explains.

'I'm glad you made the mistake. But you're a very young person to be alone at Christmas time.'

'I wouldn't go back to the country to my family. It would hold up my work. I'm a writer.'

'I see.' I can't help smiling a little. That explains his rather unusual dress. And he takes himself so seriously, this young man! 'Of course, you mustn't waste a precious moment of writing,' I say with a twinkle.

'No, not a moment! That's what my family won't see. They don't appreciate urgency.'

'Families are never appreciative of the artistic nature.'

'No, they aren't,' he agrees seriously.

'What are you writing?'

'Poetry and a diary combined. It's called *My Poems and I*, by Francis Randel. That's my name. My family say there's no point in my writing, that I'm too young. But I don't feel young. Sometimes I feel like an old man, with too much to do before he dies.'

'Revolving faster and faster on the wheel of creativeness.'

'Yes! Yes, exactly! You understand! You must read my work some time. Please read my work! Read my work!' A note of desperation in his voice, a look of fear in his eyes, makes me say:

'We're both getting much too solemn for Christmas Day. I'm going to make you some coffee. And I have a plum cake.'

I move about, clattering cups, spooning coffee into my percolator. But I must have offended him, for, when I look round, I find he has left me. I am absurdly disappointed.

I finish making coffee, however, then turn to the bookshelf in the room. It is piled high with volumes, for which the landlady has apologized profusely: 'Hope you don't mind the books, Miss, but my husband won't part with them, and there's nowhere else to put them. We charge a bit less for the room for that reason.'

'I don't mind,' I said. 'Books are good friends.'

But these aren't very friendly-looking books. I take one at random. Or does some strange fate guide my hand?

Sipping my coffee, inhaling my cigarette smoke, I begin to read the battered little book, published, I see, in Spring, 1852. It's mainly poetry – immature stuff, but vivid. Then there's a kind of diary. More realistic, less affected. Out of curiosity, to see if there are any amusing comparisons, I turn to the entry for Christmas Day, 1851. I read:

'My first Christmas Day alone. I had rather an odd experience. When I went back to my lodgings after a walk, there was a middle-aged woman in my room. I thought, at first, I'd walked into the wrong room, but this was not so, and later, after a pleasant talk, she – disappeared. I suppose she was a ghost. But I wasn't frightened. I liked her. But I do not feel well tonight. Not at all well. I have never felt ill at Christmas before.'

A publisher's note followed the last entry: FRANCIS RANDEL DIED FROM A SUDDEN HEART ATTACK ON THE NIGHT OF CHRISTMAS DAY, 1851. THE WOMAN MENTIONED IN THIS FINAL ENTRY IN HIS DIARY WAS THE LAST PERSON TO SEE HIM ALIVE. IN SPITE OF REQUESTS FOR HER TO COME FORWARD, SHE NEVER DID SO. HER IDENTITY REMAINS A MYSTERY.

JONAS LIE

Elias and the Draug

On Kvalholmen down in Helgeland there once lived a poor
fisherman, by name Elias, and his wife, Karen, who before
her marriage had worked in the parsonage at Alstadhaug.*
They lived in a little hut, which they had built, and Elias
hired out by the day in the Lofoten fisheries.

Kvalholmen was a lonely island, and there were signs at
times that it was haunted. Sometimes when her husband was
away from home, the good wife heard all sorts of unearthly
noises and cries, which surely boded no good.

Each year there came a child; when they had been married
seven years there were six children in the home. But they
were both steady and hard working people, and by the time
the last arrived, Elias had managed to put aside something
and felt that he could afford a sixern, and thereafter do his
Lofoten fishing as master in his own boat.

One day, as he was walking with a halibut harpoon in one
hand, thinking about this, he suddenly came upon a huge
seal, sunning itself in the lee of a rock near the shore, and
apparently quite as much taken by surprise as he was.

Elias meanwhile was not slow. From the rocky ledge, on
which he was standing, he plunged the long, heavy harpoon
into its back just behind the neck. But then – oh, what a

*'The Parson at Alstadhaug' was Peder Dass, author of
Norlands Trompet, a long poem descriptive of northern Norway.
He died in 1707.

struggle! Instantly the seal reared itself up, stood erect on its tail, tall as the mast of a boat, and glowered at him with a pair of bloodshot eyes, at the same time showing its teeth in a grin so fiendish and venomous that Elias almost lost his wits from fright. Then suddenly it plunged into the sea and vanished in a spray of mingled blood and water.

That was the last Elias saw of it; but that very afternoon the harpoon, broken just below the iron barb, came drifting ashore near the boat landing not far from his house.

Elias had soon forgotten all about it. He bought his sixern that same autumn, and housed it in a little boat shed he had built during the summer.

One night, as he lay thinking about his new sixern, it occurred to him that perhaps, in order to safeguard it properly, he ought to put another shore on either side underneath it. He was so absurdly fond of the boat that he thought it only fun to get up and light his lantern and go down to look it over.

As he held up his lantern to see better, he suddenly glimpsed, on a tangle of nets in one corner, a face that resembled exactly the features of the seal. It grimaced for a moment angrily towards him and the light. Its mouth seemed to open wider and wider, and before he was aware of anything further, he saw a bulky man-form vanish out the door of the boat house, not so fast however but that he managed to make out, with the aid of his lantern, a long iron prong projecting from its back.

Elias now began to put two and two together. But even so he was more concerned for the safety of his boat than he was for his own life.

On the morning, early in January, when he set out for the fishing banks, with two men in the boat beside himself, he heard a voice call to him in the darkness from a skerry directly opposite the mouth of the cove. He thought that it laughed derisively.

'Better beware, Elias, when you get your femböring!'*

Femböring, the famous Nordland fishing-boat whose form has been perfected by centuries of experimenting.

It was a long time, however, before Elias saw his way clear to get a femböring – not until his eldest son was seventeen years old.

It was in the fall of the year that Elias embarked with his whole family and went to Ranen to trade in his sixern for a femböring. At home they left only a little Lapp girl, but newly confirmed, whom they had taken into their home some years before. There was one femböring in particular which he had his eye on, a little four man boat, which the best shipwright thereabout had finished and tarred that very fall. For this boat he traded in his own sixern, paying the difference in coin.

Elias thereupon began to think of sailing home. He first stopped at the village store and laid in a supply for Christmas for himself and his family, among other things a little keg of brandy. It may be that, pleased as they were with the day's bargaining, both he and his wife had one drop too many before they left, and Bernt, their son, was given a taste too.

Whereupon they set sail for home in the new femböring. Other ballast than himself, his wife and children, and his Christmas supplies he had none. His son Bernt sat at the stem; his wife, with the assistance of the second son, managed the halyard; Elias himself sat at the tiller, while the two younger sons, twelve and fourteen respectively, were to alternate at the bailing.

They had fifty odd miles of sea before them, and they had no sooner reached the open than it was apparent that the femböring would be put to the test the very first time it was in use. A storm blew up before long, and soon white-crested waves began dashing themselves into spray. Then Elias saw what kind of a boat he had. It rode the waves like a sea gull, without so much as taking in one single drop, and he was ready to swear that he would not even have to single-reef, as any ordinary femböring would have been compelled to do in such weather.

As the day drew on, he noticed not far away another femböring, completely manned, speeding along, just as he was then, with four reefs in the sail. It seemed to follow the same course, and he thought it strange that he had not noticed it before. It seemed to want to race with him, and

when Elias realized this, he could not resist letting out a reef
again.

So they raced along at a terrific speed past headlands and
islands and skerries. To Elias it seemed that he had never
before sailed so gloriously, and the femböring proved to be
every whit that had been claimed – the best boat in Ranen.

Meanwhile the sea had risen, and already several huge
waves had rolled over them, breaking against the stem up
forward, where Bernt sat, and sweeping out to leeward near
the stern.

Ever since dusk had settled over the sea, the other boat had
kept very close to them, and they were now so near each other
that they could have thrown a bailing-dipper, one to the
other, had they wished. And so they sailed on, side by side,
all the evening, in an ever-increasing sea.

That last reef, Elias began to think, ought really to be
taken in again, but he was loath to give up the race, and made
up his mind to wait as long as possible, until the other boat
saw fit to reef in, for it was quite as hard pressed as he. And
since they now had to fight both the cold and the wet, the
brandy bottle was now and then brought forth and passed
around.

The phosphorescent light, which played on the dark sea
near his own boat, flashed eerily in the white crests around
the stranger, which appeared to be plowing a furrow of light
and throwing a fiery foam to either side. In the reflection of
this light he could even distinguish the rope ends in the other
boat. He could also make out the crew on board in their
oilskin caps, but inasmuch as they were on the leeward side
of him, they kept their backs turned and were almost hid
behind the lofty gunwale, as it rose with the seas.

Of a sudden a gigantic breaker, whose white crest Elias
had for some time seen in the darkness, crashed against the
prow of the boat, where Bernt sat. For a moment the whole
femböring seemed to come to a stop, the timbers creaked and
jarred under the strain, and then the boat, which for half a
second had balanced uncertainly, righted itself and sped
forward, while the wave rolled out again to leeward.

All the while this was happening Elias thought he heard
fiendish cries issuing from the other boat.

But when it was over, his wife, who sat at the halyard, cried out in a voice that cut him to the very soul, 'My God, Elias, that sea took Marthe and Nils!'

These were their two youngest children, the former nine, the latter seven years old, who had been sitting forward close to Bernt.

'Hold fast to the halyard, Karen, or you may lose more!' was all that Elias answered.

It was necessary now to take in the fourth reef, and Elias had no sooner done so than he thought it advisable to reef in the fifth, for the sea was steadily rising. On the other hand, if he hoped to sail his boat clear of the ever mounting waves, he dared not lessen his sail more than was absolutely necessary.

It turned out, however, to be difficult going even with the sail thus diminished. The sea raged furiously, and deluged them with spray after spray. Finally Bernt and Anton, the next oldest, who had helped his mother at the halyard, had to take hold of the yardarm, something one resorts to only when a boat is hard pressed even with the last reef in – in this case the fifth.

The rival boat, which in the meantime had disappeared from sight, bobbed up alongside them again with exactly the same amount of sail that he was carrying.

Elias now began rather to dislike the crew over there. The two men who stood holding the yardarm, and whose faces he could glimpse underneath their oilskin caps, appeared to him in the weird reflections from the spray more like spectres than human beings. They spoke ne'er a word.

A little to leeward he spied the foaming ridge of another breaker rising before him in the dark, and he prepared himself to meet it. He turned the prow slantwise towards it, and let out as much sail as he dared, to give the boat speed enough to cleave its way through.

The sea struck them with the roar of a torrent. For a moment the boat again careened uncertainly. When it was all over, and the vessel had righted itself once more, his wife no longer sat at the halyard, nor was Anton at the yardarm – they had both been washed asea.

This time, too, he thought he made out the same fiendish voices above the storm, but mingled with them he also heard his wife's agonizing cries as she called him by name. When he realized that she had been swept overboard, he muttered to himself, 'In Jesus's name!' and said no more.

He felt vaguely that he would have preferred to follow her, but he realized at the same time that it was up to him to save the other three he had on board, Bernt and the two younger sons, the one twelve, the other fourteen, who for a while had been doing the bailing, but whom he had later placed in the stern behind him.

Bernt was now left to manage the yardarm alone, and the two, father and son, had to help each other as best they could. The tiller Elias did not dare let go; he held on to it with a hand of iron, long since numb from the strain.

After a while the companion boat bobbed up again; as before it had been momentarily lost to view. He now saw more clearly than before the bulky form that sat aft, much as he was sitting, and controlled the tiller. Projecting from his neck whenever he turned his back, just below the oilskin cap, Elias could clearly discern some four inches or so of an iron prong, which he had seen before.

At that he was convinced in his innermost soul of two things: one was that it was none other than the Draug* himself who sat steering his half-boat alongside his and who had lured him on to destruction, and the other was that he was fated no doubt this night to sail the sea for the last time. For he who sees the Draug at sea is a marked man. He said nothing to the others, in order not to discourage them, but he commended his soul in silence to the Lord.

He had found it necessary, during the last hours, to bear away from his course because of the storm, and when furthermore it took to snowing heavily, he realized that he would no doubt have to postpone any attempt to land until dawn.

Meanwhile they sailed on as before.

Now and again the boys aft complained of freezing, but there was nothing to do about that, wet as they were, and

---

*The Draug is a sea monster who sails a half-boat with a crew of men lost at sea who have not received Christian burial. He who sees the Draug, according to Nordland superstition, will soon die.

furthermore Elias sat preoccupied with his own thoughts.

He had been seized with an insatiable desire to avenge himself. What he would have liked to do, had he not had the lives of his three remaining children to safeguard, was suddenly to veer about in an attempt to ram and sink the cursed boat, which still as if to mock him ran ever alongside him, and whose fiendish purpose he now fully comprehended. If the halibut harpoon had once taken effect, why might not now a knife or a gaff do likewise? He felt he would willingly give his life to deal one good blow to this monster, who had so unmercifully robbed him of all that was dearest to him on earth, and who still seemed insatiate and demanded more.

About three or four o'clock in the morning they again spied rolling towards them in the darkness the white crest of a wave, so huge that Elias for a moment surely thought they were just off shore somewhere in the neighbourhood of breakers. It was not long, however, before he understood that it really was only a colossal wave.

Then he thought he clearly heard someone laugh and cry out in the other boat.

'There goes your femböring, Elias!'

Elias, who foresaw the catastrophe, repeated loudly, 'In Jesus's name!' commanded his sons to hold fast, and told them if the boat went down to grasp the osier band in the oarlocks, and not to let go till it had come afloat again. He let the elder of the two boys go forward to Bernt; the younger he kept close to himself, caressing his cheeks furtively once or twice, and assuring himself that the child had a tight hold.

The boat was literally buried beneath the towering comber, and was then pitched up on end, its stem high above the wave, before it finally went under. When it came afloat again, its keel now in the air, Elias, Bernt, and the twelve-year-old Martin appeared too, still clinging to the osier bands. But the third of the brothers had disappeared.

It was a matter of life and death now, first of all, to get the rigging cut away on one side, that they might be rid of the mast, which would otherwise rock the boat from beneath, and then to crawl up onto the hull and let the imprisoned air out, which would otherwise have kept the boat too high afloat and prevented it riding the waves safely. After considerable difficulty they succeeded in so doing, and Elias, who had been the first to clamber up, assisted the other two to safety.

Thus they sat the long winter night through, desperately clinging with cramped hands and numb knees to the hull, as one wave after another swept over them.

After a few hours, Martin, whom the father had supported all this time as best he could, died of exhaustion and slipped into the sea.

They had several times attempted to call for help, but realizing that it was of no avail, they finally gave it up.

As the two, thus left alone, sat on the hull of the boat, Elias told Bernt he knew that he himself was fated soon to 'follow mother', but he had a firm hope that Bernt would be saved in the end, if only he stuck it out like a man. And then he told him all about the Draug – how he had wounded him in the neck with the halibut harpoon, and how the Draug was now taking his revenge and would surely not give in until they were quits.

It was towards nine o'clock in the morning before the day finally began to dawn. Elias then handed over to Bernt, who sat at his side, his silver watch with the brass chain, which he had broken in pulling it out from underneath his close-buttoned vests.

He still sat on a while longer, but as it grew lighter, Bernt saw that his father's face was ghastly pale. The hair on his head had parted in several places, as it often does just before death, and the skin on his hands was worn off from his efforts to hang on to the keel. Bernt realized that his father was near the end. He tried, as well as the pitching of the boat permitted, to edge over to him and support him. But when Elias noticed it, he waved him back.

'You stay where you are, Bernt, and hold fast! I'm going to mother! In Jesus's name!'

And so saying he threw himself backward down from the hull.

When the sea had got its own, it quieted down for a while, as everyone knows who has straddled a hull. It became easier for Bernt to maintain his hold, and with the coming of daylight new hope kindled in him. The storm moderated, and in the full light of day he thought he recognized his surroundings — that he was, in fact, drifting directly off shore from his own home, Kvalholmen.

He began crying for help again, but he really had greater faith in a tide he knew bore landward, just beyond a projection of the island, which checked the fury of the sea.

He drifted nearer and nearer shore, and finally came so close to one of the skerries that the mast, which still floated alongside the boat, grated on the rocks with the rising and falling of the surf. Stiff as his muscles and joints were from his sitting so long and holding fast to the hull, he managed with a great effort to transfer himself to the skerry, after which he hauled in the mast and finally moored the femböring.

The little Lapp girl, who was home alone, for two whole hours thought she heard cries for help, and when they persisted she mounted the hilltop to look out to sea. There she saw Bernt on the skerry, and the upturned femböring beating up and down against it. She ran instantly down to the boat house, pushed out the old rowboat, and rowed it out to the skerry, hugging the shore round the island.

Bernt lay ill, under her care, the whole winter long, and did not take part in the fishing that year. People used to say that ever after he seemed now and again a little queer. To sea he would never go again; he had come to fear it.

He married the Lapp girl, and moved up to Malingen, where he broke new ground and cleared himself a home. There he is still living and doing well.

A. M. BURRAGE

Playmates

Although everybody who knew Stephen Everton agreed that
he was the last man under Heaven who ought to have been
allowed to bring up a child, it was fortunate for Monica that
she fell into his hands; else she had probably starved or
drifted into some refuge for waifs and strays. True her
father, Sebastian Threlfall the poet, had plenty of casual
friends. Almost everybody knew him slightly, and right up
to the time of his fatal attack of *delirium tremens* he contrived
to look one of the most interesting of the regular frequenters
of the Café Royal. But people are generally not hasty to bring
up the children of casual acquaintances, particularly when
such children may be suspected of having inherited more
than a fair share of human weaknesses.

Of Monica's mother literally nothing was known. Nobody
seemed able to say if she were dead or alive. Probably she had
long since deserted Threlfall for some consort able and
willing to provide regular meals.

Everton knew Threlfall no better than a hundred others
knew him, and was ignorant of his daughter's existence until
the father's death was a new topic of conversation in literary
and artistic circles. People vaguely wondered what would
become of 'the kid', and while they were still wondering,
Everton quietly took possession of her.

Who's Who will tell you the year of Everton's birth, the
names of his *Almae Matres* (Winchester and Magdalen
College, Oxford), the titles of his books and of his

predilections for skating and mountaineering; but it is necessary to know the man a little less superficially. He was then a year or two short of fifty and looked ten years older. He was a tall, lean man, with a delicate pink complexion, an oval head, a Roman nose, blue eyes which looked out mildly through strong glasses, and thin straight lips drawn tightly over slightly protruding teeth. His high forehead was bare, for he was bald to the base of his skull. What remained of his hair was a neutral tint between black and grey, and was kept closely cropped. He contrived to look at once prim and irascible, scholarly and acute; Sherlock Holmes, perhaps, with a touch of old-maidishness.

The world knew him for a writer of books on historical crises. They were cumbersome books with cumbersome titles, written by a scholar for scholars. They brought him fame and not a little money. The money he could have afforded to be without, since he was modestly wealthy by inheritance. He was essentially a cold-blooded animal, a bachelor, a man of regular and temperate habits, fastidious, and fond of quietude and simple comforts.

Nobody is ever likely to know why Everton adopted the orphan daughter of a man whom he knew but slightly and neither liked nor respected. He was no lover of children, and his humours were sardonic rather than sentimental. I am only hazarding a guess when I suggest that, like so many childless men, he had theories of his own concerning the upbringing of children, which he wanted to see tested. Certain it is that Monica's childhood, which had been extraordinary enough before, passed from the tragic to the grotesque.

Everton took Monica from the Bloomsbury 'apartments' house, where the landlady, already nursing a bad debt, was wondering how to dispose of the child. Monica was then eight years old, and a woman of the world in her small way. She had lived with drink and poverty and squalor; had never played a game nor had a playmate; had seen nothing but the seamy side of life; and had learned skill in practising her father's petty shifts and mean contrivances. She was grave and sullen and plain and pale, this child who had never known childhood. When she spoke, which was as seldom as possible, her voice was hard and gruff. She was, poor little thing, as unattractive as her life could have made her.

She went with Everton without question or demur. She would no more have questioned anybody's ownership than if she had been an inanimate piece of luggage left in a cloak-room. She had belonged to her father. Now that he was gone to his own place she was the property of whomsoever chose to claim her. Everton took her with a cold kindness in which was neither love nor pity; in return she gave him neither love nor gratitude, but did as she was desired after the manner of a paid servant.

Everton disliked modern children, and for what he disliked in them he blamed modern schools. It may have been on this account that he did not send Monica to one; or perhaps he wanted to see how a child would contrive its own education. Monica could already read and write and, thus equipped, she had the run of his large library, in which was almost every conceivable kind of book from heavy tomes on abstruse subjects to trashy modern novels bought and left there by Miss Gribbin. Everton barred nothing, recommended nothing, but watched the tree grow naturally, untended and unpruned.

Miss Gribbin was Everton's secretary. She was the kind of hatchet-faced, flat-chested, middle-aged sexless woman who could safely share the home of a bachelor without either of them being troubled by the tongue of Scandal. To her duties was now added the instruction of Monica in certain elementary subjects. Thus Monica learned that a man named William the Conqueror arrived in England in 1066; but to find out what manner of man this William was, she had to go to the library and read the conflicting accounts of him given by the several historians. From Miss Gribbin she learned bare irrefutable facts; for the rest she was left to fend for herself. In the library she found herself surrounded by all the realms of reality and fancy, each with its door invitingly ajar.

Monica was fond of reading. It was, indeed, almost her only recreation, for Everton knew no other children of her age, and treated her as a grown-up member of the household. Thus she read everything from translations of the *Iliad* to Hans Andersen, from the Bible to the love-gush of the modern female fictionmongers.

Everton, although he watched her closely, and plied her with innocent-sounding questions, was never allowed a peep into her mind. What muddled dreams she may have had of a strange world surrounding the Hampstead house – a world of gods and fairies and demons, and strong silent men making love to sloppyminded young women – she kept to herself. Reticence was all that she had in common with normal childhood, and Everton noticed that she never played.

Unlike most young animals, she did not take naturally to playing. Perhaps the instinct had been beaten out of her by the realities of life while her father was alive. Most lonely children improvise their own games and provide themselves with a vast store of make-believe. But Monica, as sullen-seeming as a caged animal, devoid alike of the naughtiness and the charms of childhood, rarely crying and still more rarely laughing, moved about the house sedate to the verge of being wooden. Occasionally Everton, the experimentalist, had twinges of conscience and grew half afraid . . .

When Monica was twelve Everton moved his establishment from Hampstead to a house remotely situated in the middle of Suffolk, which was part of a recent legacy. It was a tall, rectangular, Queen Anne house standing on a knoll above marshy fields and wind-bowed beech woods. Once it had been the manor house, but now little land went with it. A short drive passed between rank evergreens from the heavy wrought-iron gate to a circle of grass and flower beds in front of the house. Behind was an acre and a half of rank garden, given over to weeds and marigolds. The rooms were high and well lighted, but the house wore an air of depression as if it were a live thing unable to shake off some ancient fit of melancholy.

Everton went to live in the house for a variety of reasons. For the most part of a year he had been trying in vain to let or sell it, and it was when he found that he would have no difficulty in disposing of his house at Hampstead that he made up his mind. The old house, a mile distant from a remote Suffolk village, would give him all the solitude he required. Moreover he was anxious about his health – his nervous system had never been strong – and his doctor had recommended the bracing air of East Anglia.

He was not in the least concerned to find that the house was too big for him. His furniture filled the same number of rooms as it had filled at Hampstead, and the others he left empty. Nor did he increase his staff of three indoor servants and gardener. Miss Gribbin, now less dispensable than ever, accompanied him; and with them came Monica to see another aspect of life, with the same wooden stoicism which Everton had remarked in her upon the occasion of their first meeting.

As regarded Monica, Miss Gribbin's duties were then becoming more and more of a sinecure. 'Lessons' now occupied no more than half an hour a day. The older Monica grew, the better she was able to grub for her education in the great library. Between Monica and Miss Gribbin there was neither love nor sympathy, nor was there any affectation of either. In their common duty to Everton they owed and paid certain duties to each other. Their intercourse began and ended there.

Everton and Miss Gribbin both liked the house at first. It suited the two temperaments which were alike in their lack of festivity. Asked if she too liked it, Monica said simply 'Yes,' in a tone which implied stolid and complete indifference.

All three in their several ways led much the same lives as they had led at Hampstead. But a slow change began to work in Monica, a change so slight and subtle that weeks passed before Everton or Miss Gribbin noticed it. It was late on an afternoon in early spring when Everton first became aware of something unusual in Monica's demeanor.

He had been searching in the library for one of his own books – *The Fall of the Commonwealth of England* – and having failed to find it went in search of Miss Gribbin and met Monica instead at the foot of the long oak staircase. Of her he casually inquired about the book, and she jerked up her head brightly, to answer him with an unwonted smile:

'Yes, I've been reading it. I expect I left it in the schoolroom. I'll go and see.'

It was a long speech for her to have uttered, but Everton

scarcely noticed that at the time. His attention was directed elsewhere.

'*Where* did you leave it?' he demanded.

'In the schoolroom,' she repeated.

'I know of no schoolroom,' said Everton coldly. He hated to hear anything mis-called, even were it only a room. 'Miss Gribbin generally takes you for your lessons in either the library or the dining-room. If it is one of those rooms, kindly call it by its proper name.'

Monica shook her head.

'No, I mean the schoolroom – the big empty room next to the library. That's what it's called.'

Everton knew the room. It faced north, and seemed darker and more dismal than any other room in the house. He had wondered idly why Monica chose to spend so much of her time in a room bare of furniture, with nothing better to sit on than uncovered boards or a cushionless window-seat; and put it down to her genius for being unlike anybody else.

'Who calls it that?' he demanded.

'*It's* its name,' said Monica smiling.

She ran upstairs, and presently returned with the book, which she handed to him with another smile. He was already wondering at her. It was surprising and pleasant to see her run, instead of the heavy and clumsy walk which generally moved her when she went to obey a behest. And she had smiled two or three times in the short space of a minute. Then he realized that for some little while she had been a brighter, happier creature than she had ever been at Hampstead.

'How did you come to call that room the schoolroom?' he asked, as he took the book from her hand.

'It *is* the schoolroom,' she insisted, seeking to cover her evasion by laying stress on the verb.

That was all he could get out of her. As he questioned further the smiles ceased and the pale, plain little face became devoid of any expression. He knew then that it was useless to press her, but his curiosity was aroused. He inquired of Miss Gribbin and the servant, and learned that nobody was in the habit of calling the long, empty apartment the schoolroom.

Clearly Monica had given it its name. But why? She was so altogether remote from school and schoolrooms. Some germ of imagination was active in her small mind. Everton's interest was stimulated. He was like a doctor who remarks in a patient some abnormal symptom.

'Monica seems a lot brighter and more alert than she used to be,' he remarked to Miss Gribbin.

'Yes,' agreed the secretary. 'I have noticed that. She is learning to play.'

'To play what? The piano?'

'No, no. To play childish games. Haven't you heard her dancing about and singing?'

Everton shook his head and looked interested.

'I have not,' he said. 'Possibly my presence acts as a check upon her – er – exuberance.'

'I hear her in that empty room which she insists upon calling the schoolroom. She stops when she hears my step. Of course, I have not interfered with her in any way, but I could wish that she would not talk to herself. I don't like people who do that. It is somehow – uncomfortable.'

'I didn't know she did,' said Everton slowly.

'Oh, yes, quite long conversations. I haven't actually heard what she talks about, but sometimes you would think she was in the midst of a circle of friends.'

'In that same room?'

'Generally,' said Miss Gribbin, with a nod.

Everton regarded his secretary with a slow, thoughtful smile.

'Development,' he said, 'is always extremely interesting. I am glad the place seems to suit Monica. I think it suits all of us.'

There was a doubtful note in his voice as he uttered the last words, and Miss Gribbin agreed with him with the same lack of conviction in her tone. As a fact, Everton had been doubtful of late if his health had been benefited by the move from Hampstead. For the first week or two his nerves had been the better for the change of air; but now he was conscious of the beginning of a relapse. His imagination was beginning to play him tricks, filling his mind with vague, distorted fancies. Sometimes when he sat up late, writing –

he was given to working at night on strong coffee – he became a victim of the most distressing nervous symptoms, hard to analyse and impossible to combat, which invariably drove him to bed with a sense of defeat.

That same night he suffered one of the variations of this common experience.

It was close upon midnight when he felt stealing over him a sense of discomfort which he was compelled to classify as fear. He was working in a small room leading out of the drawing-room which he had selected for his study. At first he was scarcely aware of the sensation. The effect was always cumulative; the burden was laid upon him straw by straw.

It began with his being oppressed by the silence of the house. He became more and more acutely conscious of it, until it became like a thing tangible, a prison of solid walls growing around him.

The scratching of his pen at first relieved the tension. He wrote words and erased them again for the sake of that comfortable sound. But presently that comfort was denied him, for it seemed to him that this minute and busy noise was attracting attention to himself. Yes, that was it. He was being watched.

Everton sat quite still, the pen poised an inch above the half-covered sheet of paper. This was become a familiar sensation. He was being watched. And by what? And from what corner of the room?

He forced a tremulous smile to his lips. One moment he called himself ridiculous; the next, he asked himself hopelessly how a man could argue with his nerves. Experience had taught him that the only cure – and that a temporary one – was to go to bed. Yet he sat on, anxious to learn more about himself, to coax his vague imaginings into some definite shape.

Imagination told him that he was being watched, and although he called it imagination he was afraid. That rapid beating against his ribs was his heart, warning him of fear. But he sat rigid, anxious to learn in what part of the room his fancy would place these imaginary 'watchers' – for he was conscious of the gaze of more than one pair of eyes being bent upon him.

At first the experiment failed. The rigidity of his pose, the hold he was keeping upon himself, acted as a brake upon his mind. Presently he realized this and relaxed the tension, striving to give his mind that perfect freedom which might have been demanded by a hypnotist or one experimenting in telepathy.

Almost at once he thought of the door. The eyes of his mind veered round in that direction as the needle of a compass veers to the magnetic north. With these eyes of his imagination he saw the door. It was standing half open, and the aperture was thronged with faces. What kind of faces he could not tell. They were just faces; imagination left it at that. But he was aware that these spies were timid; that they were in some wise as fearful of him as he was of them; that to scatter them he had but to turn his head and gaze at them with the eyes of his body.

The door was at his shoulder. He turned his head suddenly and gave it one swift glance out of the tail of his eye.

However imagination deceived him, it had not played him false about the door. It was standing half open although he could have sworn that he had closed it on entering the room. The aperture was empty. Only darkness, solid as a pillar, filled the space between floor and lintel. But although he saw nothing as he turned his head, he was dimly conscious of something vanishing, a scurrying noiseless and incredibly swift, like the flitting of trout in clear, shallow water.

Everton stood up, stretched himself, and brought his knuckles up to his strained eyes. He told himself that he must go to bed. It was bad enough that he must suffer these nervous attacks; to encourage them was madness.

But as he mounted the stairs he was still conscious of not being alone. Shy, timorous, ready to melt into the shadows of the walls if he turned his head, *they* were following him, whispering noiselessly, linking hands and arms, watching him with the fearful, awed curiosity of – Children.

The Vicar had called upon Everton. His name was Parslow, and he was a typical country parson of the poorer sort, a tall, rugged, shabby, worried man in the middle forties, obviously embarrassed by the eternal problem of making ends meet on an inadequate stipend.

Everton received him courteously enough, but with a certain coldness which implied that he had nothing in common with his visitor. Parslow was evidently disappointed because 'the new people' were not church-goers nor likely to take much interest in the parish. The two men made half-hearted and vain attempts to find common ground. It was not until he was on the point of leaving that the Vicar mentioned Monica.

'You have, I believe, a little girl?' he said.

'Yes. My small ward.'

'Ah! I expect she finds it lonely here. I have a little girl of the same age. She is at present away at school, but she will be home soon for the Easter holidays. I know she would be delighted if your little – er – ward would come down to the Vicarage and play with her sometimes.'

The suggestion was not particularly welcome to Everton, and his thanks were perfunctory. This other small girl, although she was a vicar's daughter, might carry the contagion of other modern children and infect Monica with the pertness and slanginess which he so detested. Altogether he was determined to have as little to do with the Vicarage as possible.

Meanwhile the child was becoming to him a study of more and more absorbing interest. The change in her was almost as marked as if she had just returned after having spent a term at school. She astonished and mystified him by using expressions which she could scarcely have learned from any member of the household. It was not the jargon of the smart young people of the day which slipped easily from her lips, but the polite family slang of his own youth. For instance, she remarked one morning that Mead, the gardener, was a whale at pruning vines.

A whale! The expression took Everton back a very long way down the level road of the spent years; took him, indeed, to a nursery in a solid respectable house in a Belgravian square, where he had heard the word used in that same sense for the first time. His sister Gertrude, aged ten, notorious in those days for picking up loose expressions, announced that she was getting to be a whale at French. Yes, in those days an expert was 'whale' or a 'don', not, as he is today, a 'stout fellow'. But who was a 'whale' nowadays? It was years since he had heard the term.

'Where did you learn to say that?' he demanded in so strange a tone that Monica stared at him anxiously.

'Isn't it right?' she asked eagerly. She might have been a child at a new school, fearful of not having acquired the fashionable phraseology of the place.

'It is a slang expression,' said the purist coldly. 'It used to mean a person who was proficient in something. How did you come to hear it?'

She smiled without answering, and her smile was mysterious, even coquettish after a childish fashion. Silence had always been her refuge, but it was no longer a sullen silence. She was changing rapidly, and in a manner to bewilder her guardian. He failed in an effort to cross-examine her, and, later in the day, consulted Miss Gribbin.

'That child,' he said, 'is reading something that we know nothing about.'

'Just at present,' said Miss Gribbin, 'she is glued to Dickens and Stevenson.'

'Then where on earth does she get her expressions?'

'I don't know,' the secretary retorted testily, 'any more than I know how she learned to play Cat's Cradle.'

'What? That game with string? Does she play that?'

'I found her doing something quite complicated and elaborate the other day. She wouldn't tell me how she learned to do it. I took the trouble to question the servants, but none of them had shown her.'

Everton frowned.

'And I know of no book in the library which tells how to perform tricks with string. Do you think she has made a clandestine friendship with any of the village children?'

Miss Gribbin shook her head.

'She is too fastidious for that. Besides, she seldom goes into the village alone.'

There, for the time, the discussion ended. Everton, with all the curiosity of the student, watched the child as carefully and closely as he was able without at the same time arousing her suspicions. She was developing fast. He had known that she must develop, but the manner of her doing so amazed and mystified him, and, likely as not, denied some preconceived theory. The untended plant was not only growing but showed signs of pruning. It was as if there were outside influences at work on Monica which could have come neither from him nor from any other member of the household.

Winter was dying hard, and dark days of rain kept Miss Gribbin, Monica and Everton within doors. He lacked no opportunities of keeping the child under observation, and once, on a gloomy afternoon, passing the room which she had named the schoolroom, he paused and listened until he became suddenly aware that his conduct bore an unpleasant resemblance to eavesdropping. The psychologist and the gentleman engaged in a brief struggle in which the gentleman temporarily got the upper hand. Everton approached the door with a heavy step and flung it open.

The sensation he received, as he pushed open the door, was vague but slightly disturbing, and it was by no means new to him. Several times of late, but generally after dark, he had entered an empty room with the impression that it had been occupied by others until the very moment of his crossing the threshold. His coming disturbed not merely one or two, but a crowd. He felt rather than heard them scattering, flying swiftly and silently as shadows to incredible hiding-places, where they held breath and watched and waited for him to go. Into the same atmosphere of tension he now walked, and looked about him as if expecting to see more than only the child who held the floor in the middle of the room, or some tell-tale trace of other children in hiding. Had the room been furnished he must have looked involuntarily for shoes protruding from under tables or settees, for ends of garments unconsciously left exposed.

The long room, however, was empty save for Monica from wainscot to wainscot and from floor to ceiling. Fronting him were the long high windows starred by fine rain. With her back to the white filtered light Monica faced him, looking up to him as he entered. He was just in time to see a smile fading from her lips. He also saw by a slight convulsive movement of her shoulders that she was hiding something from him in the hands clasped behind her back.

'Hullo,' he said, with a kind of forced geniality, 'what are you up to?'

She said: 'Nothing,' but not as sullenly as she would once have said it.

'Come,' said Everton, 'that is impossible. You were talking to yourself, Monica. You should not do that. It is an idle and very, very foolish habit. You will go mad if you continue to do that.'

She let her head droop a little.

'I wasn't talking to myself,' she said in a low, half playful but very deliberate tone.

'That's nonsense. I heard you.'

'I wasn't talking to myself.'

'But you must have been. There is nobody else here.'

'There isn't – now.'

'What do you mean? Now?'

'They've gone. You frightened them, I expect.'

'What do you mean?' he repeated, advancing a step or two towards her. 'And whom do you call "they"?'

Next moment he was angry with himself. His tone was so heavy and serious and the child was half laughing at him. It was as if she were triumphant at having inveigled him into taking a serious part in her own game of make-believe.

'You wouldn't understand,' she said.

'I understand this – that you are wasting your time and being a very silly little girl. What's that you're hiding behind your back?'

She held out her right hand at once, unclenched her fingers and disclosed a thimble. He looked at it and then into her face.

'Why did you hide that from me?' he asked. 'There was no need.'

She gave him a faint secretive smile – that new smile of hers – before replying.

'We were playing with it. I didn't want you to know.'

'*You* were playing with it, you mean. And why didn't you want me to know?'

'About them. Because I thought you wouldn't under-stand. You *don't* understand.'

He saw that it was useless to affect anger or show impatience. He spoke to her gently, even with an attempt at displaying sympathy.

'Who are "they"?' he asked.

'They're just them. Other girls.'

'I see. And they come and play with you, do they? And they run away whenever I'm about, because they don't like me. Is that it?'

She shook her head.

'It isn't that they don't like you. I think they like everybody. But they're so shy. They were shy of me for a long, long time. I knew they were there, but it was weeks and weeks before they'd come and play with me. It was weeks before I even saw them.'

'Yes? Well, what are they like?'

'Oh, they're just girls. And they're awfully, awfully nice. Some are a bit older than me and some are a bit younger. And they don't dress like other girls you see today. They're in white with longer skirts and they wear sashes.'

Everton inclined his head gravely. 'She got that out of the illustrations of books in the library,' he reflected.

'You don't happen to know their names, I suppose?' he asked, hoping that no quizzical note in his voice rang through the casual but sincere tone which he intended.

'Oh, yes. There's Mary Hewitt – I think I love her best of all – and Elsie Power and – '

'How many of them altogether?'

'Seven. It's just a nice number. And this is the schoolroom where we play games. I love games. I wish I'd learned to play games before.'

'And you've been playing with the thimble?'

'Yes. Hunt-the-thimble they call it. One of us hides it, and then the rest of us try to find it, and the one who finds it hides it again.'

'You mean you hide it yourself, and then go and find it.'

The smile left her face at once, and the look in her eyes warned him that she was done with confidences.

'Ah!' she exclaimed. 'You don't understand after all. I somehow knew you wouldn't.'

Everton, however, thought he did. His face wore a sudden

smile of relief.

'Well, never mind,' he said. 'But I shouldn't play too much if I were you.'

With that he left her. But curiosity tempted him, not in vain, to linger and listen for a moment on the other side of the door which he had closed behind him. He heard Monica whisper:

'Mary! Elsie! Come on. It's all right. He's gone now.'

At an answering whisper, very unlike Monica's, he started violently and then found himself grinning at his own discomfiture. It was natural that Monica, playing many parts, should try to change her voice with every character. He went downstairs sunk in a brown study which brought him to certain interesting conclusions. A little later he communicated these to Miss Gribbin.

'I've discovered the cause of the change in Monica. She's invented for herself some imaginary friends – other little girls, of course.'

Miss Gribbin started slightly and looked up from the newspaper which she had been reading.

'Really?' she exclaimed. 'Isn't that rather an unhealthy sign?'

'No, I should say not. Having imaginary friends is quite a common symptom of childhood, especially among young girls. I remember my sister used to have one, and was very angry when none of the rest of us would take the matter seriously. In Monica's case I should say it was perfectly normal – normal, but interesting. She must have inherited an imagination from that father of hers, with the result that she has seven imaginary friends, all properly named, if you please. You see, being lonely, and having no friends of her own age, she would naturally invent more than one "friend". They are all nicely and primly dressed, I must tell you, out of Victorian books which she has found in the library.'

'It can't be healthy,' said Miss Gribbin, pursing her lips. 'And I can't understand how she has learned certain expressions and a certain style of talking and games – '

'All out of books. And pretends to herself that "they" have taught her. But the most interesting part of the affair is this: it's given me my first practical experience of telepathy, of the existence of which I have hitherto been rather sceptical. Since Monica invented this new game, and before I was aware that she had done so, I have had at different times distinct impressions of there being a lot of little girls about the house.'

Miss Gribbin started and stared. Her lips parted as if she were about to speak, but it was as if she had changed her mind while framing the first word she had been about to utter.

'Monica,' he continued smiling, 'invented these "friends", and has been making me telepathically aware of them, too. I have lately been most concerned about the state of my nerves.'

Miss Gribbin jumped up as if in anger, but her brow was smooth and her mouth dropped at the corners.

'Mr Everton,' she said, 'I wish you had not told me all this.' Her lips worked. 'You see,' she added unsteadily, 'I don't believe in telepathy.'

Easter, which fell early that year, brought little Gladys Parslow home for the holidays to the Vicarage. The event was shortly afterwards signalized by a note from the Vicar to Everton, inviting him to send Monica down to have tea and play games with his little daughter on the following Wednesday.

The invitation was an annoyance and an embarrassment to Everton. Here was the disturbing factor, the outside influence, which might possibly thwart his experiment in the upbringing of Monica. He was free, of course, simply to decline the invitation so coldly and briefly as to make sure that it would not be repeated; but the man was not strong enough to stand on his own feet impervious to the winds of criticism. He was sensitive and had little wish to seem churlish, still less to appear ridiculous. Taking the line of least resistance he began to reason that one child, herself no older than Monica, and in the atmosphere of her own home, could make but little impression. It ended in his allowing Monica to go.

Monica herself seemed pleased at the prospect of going but expressed her pleasure in a discreet, restrained, grown-up way. Miss Gribbin accompanied her as far as the Vicarage doorstep, arriving with her punctually at half past three on a sullen and muggy afternoon, and handed her over to the woman-of-all-work who answered the summons at the door.

Miss Gribbin reported to Everton on her return. An idea which she conceived to be humorous had possession of her mind, and in talking to Everton she uttered one of her infrequent laughs.

'I only left her at the door,' she said, 'so I didn't see her meet the other little girl. I wish I'd stayed to see that. It must have been funny.'

She irritated Everton by speaking exactly as if Monica were a captive animal which had just been shown, for the first time in its life, another of its own kind. The analogy thus conveyed to Everton was close enough to make him wince. He felt something like a twinge of conscience, and it may have been then that he asked himself for the first time if he were being fair to Monica.

It had never once occurred to him to ask himself if she were happy. The truth was that he understood children so little as to suppose that physical cruelty was the one kind of cruelty from which they were capable of suffering. Had he ever before troubled to ask himself if Monica were happy, he had probably given the question a curt dismissal with the thought that she had no right to be otherwise. He had given her a good home, even luxuries, together with every opportunity to develop her mind. For companions she had himself, Miss Gribbin, and, to a limited extent, the servants . . .

Ah, but that picture, conjured up by Miss Gribbin's words with their accompaniment of unreasonable laughter! The little creature meeting for the first time another little creature of its own kind and looking bewildered, knowing neither what to do nor what to say. There was pathos in that – uncomfortable pathos for Everton. Those imaginary friends – did they really mean that Monica had needs of which he knew nothing, of which he had never troubled to learn?

He was not an unkind man, and it hurt him to suspect that he might have committed an unkindness. The modern children whose behaviour and manners he disliked, were perhaps only obeying some inexorable law of evolution. Suppose in keeping Monica from their companionship he were actually flying in the face of Nature? Suppose, after all, if Monica were to be natural, she must go unhindered on the tide of her generation?

He compromised with himself, pacing the little study. He would watch Monica much more closely, question her when he had the chance. Then, if he found she was not happy, and really needed the companionship of other children, he would see what could be done.

But when Monica returned home from the Vicarage it was quite plain that she had not enjoyed herself. She was subdued, and said very little about her experience. Quite obviously the two little girls had not made very good friends. Questioned, Monica confessed that she did not like Gladys – much. She said this very thoughtfully with a little pause before the adverb.

'Why don't you like her?' Everton demanded bluntly.

'I don't know. She's so funny. Not like other girls.'

'And what do you know about other girls?' he demanded, faintly amused.

'Well, she's not a bit like – '

Monica paused suddenly and lowered her gaze.

'Not like your "friends", you mean?' Everton asked.

She gave him a quick, penetrating little glance and then lowered her gaze once more.

'No,' she said, 'not a bit.'

She wouldn't be, of course. Everton teased the child with no more questions for the time being, and let her go. She ran off at once to the great empty room, there to seek that uncanny companionship which had come to suffice her.

For the moment Everton was satisfied. Monica was perfectly happy as she was, and had no need of Gladys or, probably, any other child friends. His experiment with her was shaping successfully. She had invented her own young friends, and had gone off eagerly to play with the creations of her own fancy.

This seemed very well at first. Everton reflected that it was just what he would have wished, until he realized suddenly with a little shock of discomfort that it was not normal and it was not healthy.

Although Monica plainly had no great desire to see any more of Gladys Parslow, common civility made it necessary for the Vicar's little daughter to be asked to pay a return visit. Most likely Gladys Parslow was as unwilling to come as was Monica to entertain her. Stern discipline, however, presented her at the appointed time on an afternoon pre-arranged by correspondence, when Monica received her coldly and with dignity, tempered by a sort of grown-up graciousness.

Monica bore her guest away to the big empty room, and that was the last of Gladys Parslow seen by Everton or Miss Gribbin that afternoon. Monica appeared alone when the gong sounded for tea, and announced in a subdued tone that Gladys had already gone home.

'Did you quarrel with her?' Miss Gribbin asked quickly.

'No-o.'

'Then why has she gone like this?'

'She was stupid,' said Monica, simply. 'That's all.'

'Perhaps it was you who was stupid. Why did she go?'

'She got frightened.'

'Frightened!'

'She didn't like my friends.'

Miss Gribbin exchanged glances with Everton.

'She didn't like a silly little girl who talks to herself and imagines things. No wonder she was frightened.'

'She didn't think they were real at first, and laughed at me,' said Monica, sitting down.

'Naturally!'

'And then when she saw them – '

Miss Gribbin and Everton interrupted her simultaneously, repeating in unison and with well-matched astonishment, her two last words.

'And when she saw them,' Monica continued, unperturbed, 'she didn't like it. I think she was frightened. Anyhow, she said she wouldn't stay and went straight off home. I think she's a stupid girl. We all had a good laugh about her after she was gone.'

She spoke in her ordinary matter-of-fact tones, and if she were secretly pleased at the state of perturbation into which her last words had obviously thrown Miss Gribbin she gave no sign of it. Miss Gribbin immediately exhibited outward signs of anger.

'You are a very naughty child to tell such untruths. You know perfectly well that Gladys couldn't have *seen* your "friends". You have simply frightened her by pretending to talk to people who weren't there, and it will serve you right if she never comes to play with you again.'

'She won't,' said Monica. 'And she *did* see them, Miss Gribbin.'

'How do you know?' Everton asked.

'By her face. And she spoke to them too, when she ran to the door. They were very shy at first because Gladys was there. They wouldn't come for a long time, but I begged them, and at last they did.'

Everton checked another outburst from Miss Gribbin with a look. He wanted to learn more, and to that end he applied some show of patience and gentleness.

'Where did they come from?' he asked. 'From outside the door?'

'Oh, no. From where they always come.'

'And where's that?'

'I don't know. They don't seem to know themselves. It's always from some direction where I'm not looking. Isn't it strange?'

'Very! And do they disappear in the same way?'

Monica frowned very seriously and thoughtfully.

'It's so quick you can't tell where they go. When you or Miss Gribbin come in — '

'They always fly on our approach, of course. But why?'

'Because they're dreadfully, dreadfully shy. But not so shy as they were. Perhaps soon they'll get used to you and not mind at all.'

'That's a comforting thought!' said Everton with a dry laugh.

When Monica had taken her tea and departed, Everton turned to his secretary.

'You are wrong to blame the child. These creatures of her

fancy are perfectly real to her. Her powers of suggestion have been strong enough to force them to some extent on me. The little Parslow girl, being younger and more receptive, actually *sees* them. It is a clear case of telepathy and auto-suggestion. I have never studied such matters, but I should say that these instances are of some scientific interest.'

Miss Gribbin's lips tightened and he saw her shiver slightly.

'Mr Parslow will be angry,' was all she said.

'I really cannot help that. Perhaps it is all for the best. If Monica does not like his little daughter they had better not be brought together again.'

For all that, Everton was a little embarrassed when on the following morning he met the Vicar out walking. If the Rev. Parslow knew that his little daughter had left the house so unceremoniously on the preceding day, he would either wish to make an apology, or perhaps require one, according to his view of the situation. Everton did not wish to deal in apologies one way or the other, he did not care to discuss the vagaries of children, and altogether he wanted to have as little to do with Mr Parslow as was conveniently possible. He would have passed with a brief acknowledgment of the Vicar's existence, but, as he had feared, the Vicar stopped him.

'I had been meaning to come and see you,' said the Rev. Parslow.

Everton halted and sighed inaudibly, thinking that perhaps this casual meeting out of doors might after all have saved him something.

'Yes?' he said.

'I will walk in your direction if I may.' The Vicar eyed him anxiously. 'There is something you must certainly be told. I don't know if you guess, or if you already know. If not, I don't know how you will take it. I really don't.'

Everton looked puzzled. Whichever child the Vicar might blame for the hurried departure of Gladys, there seemed no cause for such a portentous face and manner.

'Really?' he asked. 'Is it something serious?'

'I think so, Mr Everton. You are aware, of course, that my little girl left your house yesterday afternoon with some lack of ceremony.'

'Yes, Monica told us she had gone. If they could not agree it was surely the best thing she could have done, although it may sound inhospitable of me to say it. Excuse me, Mr Parslow, but I hope you are not trying to embroil me in a quarrel between children?'

The Vicar stared in his turn.

'I am not,' he said, 'and I am unaware that there was any quarrel. I was going to ask you to forgive Gladys. There was some excuse for her lack of ceremony. She was badly frightened, poor child.'

'Then it is my turn to express regret. I had Monica's version of what happened. Monica has been left a great deal to her own resources, and, having no playmates of her own age, she seems to have invented some.'

'Ah!' said the Rev. Parslow, drawing a deep breath.

'Unfortunately,' Everton continued, 'Monica has an uncomfortable gift for impressing her fancies on other people. I have often thought I felt the presence of children about the house, and so, I am almost sure, has Miss Gribbin. I am afraid that when your little girl came to play with her yesterday afternoon, Monica scared her by introducing her invisible "friends" and by talking to imaginary and therefore invisible little girls.'

The Vicar laid a hand on Everton's arm.

'There is something more in it than that. Gladys is not an imaginative child; she is, indeed, a practical little person. I have never yet known her to tell me a lie. What would you say, Mr Everton, if I were to tell you that Gladys positively asserts that she *saw* those other children?'

Something like a cold draught went through Everton. An ugly suspicion, vague and almost shapeless, began to move in dim recesses of his mind. He tried to shake himself free of it, to smile and to speak lightly.

'I shouldn't be in the least surprised. Nobody knows the limits of telepathy and auto-suggestion. If I can feel the presence of children whom Monica has created out of her own imagination, why shouldn't your daughter, who is probably more receptive and impressionable than I am, be able to see them?'

The Rev. Parslow shook his head.

'Do you really mean that?' he asked. 'Doesn't it seem to you a little far-fetched?'

'Everything we don't understand must seem far-fetched. If one had dared to talk of wireless thirty years ago – '

'Mr Everton, do you know that your house was once a girl's school?'

Once more Everton experienced that vague feeling of discomfiture.

'I didn't know,' he said, still indifferently.

'My aunt, whom I never saw, was there. Indeed she died there. There were seven who died. Diphtheria broke out there many years ago. It ruined the school which was shortly afterwards closed. Did you know that, Mr Everton? My aunt's name was Mary Hewitt – '

'Good God!' Everton cried out sharply. 'Good God!'

'Ah!' said Parslow. 'Now do you begin to see?'

Everton, suddenly a little giddy, passed a hand across his forehead.

'That is – one of the names Monica told me,' he faltered. 'How could she know?'

'How indeed? Mary Hewitt's great friend was Elsie Power. They died within a few hours of each other.'

'That name too . . . she told me . . . and there were seven. How could she have known? Even the people around here wouldn't have remembered names after all these years.'

'Gladys knew them. But that was only partly why she was afraid. Yet I think she was more awed than afraid, because she knew instinctively that the children who came to play with little Monica, although they were not of this world, were good children, blessed children.'

'What are you telling me?' Everton burst out.

'Don't be afraid, Mr Everton. You are not afraid, are you? If those whom we call dead still remain close to us, what more natural than these children should come back to play with a lonely little girl who lacked human playmates? It may seem inconceivable, but how else explain it? How could little Monica have invented those two names? How could she have learned that seven little girls once died in your house? Only the very old people about here remember it, and even they could not tell you how many died or the name of any one of the little victims. Haven't you noticed a change in your ward since first she began to – imagine them, as you thought?'

Everton nodded heavily.

'Yes,' he said, almost unwittingly, 'she learned all sorts of tricks of speech, childish gestures she never had before, and games . . . I couldn't understand. Mr Parslow, what in God's name am I to do?'

The Rev. Parslow still kept a hand on Everton's arm.

'If I were you I should send her off to school. It may not be very good for her.'

'Not good for her! But the children, you say – '

'Children? I might have said angels. *They* will never harm her. But Monica is developing a gift of seeing and conversing with – with beings that are invisible and inaudible to others. It is not a gift to be encouraged. She may in time see and converse with others – wretched souls who are not God's children. She may lose the faculty if she mixes with others of her age. Out of her need, I am sure, these came to her.'

'I must think,' said Everton.

He walked on dazedly. In a moment or two the whole aspect of life had changed, had grown clearer, as if he had been blind from birth and was now given the first glimmerings of light. He looked forward no longer into the face of a blank and featureless wall, but through a curtain beyond which life manifested itself vaguely but at least perceptibly. His footfalls on the ground beat out the words: 'There is no death. There is no death.'

That evening after dinner he sent for Monica and spoke to her in an unaccustomed way. He was strangely shy of her, and his hand, which he rested on one of her slim shoulders, lay there awkwardly.

'Do you know what I'm going to do with you, young woman?' he said. 'I'm going to pack you off to school.'

'O-oh!' she stared at him, half smiling. 'Are you really?'

'Do you want to go?'

She considered the matter, frowning and staring at the tips of her fingers.

'I don't know. I don't want to leave *them*.'

'Who?' he asked.

'Oh, you know!' she said, and turned her head half shyly.

'What? Your – friends, Monica?'

'Yes.'

'Wouldn't you like other playmates?'

'I don't know. I love *them*, you see. But they said – they said I ought to go to school if you ever sent me. They might be angry with me if I was to ask you to let me stay. They wanted me to play with other girls who aren't – what aren't like they are. Because you know, they are *different* from children that everybody can see. And Mary told me not to – not to encourage anybody else who was different, like them.'

Everton drew a deep breath.

'We'll have a talk tomorrow about finding a school for you, Monica,' he said. 'Run off to bed, now. Good night, my dear.'

He hesitated, then touched her forehead with his lips. She ran from him, nearly as shy as Everton himself, tossing back her long hair, but from the door she gave him the strangest little brimming glance, and there was that in her eyes which he had never seen before.

Late that night Everton entered the great empty room which Monica had named the schoolroom. A flag of moonlight from the window lay across the floor, and it was empty to the gaze. But the deep shadows hid little shy presences of which some unnamed and undeveloped sense in the man was acutely aware.

'Children!' he whispered. 'Children!'

He closed his eyes and stretched out his hands. Still they were shy and held aloof, but he fancied that they came a little nearer.

'Don't be afraid,' he whispered. 'I'm only a very lonely man. Be near me after Monica is gone.'

He paused, waiting. Then as he turned away he was aware of little caressing hands upon his arm. He looked around at once, but the time had not yet come for him to see. He saw only the barred window, the shadows on either wall and the flag of moonlight.

ROBERT AICKMAN

Ringing the Changes

He had never been among those many who deeply dislike church bells, but the ringing that evening at Holihaven changed his view. Bells could certainly get on one's nerves, he felt, although he had only just arrived in the town.

He had been too well aware of the perils attendant upon marrying a girl twenty-four years younger than himself to add to them by a conventional honeymoon. The strange force of Phrynne's love had borne both of them away from their previous selves: in him a formerly haphazard and easy-going approach to life had been replaced by much deep planning to wall in happiness; and she, though once thought cold and choosy, would now agree to anything as long as she was with him. He had said that if they were to marry in June, it would be at the cost of not being able to honeymoon until October. Had they been courting longer, he had explained, gravely smiling, special arrangements could have been made; but, as it was, business claimed him. This, indeed, was true; because his business position was less influential than he had led Phrynne to believe. Finally, it would have been impossible for them to have courted longer, because they had courted from the day they met, which was less than six weeks before the day they married.

' "A village",' he had quoted as they entered the branch line train at the junction (itself sufficiently remote), ' "from which (it was said) persons of sufficient longevity might hope

to reach Liverpool Street." ' By now he was able to make
jokes about age, although perhaps he did so rather too often.

'Who said that?'

'Bertrand Russell.'

She had looked at him with her big eyes in her tiny face.

'Really.' He had smiled confirmation.

'I'm not arguing.' She had still been looking at him. The
romantic gas light in the charming period compartment had
left him uncertain whether she was smiling back or not. He
had given himself the benefit of the doubt, and kissed her.

The guard had blown his whistle and they rumbled into
the darkness. The branch line swung so sharply away from
the main line that Phrynne had been almost toppled from her
seat.

'Why do we go so slowly when it's so flat?'

'Because the engineer laid the line up and down the hills
and valleys such as they are, instead of cutting through and
embanking over them.' He liked being able to inform her.

'How do you know? Gerald! You said you hadn't been to
Holihaven before.'

'It applies to most of the railways in East Anglia.'

'So that even though it's flatter, it's slower?'

'Time matters less.'

'I should have hated going to a place where time mattered
or that you'd been to before. You'd have had nothing to
remember me by.'

He hadn't been quite sure that her words exactly expressed
her thought, but the thought had lightened his heart.

Holihaven station could hardly have been built in the days of
the town's magnificence, for they were in the Middle Ages;
but it still implied grander functions than came its way now.
The platforms were long enough for visiting London
expresses, which had since gone elsewhere; and the
architecture of the waiting rooms would have been not
insufficient for occasional use by Foreign Royalty. Oil lamps
on perches like those occupied by macaws, lighted the
uniformed staff, who numbered two, and, together with
every other native of Holihaven, looked like storm-
habituated mariners.

The station-master and porter, as Gerald took them to be, watched him approach down the platform, with a heavy suitcase in each hand and Phrynne walking deliciously by his side. He saw one of them address a remark to the other, but neither offered to help. Gerald had to put down the cases in order to give up their tickets. The other passengers had already disappeared.

'Where's the Bell?'

Gerald had found the hotel in a reference book. It was the only one the book allotted in Holihaven. But as Gerald spoke, and before the ticket collector could answer, the sudden deep note of an actual bell rang through the darkness. Phrynne caught hold of Gerald's sleeve.

Ignoring Gerald, the station-master, if such he was, turned to his colleague. 'They're starting early.'

'Every reason to be in good time,' said the other man.

The station-master nodded, and put Gerald's tickets indifferently in his jacket pocket.

'Can you please tell me how I get to the Bell Hotel?'

The station-master's attention returned to him. 'Have you a room booked?'

'Certainly.'

'Tonight?' The station-master looked inappropriately suspicious.

'Of course.'

Again the station-master looked at the other man.

'It's them Pascoes.'

'Yes,' said Gerald. 'That's the name. Pascoe.'

'We don't use the Bell,' explained the station-master. 'But you'll find it in Wrack Street.' He gesticulated vaguely and unhelpfully. 'Straight ahead. Down Station Road. Then down Wrack Street. You can't miss it.'

'Thank you.'

As soon as they entered the town, the big bell began to boom regularly.

'What narrow streets!' said Phrynne.

'They follow the lines of the mediaeval city. Before the river silted up, Holihaven was one of the most important seaports in Great Britain.'

'Where's everybody got to?'

Although it was only six o'clock, the place certainly seemed deserted.

'Where's the hotel got to?' rejoined Gerald.

'Poor Gerald! Let me help.' She laid her hand beside his on the handle of the suitcase nearest to her, but as she was about fifteen inches shorter than he, she could be of little assistance. They must already have gone more than a quarter of a mile. 'Do you think we're in the right street?'

'Most unlikely, I should say. But there's no one to ask.'

'Must be early closing day.'

The single deep notes of the bell were now coming more frequently.

'Why are they ringing that bell? Is it a funeral?'

'Bit late for a funeral.'

She looked at him a little anxiously.

'Anyway it's not cold.'

'Considering we're on the east coast it's quite astonishingly warm.'

'Not that I care.'

'I hope that bell isn't going to ring all night.'

She pulled on the suitcase. His arms were in any case almost parting from his body. 'Look! We've passed it.'

They stopped, and he looked back. 'How could we have done that?'

'Well, we have.'

She was right. He could see a big ornamental bell hanging from a bracket attached to a house about a hundred yards behind them.

They retraced their steps and entered the hotel. A woman dressed in a navy blue coat and skirt, with a good figure but dyed red hair and a face ridged with make-up, advanced upon them.

'Mr and Mrs Banstead? I'm Hilda Pascoe. Don, my husband, isn't very well.'

Gerald felt full of doubts. His arrangements were not going as they should. Never rely on guide book recommendations. The trouble lay partly in Phrynne's insistence that they go somewhere he did not know. 'I'm sorry to hear that,' he said.

'You know what men are like when they're ill?' Mrs Pascoe

spoke understandingly to Phrynne.

'Impossible,' said Phrynne. 'Or very difficult.'

'Talk about Woman in our hours of ease.'

'Yes,' said Phrynne. 'What's the trouble?'

'It's always the same trouble with Don,' said Mrs Pascoe, then checked herself. 'It's his stomach,' she said. 'Ever since he was a kid, Don's had trouble with the lining of his stomach.'

Gerald interrupted. 'I wonder if we could see our room?'

'So sorry,' said Mrs Pascoe. 'Will you register first?' She produced a battered volume bound in peeling imitation leather. 'Just the name and address.' She spoke as if Gerald might contribute a résumé of his life.

It was the first time he and Phrynne had ever registered in a hotel; but his confidence in the place was not increased by the long period which had passed since the registration above.

'We're always quiet in October,' remarked Mrs Pascoe, her eyes upon him. Gerald noticed that her eyes were slightly bloodshot. 'Except sometimes for the bars, of course.'

'We wanted to come out of the season,' said Phrynne soothingly.

'Quite,' said Mrs Pascoe.

'Are we alone in the house?' inquired Gerald. After all the woman was probably doing her best.

'Except for Commandant Shotcroft. You won't mind him, will you? He's a regular.'

'I'm sure we shan't,' said Phrynne.

'People say the house wouldn't be the same without Commandant Shotcroft.'

'I see.'

'What's that bell?' asked Gerald. Apart from anything else, it really was much too near.

Mrs Pascoe looked away. He thought she looked shifty under her entrenched make-up. But she only said, 'Practice.'

'Do you mean there will be more of them later?'

She nodded. 'But never mind,' she said encouragingly. 'Let me show you to your room. Sorry there's no porter.'

Before they had reached the bedroom, the whole peal had commenced.

'Is this the quietest room you have?' inquired Gerald. 'What about the other side of the house?'

'This *is* the other side of the house. Saint Guthlac's is over there.' She pointed out through the bedroom door.

'Darling,' said Phrynne, her hand on Gerald's arm, 'they'll soon stop. They're only practising.'

Mrs Pascoe said nothing. Her expression indicated that she was one of those people whose friendliness has a precise and seldom exceeded limit.

'If *you* don't mind,' said Gerald to Phrynne, hesitating.

'They have ways of their own in Holihaven,' said Mrs Pascoe. Her undertone of militancy implied, among other things, that if Gerald and Phrynne chose to leave, they were at liberty to do so. Gerald did not care for that either: her attitude would have been different, he felt, had there been anywhere else for them to go. The bells were making him touchy and irritable.

'It's a very pretty room,' said Phrynne. 'I adore four-posters.'

'Thank you,' said Gerald to Mrs Pascoe. 'What time's dinner?'

'Seven-thirty. You've time for a drink in the bar first.' She went.

'We certainly have,' said Gerald when the door was shut. 'It's only just six.'

'Actually,' said Phrynne, who was standing by the window looking down into the street, 'I *like* church bells.'

'All very well,' said Gerald, 'but on one's honeymoon they distract the attention.'

'Not mine,' said Phrynne simply. Then she added, 'There's still no one about.'

'I expect they're all in the bar.'

'I don't want a drink. I want to explore the town.'

'As you wish. But hadn't you better unpack?'

'I ought to, but I'm not going to. Not until after I've seen the sea.' Such small shows of independence in her enchanted Gerald.

Mrs Pascoe was not about when they passed through the Lounge, nor was there any sound of activity in the establishment.

Outside, the bells seemed to be booming and bounding immediately over their heads.

'It's like warriors fighting in the sky,' shouted Phrynne. 'Do you think the sea's down there?' She indicated the direction from which they had previously retraced their steps.

'I imagine so. The street seems to end in nothing. That would be the sea.'

'Come on. Let's run.' She was off, before he could even think about it. Then there was nothing to do but run after her. He hoped there were not eyes behind blinds.

She stopped, and held her arms to catch him. The top of her head hardly came up to his chin. He knew she was silently indicating that his failure to keep up with her was not a matter for self-consciousness.

'Isn't it beautiful?'

'The sea?' There was no moon; and little was discernible beyond the end of the street.

'Not only.'

'Everything but the sea. The sea's invisible.'

'You can smell it.'

'I certainly can't hear it.'

She slackened her embrace and cocked her head away from him. 'The bells echo so much, it's as if there were two churches.'

'I'm sure there are more than that. There always are in old towns like this.' Suddenly he was struck by the significance of his words in relation to what she had said. He shrank into himself, tautly listening.

'Yes,' cried Phrynne delightedly. 'It *is* another church.'

'Impossible,' said Gerald. 'Two churches wouldn't have practice ringing on the same night.'

'I'm quite sure. I can hear one lot of bells with my left ear, and another lot with my right.'

They had still seen no one. The sparse gas lights fell on the furnishings of a stone quay, small but plainly in regular use.

'The whole population must be ringing the bells.' His own remark discomfited Gerald.

'Good for them.' She took his hand. 'Let's go down on the beach and look for the sea.'

They descended a flight of stone steps at which the sea had sucked and bitten. The beach was as stony as the steps, but lumpier.

'We'll just go straight on,' said Phrynne. 'Until we find it.'

Left to himself, Gerald would have been less keen. The stones were very large and very slippery, and his eyes did not seem to be becoming accustomed to the dark.

'You're right, Phrynne, about the smell.'

'Honest sea smell.'

'Just as you say.' He took it rather to be the smell of dense rotting weed; across which he supposed they must be slithering. It was not a smell he had previously encountered in such strength.

Energy could hardly be spared for talking, and advancing hand in hand was impossible.

After various random remarks on both sides and the lapse of what seemed a very long time, Phrynne spoke again. 'Gerald, where is it? What sort of seaport is it that has no sea?'

She continued onwards, but Gerald stopped and looked back. He had thought the distance they had gone overlong, but was startled to see how great it was. The darkness was doubtless deceitful, but the few lights on the quay appeared as on a distant horizon.

The far glimmering specks still in his eyes, he turned and looked after Phrynne. He could barely see her. Perhaps she was progressing faster without him.

'Phrynne! Darling!'

Unexpectedly she gave a sharp cry.

'Phrynne!'

She did not answer.

'Phrynne!'

Then she spoke more or less calmly. 'Panic over. Sorry, darling. I stood on something.'

He realized that a panic it had indeed been; at least in him.

'You're all right?'

'Think so.'

He struggled up to her. 'The smell's worse than ever.' It was overpowering.

'I think it's coming from what I stepped on. My foot went right in, and then there was the smell.'

'I've never known anything like it.'

'Sorry, darling,' she said gently mocking him. 'Let's go away.'

'Let's go back. Don't you think?'

'Yes,' said Phrynne. 'But I must warn you I'm very disappointed. I think that seaside attractions should include the sea.'

He noticed that as they retreated, she was scraping the sides of one shoe against the stones, as if trying to clean it.

'I think the whole place is a disappointment,' he said. 'I really must apologize. We'll go somewhere else.'

'I like the bells,' she replied, making a careful reservation.

Gerald said nothing.

'I don't want to go somewhere where you've been before.'

The bells rang out over the desolate, unattractive beach. Now the sound seemed to be coming from every point along the shore.

'I suppose all the churches practise on the same night in order to get it over with,' said Gerald.

'They do it in order to see which can ring the loudest,' said Phrynne.

'Take care you don't twist your ankle.'

The din as they reached the rough little quay was such as to suggest that Phrynne's idea was literally true.

The Coffee Room was so low that Gerald had to dip beneath a sequence of thick beams.

'Why "Coffee Room"?' asked Phrynne, looking at the words on the door. 'I saw a notice that coffee will only be served in the Lounge.'

'It's the *lucus a non lucendo* principle.'

'That explains everything. I wonder where we sit.' A single electric lantern, mass produced in an antique pattern, had been turned on. The bulb was of that limited wattage which is peculiar to hotels. It did little to penetrate the shadows.

'The *lucus a non lucendo* principle is the principle of calling white black.'

'Not at all,' said a voice from the darkness. 'On the contrary the word black comes from the ancient root which means "to bleach".'

They had thought themselves alone, but now saw a small man seated by himself at an unlighted corner table. In the darkness he looked like a monkey.

'I stand corrected,' said Gerald.

They sat at the table under the lantern.

The man in the corner spoke again. 'Why are you here at all?'

Phrynne looked frightened, but Gerald replied quietly. 'We're on holiday. We prefer it out of the season. I presume you are Commandant Shotcroft?'

'No need to presume.' Unexpectedly the Commandant switched on the antique lantern which was nearest to him. His table was littered with a finished meal. It struck Gerald that he must have switched off the light when he heard them approach the Coffee Room. 'I'm going anyway.'

'Are we late?' asked Phrynne, always the assuager of situations.

'No, you're not late,' said the Commandant in a deep, moody voice. 'My meals are prepared half an hour before the time the rest come in. I don't like eating in company.' He had risen to his feet. 'So perhaps you'll excuse me.'

Without troubling about an answer, he stepped quickly out of the Coffee Room. He had cropped white hair; tragic, heavy-lidded eyes; and a round face which was yellow and lined.

A second later his head reappeared round the door.

'Ring,' he said; and again withdrew.

'Too many other people ringing,' said Gerald. 'But I don't see what else we can do.'

The Coffee Room bell, however, made a noise like a fire alarm.

Mrs Pascoe appeared. She looked considerably the worse for drink.

'Didn't see you in the Bar.'

'Must have missed us in the crowd,' said Gerald amiably.

'Crowd?' inquired Mrs Pascoe drunkenly. Then, after a difficult pause, she offered them a hand-written menu.

They ordered; and Mrs Pascoe served them throughout. Gerald was apprehensive lest her indisposition increase during the course of the meal; but her insobriety, like her affability, seemed to have an exact and definite limit.

'All things considered, the food might be worse,' remarked Gerald, towards the end. It was a relief that something was going reasonably well. 'Not much of it, but at least the dishes are hot.'

When Phrynne translated this into a compliment to the cook, Mrs Pascoe said, 'I cooked it all myself, although I shouldn't be the one to say so.'

Gerald felt really surprised that she was in a condition to have accomplished this. Possibly, he reflected with alarm, she had had much practice under similar conditions.

'Coffee is served in the Lounge,' said Mrs Pascoe.

They withdrew. In a corner of the Lounge was a screen decorated with winning Elizabethan ladies in ruffs and hoops. From behind it projected a pair of small black boots. Phrynne nudged Gerald and pointed to them. Gerald nodded. They felt themselves constrained to talk about things which bored them.

The hotel was old and its walls thick. In the empty Lounge the noise of the bells would not prevent conversation being overheard, but still came from all around, as if the hotel were a fortress beleaguered by surrounding artillery.

After their second cups of coffee, Gerald suddenly said he couldn't stand it.

'Darling, it's not doing us any harm. I think it's rather cosy.' Phrynne subsided in the wooden chair with its sloping back and long mud-coloured mock-velvet cushions; and opened her pretty legs to the fire.

'Every church in the town must be ringing its bells. It's been going on for two and a half hours and they never seem to take the usual breathers.'

'We wouldn't hear. Because of all the other bells ringing. I think it's nice of them to ring the bells for us.'

Nothing further was said for several minutes. Gerald was beginning to realize that they had yet to evolve a holiday routine.

'I'll get you a drink. What shall it be?'

'Anything you like. Whatever *you* have.' Phrynne was immersed in female enjoyment of the fire's radiance on her body.

Gerald missed this, and said, 'I don't quite see why they have to keep the place like a hothouse. When I come back, we'll sit somewhere else.'

'Men wear too many clothes, darling,' said Phrynne drowsily.

Contrary to his assumption, Gerald found the Lounge Bar as empty as everywhere else in the hotel and the town. There was not even a person to dispense.

Somewhat irritably, Gerald struck a brass bell which stood on the counter. It rang out sharply as a pistol shot.

Mrs Pascoe appeared at a door among the shelves. She had taken off her jacket, and her make-up had begun to run.

'A cognac, please. Double. And a Kümmel.'

Mrs Pascoe's hands were shaking so much that she could not get the cork out of the brandy bottle.

'Allow me.' Gerald stretched his arm across the bar.

Mrs Pascoe stared at him blearily. 'O.K. But I must pour it.'

Gerald extracted the cork and returned the bottle. Mrs Pascoe slopped a far from precise dose into a balloon.

Catastrophe followed. Unable to return the bottle to the high shelf where it resided, Mrs Pascoe placed it on a waist-level ledge. Reaching for the alembic of Kümmel, she swept the three-quarters full brandy bottle on to the tiled floor. The stuffy air became fogged with the fumes of brandy from behind the bar.

At the door from which Mrs Pascoe had emerged appeared a man from the inner room. Though still youngish, he was puce and puffy, and in his braces, with no collar. Streaks of sandy hair laced his vast red scalp. Liquor oozed all over him, as if from a perished gourd. Gerald took it that this was Don.

The man was too drunk to articulate. He stood in the doorway clinging with each red hand to the ledge, and savagely struggling to flay his wife with imprecations.

'How much?' said Gerald to Mrs Pascoe. It seemed useless to try for the Kümmel. The hotel must have another Bar.

'Three and six,' said Mrs Pascoe, quite lucidly; but Gerald saw that she was about to weep.

He had the exact sum. She turned her back on him and

flicked the cash register. As she returned from it, he heard the fragmentation of glass as she stepped on a piece of the broken bottle. Gerald looked at her husband out of the corner of his eye. The sagging, loose-mouthed figure made him shudder. Something moved him.

'I'm sorry about the accident,' he said to Mrs Pascoe. He held the balloon in one hand, and was just going.

Mrs Pascoe looked at him. The slow tears of desperation were edging down her face, but she now seemed quite sober. 'Mr Banstead,' she said in a flat, hurried voice. 'May I come and sit with you and your wife in the Lounge? Just for a few minutes.'

'Of course.' It was certainly not what he wanted, and he wondered what would become of the Bar, but he felt unexpectedly sorry for her, and it was impossible to say no.

To reach the flap of the bar she had to pass her husband. Gerald saw her hesitate for a second; then she advanced resolutely and steadily, and looking straight before her. If the man had let go with his hands, he would have fallen; but as she passed him, he released a great gob of spit. He was far too incapable to aim, and it fell on the side of his own trousers. Gerald lifted the flap for Mrs Pascoe and stood back to let her precede him from the Bar. As he followed her, he heard her husband maundering off into unintelligible inward searchings.

'The Kümmel!' said Mrs Pascoe, remembering in the doorway.

'Never mind,' said Gerald. 'Perhaps I could try one of the other Bars?'

'Not tonight. They're shut. I'd better go back.'

'No. We'll think of something else.' It was not yet nine o'clock, and Gerald wondered about the Licensing Justices.

But in the Lounge was another unexpected scene. Mrs Pascoe stopped as soon as they entered, and Gerald, caught between two imitation-leather armchairs, looked over her shoulder.

Phrynne had fallen asleep. Her head was slightly on one side, but her mouth was shut, and her body no more than gracefully relaxed, so that she looked most beautiful, and Gerald thought, a trifle unearthly, like a dead girl in an early picture by Millais.

The quality of her beauty seemed also to have impressed Commandant Shotcroft; for he was standing silently behind her and looking down at her, his sad face transfigured. Gerald noticed that a leaf of the pseudo-Elizabethan screen had been folded back, revealing a small cretonne-covered chair, with an open tome face downward in its seat.

'Won't you join us?' said Gerald boldly. There was that in the Commandant's face which boded no hurt. 'Can I get you a drink?'

The Commandant did not turn his head, and seemed unable to speak. Then in a low voice he said, 'For a moment only.'

'Good,' said Gerald. 'Sit down. And you, Mrs Pascoe.' Mrs Pascoe was dabbing at her face. Gerald addressed the Commandant. 'What shall it be?'

'Nothing to drink,' said the Commandant in the same low mutter. It occurred to Gerald that if Phrynne awoke, the Commandant would go.

'What about you?' Gerald looked at Mrs Pascoe, earnestly hoping she would decline.

'No, thanks.' She was glancing at the Commandant. Clearly she had not expected him to be there.

Phrynne being asleep, Gerald sat down too. He sipped his brandy. It was impossible to romanticize the action with a toast.

The events in the Bar had made him forget about the bells. Now, as they sat silently round the sleeping Phrynne, the tide of sound swept over him once more.

'You mustn't think,' said Mrs Pascoe, 'that he's always like that.' They all spoke in hushed voices. All of them seemed to have reason to do so. The Commandant was again gazing sombrely at Phrynne's beauty.

'Of course not.' But it was hard to believe.

'The licensed business puts temptations in a man's way.'

'It must be very difficult.'

'We ought never to have come here. We were happy in South Norwood.'

'You must do good business during the season.'

'Two months,' said Mrs Pascoe bitterly, but still softly.

'Two and a half at the very most. The people who come during the season have no idea what goes on out of it.'

'What made you leave South Norwood?'

'Don's stomach. The doctor said the sea air would do him good.'

'Speaking of that, doesn't the sea go too far out? We went down on the beach before dinner, but couldn't see it anywhere.'

On the other side of the fire, the Commandant turned his eyes from Phrynne and looked at Gerald.

'I wouldn't know,' said Mrs Pascoe. 'I never have time to look from one year's end to the other.' It was a customary enough answer, but Gerald felt that it did not disclose the whole truth. He noticed that Mrs Pascoe glanced uneasily at the Commandant, who by now was staring neither at Phrynne nor at Gerald but at the toppling citadels in the fire.

'And now I must get on with my work,' continued Mrs Pascoe, 'I only came in for a minute.' She looked Gerald in the face. 'Thank you,' she said, and rose.

'Please stay a little longer,' said Gerald. 'Wait till my wife wakes up.' As he spoke, Phrynne slightly shifted.

'Can't be done,' said Mrs Pascoe, her lips smiling. Gerald noticed that all the time she was watching the Commandant from under her lids, and knew that were he not there, she would have stayed.

As it was, she went. 'I'll probably see you later to say good night. Sorry the water's not very hot. It's having no porter.'

The bells showed no sign of flagging.

When Mrs Pascoe had closed the door, the Commandant spoke.

'He was a fine man once. Don't think otherwise.'

'You mean Pascoe?'

The Commandant nodded seriously.

'Not my type,' said Gerald.

'DSO and bar. DFC and bar.'

'And now bar only. Why?'

'You heard what she said. It was a lie. They didn't leave South Norwood for the sea air.'

'So I supposed.'

'He got into trouble. He was fixed. He wasn't the kind of

man to know about human nature and all its rottenness.'

'A pity,' said Gerald. 'But perhaps, even so, this isn't the best place for him?'

'It's the worst,' said the Commandant, a dark flame in his eyes. 'For him or anyone else.'

Again Phrynne shifted in her sleep: this time more convulsively, so that she nearly awoke. For some reason the two men remained speechless and motionless until she was again breathing steadily. Against the silence within, the bells sounded louder than ever. It was as if the tumult were tearing holes in the roof.

'It's certainly a very noisy place,' said Gerald, still in an undertone.

'Why did you have to come tonight of all nights?' The Commandant spoke in the same undertone, but his vehemence was extreme.

'This doesn't happen often?'

'Once every year.'

'They should have told us.'

'They don't usually accept bookings. They've no right to accept them. When Pascoe was in charge they never did.'

'I expect that Mrs Pascoe felt they were in no position to turn away business.'

'It's not a matter that should be left to a woman.'

'Not much alternative surely?'

'At heart women are creatures of darkness all the time.'

The Commandant's seriousness and bitterness left Gerald without a reply.

'My wife doesn't mind the bells,' he said after a moment. 'In fact she rather likes them.' The Commandant really was converting a nuisance, though an acute one, into a melodrama.

The Commandant turned and gazed at him. It struck Gerald that what he had just said in some way, for the Commandant, placed Phrynne also in a category of the lost.

'Take her away, man,' said the Commandant, with scornful ferocity.

'In a day or two perhaps,' said Gerald, patiently polite. 'I admit that we are disappointed with Holihaven.'

'Now. While there's still time. This *instant*.'

There was an intensity of conviction about the Commandant which was alarming.

Gerald considered. Even the empty Lounge, with its dreary decorations and commonplace furniture seemed inimical. 'They can hardly go on practising all night,' he said. But now it was fear that hushed his voice.

'Practising!' The Commandant's scorn flickered coldly through the overheated room.

'What else?'

'They're ringing to wake the dead.'

A tremor of wind in the flue momentarily drew on the already roaring fire. Gerald had turned very pale.

'That's a figure of speech,' he said, hardly to be heard.

'Not in Holihaven.' The Commandant's gaze had returned to the fire.

Gerald looked at Phrynne. She was breathing less heavily. His voice dropped to a whisper. 'What happens?'

The Commandant also was nearly whispering. 'No one can tell how long they have to go on ringing. It varies from year to year. I don't know why. You should be all right up to midnight. Probably for some while after. In the end the dead awake. First one or two: then all of them. Tonight even the sea draws back. You have seen that for yourself. In a place like this there are always several drowned each year. This year there've been more than several. But even so that's only a few. Most of them come not from the water but from the earth. It is not a pretty sight.'

'Where do they go?'

'I've never followed them to see. I'm not stark staring mad.' The red of the fire reflected in the Commandant's eyes. There was a long pause.

'I don't believe in the resurrection of the body,' said Gerald. As the hour grew later, the bells grew louder. 'Not of the body.'

'What other kind of resurrection is possible? Everything else is only theory. You can't even imagine it. No one can.'

Gerald had not argued such a thing for twenty years. 'So,' he said, 'you advise me to go. Where?'

'Where doesn't matter.'

'I have no car.'

'Then you'd better walk.'

'With her?' He indicated Phrynne only with his eyes.

'She's young and strong.' A forlorn tenderness lay within the Commandant's words. 'She's twenty years younger than you and therefore twenty years more important.'

'Yes,' said Gerald. 'I agree . . . What about you? What will you do?'

'I've lived here some time now. I know what to do.'

'And the Pascoes?'

'He's drunk. There is nothing in the world to fear if you're thoroughly drunk. DSO and bar. DFC and bar.'

'But you're not drinking yourself?'

'Not since I came to Holihaven. I lost the knack.'

Suddenly Phrynne sat up. 'Hullo,' she said to the Commandant; not yet fully awake. Then she said, 'What fun! The bells are still ringing.'

The Commandant rose, his eyes averted. 'I don't think there's anything more to say,' he remarked, addressing Gerald. 'You've still got time.' He nodded slightly to Phrynne, and walked out of the Lounge.

'What have you still got time for?' asked Phrynne, stretching. 'Was he trying to convert you? I'm sure he's an Anabaptist.'

'Something like that,' said Gerald, trying to think.

'Shall we go to bed? Sorry, I'm so sleepy.'

'Nothing to be sorry about.'

'Or shall we go for another walk? That would wake me up. Besides the tide might have come in.'

Gerald, although he half-despised himself for it, found it impossible to explain to her that they should leave at once; without transport or a destination; walk all night if necessary. He said to himself that probably he would not go even were he alone.

'If you're sleepy, it's probably a *good* thing.'

'Darling!'

'I mean with these bells. God knows when they will stop.' Instantly he felt a new pang of fear at what he had said.

Mrs Pascoe had appeared at the door leading to the Bar, and opposite to that from which the Commandant had departed. She bore two steaming glasses on a tray. She looked about, possibly to confirm that the Commandant had really gone.

'I thought you might both like a nightcap. Ovaltine, with something in it.'

'Thank you,' said Phrynne. 'I can't think of anything nicer.'

Gerald set the glasses on a wicker table, and quickly finished his cognac.

Mrs Pascoe began to move chairs and slap cushions. She looked very haggard.

'Is the Commandant an Anabaptist?' asked Phrynne over her shoulder. She was proud of her ability to outdistance Gerald in beginning to consume a hot drink.

Mrs Pascoe stopped slapping for a moment. 'I don't know what that is,' she said.

'He's left his book,' said Phrynne, on a new tack.

Mrs Pascoe looked at it indifferently across the Lounge.

'I wonder what he's reading,' continued Phrynne. 'Fox's *Lives of the Martyrs,* I expect.' A small unusual devil seemed to have entered into her.

But Mrs Pascoe knew the answer. 'It's always the same,' she said, contemptuously. 'He only reads one. It's called *Fifteen Decisive Battles of the World.* He's been reading it ever since he came here. When he gets to the end, he starts again.'

'Should I take it up to him?' asked Gerald. It was neither courtesy nor inclination, but rather a fear lest the Commandant return to the Lounge: a desire, after those few minutes of reflection, to cross-examine.

'Thanks very much,' said Mrs Pascoe, as if relieved of a similar apprehension. 'Room One. Next to the suit of Japanese armour.' She went on tipping and banging. To Gerald's inflamed nerves, her behaviour seemed too consciously normal.

He collected the book and made his way upstairs. The volume was bound in real leather, and the tops of its pages were gilded: apparently a presentation copy. Outside the Lounge, Gerald looked at the fly leaf: in a very large hand was written 'To my dear Son, Raglan, on his being honoured by the Queen. From his proud Father, B. Shotcroft,

Major-General.' Beneath the inscription a very ugly military crest had been appended by a stamper of primitive type.

The suit of Japanese armour lurked in a dark corner as the Commandant himself had done when Gerald had first encountered him. The wide brim of the helmet concealed the black eyeholes in the headpiece; the moustache bristled realistically. It was exactly as if the figure stood guard over the door behind it. On this door was no number, but, there being no other in sight, Gerald took it to be the door of Number One. A short way down the dim empty passage was a window, the ancient sashes of which shook in the din and blast of the bells. Gerald knocked sharply.

If there was a reply, the bells drowned it; and he knocked again. When to the third knocking there was still no answer, he gently opened the door. He really had to know whether all would, or could, be well if Phrynne, and doubtless he also, were at all costs to remain in their room until it was dawn. He looked in the room and caught his breath.

There was no artificial light, but the curtains, if there were any, had been drawn back from the single window, and the bottom sash forced up as far as it would go. On the floor by the dusky void, a maelstrom of sound, knelt the Commandant, his cropped white hair faintly catching the moonless glimmer, as his head lay on the sill, like that of a man about to be guillotined. His face was in his hands, but slightly sideways, so that Gerald received a shadowy distorted idea of his expression. Some might have called it ecstatic, but Gerald found it agonized. It frightened him more than anything which had yet happened. Inside the room the bells were like plunging roaring lions.

He stood for some considerable time quite unable to move. He could not determine whether or not the Commandant knew he was there. The Commandant gave no direct sign of it, but more than once he writhed and shuddered in Gerald's direction, like an unquiet sleeper made more unquiet by an interloper. It was a matter of doubt whether Gerald should leave the book; and he decided to do so mainly because the thought of further contact with it displeased him. He crept into the room and softly laid it on a hardly visible wooden trunk at the foot of the plain metal bedstead. There seemed no other furniture in the room. Outside the door, the hanging mailed fingers of the Japanese figure touched his wrist.

He had not been away from the Lounge for long, but it was long enough for Mrs Pascoe to have begun again to drink. She had left the tidying up half-completed, or rather the room half-disarranged; and was leaning against the over-mantel, drawing heavily on a dark tumbler of whisky. Phrynne had not yet finished her Ovaltine.

'How long before the bells stop?' asked Gerald as soon as he opened the Lounge door. Now he was resolved that, come what might, they must go. The impossibility of sleep should serve as excuse.

'I don't expect Mrs Pascoe can know any more than we can,' said Phrynne.

'You should have told us about this – this annual event – before accepting our booking.'

Mrs Pascoe drank some more whisky. Gerald suspected that it was neat. 'It's not always the same night,' she said throatily, looking at the floor.

'We're not staying,' said Gerald wildly.

'Darling!' Phrynne caught him by the arm.

'Leave this to me, Phrynne.' He addressed Mrs Pascoe. 'We'll pay for the room, of course. Please order me a car.'

Mrs Pascoe was now regarding him stonily. When he asked for a car, she gave a very short laugh. Then her face changed. She made an effort, and she said, 'You mustn't take the Commandant so seriously, you know.'

Phrynne glanced quickly at her husband.

The whisky was finished. Mrs Pascoe placed the empty glass on the plastic overmantel with too much of a thud. 'No one takes Commandant Shotcroft seriously,' she said. 'Not even his nearest and dearest.'

'Has he any?' asked Phrynne. 'He seemed so lonely and pathetic.'

'He's Don and I's mascot,' she said, the drink interfering with her grammar. But not even the drink could leave any doubt about her rancour.

'I thought he had personality,' said Phrynne.

'That and a lot more no doubt,' said Mrs Pascoe. 'But they

pushed him out, all the same.'

'Out of what?'

'Cashiered, court-martialled, badges of rank stripped off, sword broken in half, muffled drums, the works.'

'Poor old man. I'm sure it was a miscarriage of justice.'

'That's because you don't know him.'

Mrs Pascoe looked as if she were waiting for Gerald to offer her another whisky.

'It's a thing he could never live down,' said Phrynne, brooding to herself, and tucking her legs beneath her. 'No wonder he's so queer if all the time it was a mistake.'

'I just told you it was not a mistake,' said Mrs Pascoe insolently.

'How can we possibly know?'

'*You* can't. *I* can. No one better.' She was at once aggressive and tearful.

'If you want to be paid,' cried Gerald, forcing himself in, 'make out your bill. Phrynne, come upstairs and pack.' If only he hadn't made her unpack between their walk and dinner.

Slowly Phrynne uncoiled and rose to her feet. She had no intention of either packing or departing, nor was she going to argue. 'I shall need your help,' she said. 'If I'm going to pack.'

In Mrs Pascoe there was another change. Now she looked terrified. 'Don't go. Please don't go. Not now. It's too late.'

Gerald confronted her. 'Too late for what?' he asked harshly.

Mrs Pascoe looked paler than ever. 'You said you wanted a car,' she faltered. 'You're too late.' Her voice trailed away.

Gerald took Phrynne by the arm. 'Come on up.'

Before they reached the door, Mrs Pascoe made a further attempt. 'You'll be all right if you stay. Really you will.' Her voice, normally somewhat strident, was so feeble that the bells obliterated it. Gerald observed that from somewhere she had produced the whisky bottle and was refilling her tumbler.

With Phrynne on his arm he went first to the stout front door. To his surprise it was neither locked nor bolted, but opened at a half-turn of the handle. Outside the building the whole sky was full of bells, the air an inferno of ringing.

He thought that for the first time Phrynne's face also seemed strained and crestfallen. 'They've been ringing too long,' she said, drawing close to him. 'I wish they'd stop.'

'We're packing and going. I needed to know whether we could get out this way. We must shut the door quietly.'

It creaked a bit on its hinges, and he hesitated with it half-shut, uncertain whether to rush the creak or to ease it. Suddenly, something dark and shapeless, with its arm seeming to hold a black vesture over its head, flitted, all sharp angles, like a bat, down the narrow ill-lighted street, the sound of its passage audible to none. It was the first being that either of them had seen in the streets of Holihaven; and Gerald was acutely relieved that he alone had set eyes upon it. With his hand trembling, he shut the door much too sharply.

But no one could possibly have heard, although he stopped for a second outside the Lounge. He could hear Mrs Pascoe now weeping hysterically; and again was glad that Phrynne was a step or two ahead of him. Upstairs the Commandant's door lay straight before them: they had to pass close beside the Japanese figure, in order to take the passage to the left of it.

But soon they were in their room, with the key turned in the big rim lock.

'Oh God,' cried Gerald, sinking on the double bed. 'It's pandemonium.' Not for the first time that evening he was instantly more frightened than ever by the unintended appositeness of his own words.

'It's pandemonium all right,' said Phrynne, almost calmly. 'And we're not going out in it.'

He was at a loss to divine how much she knew, guessed, or imagined; and any word of enlightenment from him might be inconceivably dangerous. But he was conscious of the strength of her resistance, and lacked the reserves to battle with it.

She was looking out of the window into the main street. 'We might *will* them to stop,' she suggested wearily.

Gerald was now far less frightened of the bells continuing than of their ceasing. But that they should go on ringing until day broke seemed hopelessly impossible.

Then one peal stopped. There could be no other explanation for the obvious diminution in sound.

'You see!' said Phrynne.

Gerald sat up straight on the side of the bed.

Almost at once further sections of sound subsided, quickly one after the other, until only a single peal was left, that which had begun the ringing. Then the single peal tapered off into a single bell. The single bell tolled on its own, disjointedly, five or six or seven times. Then it stopped, and there was nothing.

Gerald's head was a cave of echoes, mountingly muffled by the noisy current of his blood.

'Oh goodness,' said Phrynne, turning from the window and stretching her arms above her head. 'Let's go somewhere else tomorrow.' She began to take off her dress.

Sooner than usual they were in bed, and in one another's arms. Gerald had carefully not looked out of the window, and neither of them suggested that it should be opened, as they usually did.

'As it's a four-poster, shouldn't we draw the curtains?' asked Phrynne. 'And be really snug? After those damned bells?'

'We should suffocate.'

'Did they suffocate when everyone had four-posters?'

'They only drew the curtains when people were likely to pass through the room.'

'Darling, you're shivering. I think we *should* draw them.'

'Lie still instead and love me.'

But all his nerves were straining out into the silence. There was no sound of any kind, beyond the hotel or within it; not a creaking floorboard or a prowling cat or a distant owl. He had been afraid to look at his watch when the bells stopped, or since; the number of the dark hours before they could leave Holihaven, weighed on him. The vision of the Commandant kneeling in the dark window was clear before his eyes, as if the intervening panelled walls were made of stage gauze; and the thing he had seen in the street darted on its angular way back and forth through memory.

Then passion began to open its petals within him, layer

upon slow layer; like an illusionist's red flower which, without soil or sun or sap, grows as it is watched. The languor of tenderness began to fill the musty room with its texture and perfume. The transparent walls became again opaque, the old man's vaticinations mere obsession. The street must have been empty, as it was now; the eye deceived.

But perhaps rather it was the boundless sequacity of love that deceived, and most of all in the matter of the time which had passed since the bells stopped ringing; for suddenly Phrynne drew very close to him, and he heard steps in the thoroughfare outside, and a voice calling. These were loud steps, audible from afar even through the shut window; and the voice had the possessed stridency of the street evangelist.

'The dead are awake!'

Not even the thick bucolic accent, the guttural vibrato of emotion, could twist or mask the meaning. At first Gerald lay listening with all his body, and concentrating the more as the noise grew; then he sprang from the bed and ran to the window.

A burly, long-limbed man in a seaman's jersey was running down the street, coming clearly into view for a second at each lamp, and between them lapsing into a swaying lumpy wraith. As he shouted his joyous message, he crossed from side to side and waved his arms like a negro. By flashes, Gerald could see that his weatherworn face was transfigured.

'The dead are awake!'

Already, behind him, people were coming out of their houses, and descending from the rooms above shops. There were men, women, and children. Most of them were fully dressed, and must have been waiting in silence and darkness for the call; but a few were dishevelled in night attire or the first garments which had come to hand. Some formed themselves into groups, and advanced arm in arm, as if towards the conclusion of a Blackpool beano. More came singly, ecstatic and waving their arms above their heads, as the first man had done. All cried out, again and again, with no cohesion or harmony. 'The dead are awake! The dead are awake!'

Gerald became aware that Phrynne was standing behind him.

'The Commandant warned me,' he said brokenly. 'We should have gone.'

Phrynne shook her head and took his arm. 'Nowhere to go,' she said. But her voice was soft with fear, and her eyes blank. 'I don't expect they'll trouble *us*.'

Swiftly Gerald drew the thick plush curtains, leaving them in complete darkness. 'We'll sit it out,' he said, slightly histrionic in his fear. 'No matter what happens.'

He scrambled across to the switch. But when he pressed it, light did not come. 'The current's gone. We must get back into bed.'

'Gerald! Come and help me.' He remembered that she was curiously vulnerable in the dark. He found his way to her, and guided her to the bed.

'No more love,' she said ruefully and affectionately, her teeth chattering.

He kissed her lips with what gentleness the total night made possible.

'They were going towards the sea,' she said timidly.

'We must think of something else.'

But the noise was still growing. The whole community seemed to be passing down the street, yelling the same dreadful words again and again.

'Do you think we can?'

'Yes,' said Gerald. 'It's only until tomorrow.'

'They can't be actually dangerous,' said Phrynne. 'Or it would be stopped.'

'Yes, of course.'

By now, as always happens, the crowd had amalgamated their utterances and were beginning to shout in unison. They were like agitators bawling a slogan, or massed trouble-makers at a football match. But at the same time the noise was beginning to draw away. Gerald suspected that the entire population of the place was on the march.

Soon it was apparent that a processional route was being followed. The tumult could be heard winding about from quarter to quarter; sometimes drawing near, so that Gerald and Phrynne were once more seized by the first chill of panic, then again almost fading away. It was possibly this great variability in the volume of the sound which led Gerald to believe that there were distinct pauses in the massed shouting; periods when it was superseded by far, disorderly cheering. Certainly it began also to seem that the thing shouted had changed; but he could not make out the new cry, although unwillingly he strained to do so.

'It's extraordinary how frightened one can be,' said Phrynne, 'even when one is not directly menaced. It must prove that we all belong to one another, or whatever it is, after all.'

In many similar remarks they discussed the thing at one remove. Experience showed that this was better than not discussing it at all.

In the end there could be no doubt that the shouting had stopped, and that now the crowd was singing. It was no song that Gerald had ever heard, but something about the way it was sung convinced him that it was a hymn or psalm set to an out-of-date popular tune. Once more the crowd was approaching; this time steadily, but with strange, interminable slowness.

'What the *hell* are they doing now?' asked Gerald of the blackness, his nerves wound so tight that the foolish question was forced out of them.

Palpably the crowd had completed its peregrination, and was returning up the main street from the sea. The singers seemed to gasp and fluctuate, as if worn out with gay exercise, like children at a party. There was a steady undertow of scraping and scuffling. Time passed and more time.

Phrynne spoke. 'I believe they're *dancing*.'

She moved slightly, as if she thought of going to see.

'No, no,' said Gerald, and clutched her fiercely.

There was a tremendous concussion on the ground floor below them. The front door had been violently thrown back. They could hear the hotel filling with a stamping, singing mob.

Doors banged everywhere, and furniture was overturned, as the beatific throng surged and stumbled through the involved darkness of the old building. Glasses went and china and Birmingham brass warming pans. In a moment, Gerald heard the Japanese armour crash to the boards. Phrynne screamed. Then a mighty shoulder, made strong by the sea's assault, rammed at the panelling and their door was down.

'The living and the dead dance together.
Now's the time. Now's the place. Now's the weather.'

At last Gerald could make out the words.

The stresses in the song were heavily beaten down by much repetition.

Hand in hand, through the dim grey of the doorway, the dancers lumbered and shambled in, singing frenziedly but brokenly; ecstatic but exhausted. Through the stuffy blackness they swayed and shambled, more and more of them, until the room must have been packed tight with them.

Phrynne screamed again. 'The smell. Oh God, the smell.'

It was the smell they had encountered on the beach; in the congested room, no longer merely offensive, but obscene, unspeakable.

Phrynne was hysterical. All self-control gone, she was scratching and tearing, and screaming again and again. Gerald tried to hold her, but one of the dancers in the darkness struck him so hard that she was jolted out of his arms. Instantly it seemed that she was no longer there at all.

The dancers were thronging everywhere, their limbs whirling, their lungs bursting with the rhythm of the song. It was difficult for Gerald even to call out. He tried to struggle after Phrynne, but immediately a blow from a massive elbow knocked him to the floor, an abyss of invisible trampling feet.

But soon the dancers were going again; not only from the room, but, it seemed, from the building also. Crushed and tormented though he was, Gerald could hear the song being resumed in the street, as the various frenzied groups debouched and reunited. Within, before long there was nothing but the chaos, the darkness, and the putrescent odour. Gerald felt so sick that he had to battle with unconsciousness. He could not think or move, despite the desperate need.

Then he struggled into a sitting position, and sank his head on the torn sheets of the bed. For an uncertain period he was insensible to everything: but in the end he heard steps approaching down the dark passage. His door was pushed back, and the Commandant entered gripping a lighted candle. He seemed to disregard the flow of hot wax which had already congealed on much of his knotted hand.

'She's safe. Small thanks to you.'

The Commandant stared icily at Gerald's undignified figure. Gerald tried to stand. He was terribly bruised, and so giddy that he wondered if this could be concussion. But relief rallied him.

'Is it thanks to *you?*'

'She was caught up in it. Dancing with the rest.' The Commandant's eyes glowed in the candle-light. The singing and dancing had almost died away.

Still Gerald could do no more than sit up on the bed. His voice was low and indistinct, as if coming from outside his body. 'Were they . . . were some of them . . .?'

The Commandant replied more scornful than ever of his weakness. 'She was between two of them. Each had one of her hands.'

Gerald could not look at him. 'What did you do?' he asked in the same remote voice.

'I did what had to be done. I hope I was in time.' After the slightest possible pause he continued. 'You'll find her downstairs.'

'I'm grateful. Such a silly thing to say, but what else is there?'

'Can you walk?'

'I think so.'

'I'll light you down.' The Commandant's tone was as uncompromising as always.

There were two more candles in the Lounge, and Phrynne, wearing a woman's belted overcoat which was not hers, sat between them drinking. Mrs Pascoe, fully dressed but with eyes averted, pottered about the wreckage. It seemed hardly more than as if she were completing the task which earlier she had left unfinished.

'Darling, look at you!' Phrynne's words were still hysterical, but her voice was as gentle as it usually was.

Gerald, bruises and thoughts of concussion forgotten, dragged her into his arms. They embraced silently for a long time: then he looked into her eyes.

'Here I am,' she said, and looked away. 'Not to worry.'

Silently and unnoticed, the Commandant had already retreated.

Without returning his gaze, Phrynne finished her drink as she stood there. Gerald supposed that it was one of Mrs Pascoe's concoctions.

It was so dark where Mrs Pascoe was working that her labours could have been achieving little; but she said nothing to her visitors, nor they to her. At the door Phrynne unexpectedly stripped off the overcoat and threw it on a chair. Her nightdress was so torn that she stood almost naked. Dark though it was, Gerald saw Mrs Pascoe regarding Phrynne's pretty body with a stare of animosity.

'May we take one of the candles?' he said, normal standards reasserting themselves in him.

But Mrs Pascoe continued to stand silently staring; and they lighted themselves through the wilderness of broken furniture to the ruins of their bedroom. The Japanese figure was still prostrate, and the Commandant's door shut. And the smell had almost gone.

Even by seven o'clock the next morning surprisingly much had been done to restore order. But no one seemed to be about, and Gerald and Phrynne departed without a word.

In Wrack Street a milkman was delivering, but Gerald noticed that his cart bore the name of another town. A minute boy whom they encountered later on an obscure purposeful errand might, however, have been indigenous; and when they reached Station Road, they saw a small plot of land on which already men were silently at work with spades in their hands. They were as thick as flies on a wound, and as black. In the darkness of the previous evening, Gerald and Phrynne had missed the place. A board named it the New Municipal Cemetery.

In the mild light of an autumn morning the sight of the

black and silent toilers was horrible; but Phrynne did not seem to find it so. On the contrary, her cheeks reddened and her soft mouth became fleetingly more voluptuous still.

She seemed to have forgotten Gerald, so that he was able to examine her closely for a moment. It was the first time he had done so since the night before. Then, once more, she became herself. In those previous seconds Gerald had become aware of something dividing them which neither of them would ever mention or ever forget.

MARY TREADGOLD

The Telephone

'*If you would catch the spleen and laugh yourselves into stitches, follow me,*' I called to Sir Toby – and as I ran across the stage caught the eye of the whitehaired man in the V.I.P.'s row. The light from the stage streamed out over the darkened theatre. He was leaning forward, amused, laughing – and as Sir Toby chased after me I laughed back. I had fallen in love with him at sight – there, from the middle of the stage at an end-of-term Dramatic School performance of *Twelfth Night*.

We met at the party after the show – and met again – and again – and then we began to meet in backstreet Soho restaurants, and then in my tiny London flat. I loved him desperately. I had never been in love before, and Allan had not been in love for over thirty years – not since he had married Katherine, he told me, in some queer little snowbound Canadian township. 'I never meant this to happen. I've never felt like this about any woman before. I don't understand myself,' he said restlessly.

All through that winter I clung to Allan. We kept the long secret winter afternoons and evenings together. There was so much that he wanted to give me – the things that I wanted for myself, more than wanted, believed that I must have. 'I want to give you kindness – and shelter – and love,' he said. He and Katherine had had no children.

But it could not go on like that. Every time he came to my flat the conflict in him deepened. It was like the deepening rift splitting a tree-trunk down to its roots. He would turn wearily towards me. 'How can I hurt her?' he would ask me. 'Katherine and I – we've been together all these years. Long before you were even born. Why, I knew her when she was a school girl – a child. Look at what we've done together – look at our work.'

I tried to understand. But I seemed to see only a grey ghostly marriage, a kind of deadly, intellectual middle-aged companionship stretching back down the years. There was nothing there, I thought, that should be preserved. It would be so different for *us*, I thought, and I clung the more desperately. 'I cannot live without you,' I said, believing that I could not.

Our dilemma, Allan's agony, was resolved by Katherine finding out. There was no drama, no scenes. During the next few months I never knew what passed between them. I dared not ask. I felt like a child whose parents are gravely discussing in the next room portents beyond its comprehension. But presently Katherine went unobtrusively back to Canada without Allan . . .

Allan shut up the house in Hampstead, and talked of selling it. We neither of us wanted to live there. Immediately after our marriage we came up to this cottage in the Western Highlands which we rented through an advertisement in the *Times*. That year Scotland had one of its rare perfect summers. We bathed and fished, and the long halcyon days passed over us with scarcely a break in the weather. I was blissfully happy. Free from the conflicts and indecisions of the past months, we turned again to each other, discovering new releases, a new and deepening absorption. Our cottage lay by the shore in a curve of the hills, and whenever I remember that summer it seems as if the falling tides of the Atlantic were always in our ears, and as if the white sands were always warm under our bare feet.

But again, it could not last. One scorching day in early September I came round the cottage at lunchtime, carrying a pot-roast over to the table under our rowan-tree. I found Allan sitting staring down at an open airmail letter that the postman had just delivered. He looked up as I put the pot-roast down. His face was dazed, and his hands were shaking.

'Katherine is dead,' he said incredulously. 'Dead . . . This letter's from her sister in Toronto . . . She says – ' and he stared again at the letter as though they were lying words, 'she says – heart failure. Very peacefully, she says.'

His eyes went past mine to the open sea. Then he got up and went into the house, while I – I stayed, pleating the gingham cloth between my fingers. Once more I felt like the child who had inadvertently witnessed a parent's distress – shocked yes, but horribly embarrassed. Then I followed Allan into the cottage, and I put my arms round him. All that day I watched over him in my heart as he moved about the place. But we did not mention Katherine – nor the next day – and, although I waited for Allan to speak, her name never passed our lips during the next three weeks.

Three weeks later to the day, among other letters forwarded from London by the Post Office, arrived the telephone bill for the Hampstead house – the second demand. We had forgotten about the first.

'Damn,' said Allan – we were once again eating our lunch in the garden – 'damn, I ought to have had the thing disconnected before we ever left London.'

I picked up the envelope and looked at the date of forwarding. 'They'll probably have cut you off themselves by now,' I said. But Allan was already crossing the grass to collect the pudding from the kitchen oven. 'Go in by the hall,' I called after him. 'You can find out if it's still connected by ringing the number. If you hear it ringing away at the London end you'll know it's still on.'

And I lay back in my deck-chair, staring up at the scarlet rowan-berries against the sky and thinking that Allan was beginning to hump his shoulders like an old man, and that his skin looked somehow as if the sea-salt were drying it out . . .

'Well?' I said. 'Still connected?' Perhaps I invented the slight pause before Allan carefully set down the apple-pie, and replied, 'Yes – still connected.'

That evening I went up to bed alone, because Allan said he wanted to trim the lamps in the kitchen. I was sitting in the window in the late Highland dusk, brushing my hair and looking out over the sea, when I heard a light tinkle in the hall

below. I turned my head. But the house lay silent. I went
over to the door.

'Hampstead 96843.' Allan's voice – low – strained – came
up the stairs.

There was a long silence. And then my heart turned over,
for I heard his voice again, whispering:

'Oh, my dear – my dear – '

But the words broke off – and from the dark well of the
hall came a low sob. I suppose I moved, and a floorboard
creaked. Because I heard the receiver laid down, and I saw
Allan's shadow move heavily across the wall at the foot of the
stairs.

We lay side by side that night, and we never spoke. But I
know that it was daybreak before Allan slept.

During the next few days I became terribly afraid. I began
to watch over Allan with new eyes, those of a mother. For the
first time I knew a quite different tenderness, one that nearly
choked me with its burden of grief and fear for him as he
moved above the cottage like a sleepwalker, trying patheti-
cally to keep up appearances before me, his face, as it
seemed, ageing hourly in its weariness. I became frightened,
too, for myself. I kept telling myself that nothing – nothing
– had happened. But in the daytime I avoided looking at the
dead black telephone inert on its old-fashioned stand in the
hall. At night I lay awake, trying not to picture that
telephone wire running tautly underground away from our
cottage, running steadily south, straight down through the
border hills, down through England . . . During that week I
tried never to leave Allan's side. But once I had to go off
unexpectedly to the village shop. When I returned I had to
pretend that I hadn't seen him through the half-open door,
gently laying down the receiver. And twice more in the
evening – and there must have been other times – when I
was cooking our supper, he slipped out of the kitchen, and I
heard that faint solitary tinkle in the hall . . .

I could have rung up the telephone people, and begged
them to cut off the Hampstead number. But with what
excuse? I could have taken pliers and wrenched our own
telephone out of its socket. I knew that nothing would be
solved with pliers. But by the weekend I did know what I

could try to do, for sanity's sake, to prevent us from going down into the solitudes of our guilt.

On Friday afternoon – after tea – my opportunity came. It was a glorious evening – golden, with the sand blowing lightly along the shore, and a racing tide. I persuaded Allan to take the boat out to troll for mackerel on the turn. I watched him go off from the doorway. I waited until I actually saw him push the boat off from our small jetty. Then I turned back into the cottage, and closed the door behind me. I had shut out all the evening sunlight so that I could hardly see the telephone. But I walked over to it. I took it up in both my hands. I drew a long deep breath, and I gave the Hampstead number. All that I had been told of Katherine during those bad months in London had been of kindness and gentleness and goodness – nothing of revenge. To this I clung, and upon it I was banking. My teeth were chattering, and I was shaking all over when the bell down in London began to ring. I suppose at that moment I lost my head. I thought – I could have sworn – I heard the receiver softly raised at the far end. But I suppose I should have waited instead of bursting into words. Now I shall never *know*. And they were not even the words I'd planned. I suppose I reverted, being so frightened, to the kind of prayer one blurts out in childhood:

'Please – please – ' I said down the mouthpiece. 'Please let me have him now. I know everything I've done's been wrong. It's too late about that. But I won't be a child anymore. I'll look after him, like you've always done,' I said. 'Only please let me have him now. I'll be a wife to him. I promise you – if that's what you are wanting. I can get him right again, and I'll take care of him. Now and forever more,' I said.

And I banged the receiver down, and fled upstairs to our bedroom. Through the window I could see the little boat bobbing about on the sea. I sat down in the window in the full evening sun, and I shook all over, and I cried and cried . . .

In the small hours of the morning came the crisis. I woke – it must have been about half past four. The bed was empty. In an instant I was wide awake, because down in the hall I could hear the insistent tinkle of the telephone receiver, struck over and over again, and above it, mingled with it, Allan's voice. Somehow I got the lamp lighted. The shadows tilted all over the ceiling and I could hear the paraffin sloshing round the bowl as I stumbled out to the head of the stairs.

'Katherine – Katherine – '

He was shaking the receiver, and babbling down the mouthpiece when my light from the staircase fell upon him. He let the receiver drop, and stood looking up at me.

'I can't get her,' he said. 'I wanted her to forgive me. But she doesn't answer. I can't reach her.'

I brought him up the stairs. I can remember shivering with the little dawn sea-wind blowing through my cotton nightdress from the open window. I made him tea, while he sat in the window, staring up at the grey clouds of the morning. At last he said:

'You must book yourself a room at one of the hotels in Oban. Only for a couple of nights. I'll come back – probably tomorrow, or the next day. You see – ' and he began to explain carefully, politely as if to a foreigner, 'you see, I've got to find Katherine, and so I have to go down unexpectedly to London – '

From our remote part of the Highlands there are only two trains a day. Allan went on the early morning one. I had, of course, no intention of going to any hotel. I knew where my promise to Katherine lay, where lay my love. I said 'Yes – yes' to everything Allan said, and stayed in the cottage all that day. And then I caught the evening train.

There was no chance of a sleeper. I huddled in the corner of a carriage packed with returning holidaymakers, my face turned first to the twilight, and then to the darkness rushing past the window. In the dead cold hours, when the other passengers sprawled and snored, the terror for Allan nearly throttled me. Once I dozed off, and woke, biting back a scream because I thought I saw the telephone wire running alongside the train, stretched and singing, 'You'll never know. You'll never know . . . '

Euston in the morning loomed gaunt and monstrous. The London streets were dripping with autumn rain. I told the taxi-man to drive as fast as possible up to Hampstead. When he pulled up in Allan's road before a gate set in a high wall, I was already half out of the taxi. I pushed the fare at him, slapped open the gate, and ran up the short drive. I just had time to notice that the white Regency house was more or less what I had pictured, before I was up the flight of steps and tugging at the iron bell-pull. I was tired – deadly tired, deadly afraid. What courage I had ever had seemed to have fled. 'I promise. I promise. Oh, if you've ever really been here, please have gone,' I gabbled, while the London rain poured over me, and the bell reverberated through the house.

At last I heard a movement inside the house, and then footsteps slowly drawing towards the door. For a second Allan and I stood gazing at each other. Then – suddenly – I was over the threshold, and in his arms. While the door swung gently to behind us, I drew him over to the staircase, drew him down, knelt beside him as he sat there on the second stair. He turned his face against my shoulder, and heaved a sigh.

After a little while, I raised my head and looked about me. We were in a large white-panelled hall, with a window through which I could see a plane-tree, its quiet branches stroking the glass. The only thing in common with our hall up in Scotland was the telephone, standing on a mahogany table against the wall. For some moments I gazed at it. My terror was wholly gone – like a dream at morning. But I became aware of a new emotion – disquieting, faintly discreditable. I looked suspiciously down at Allan, I wanted to *know*. Cautiously I began to frame my question. He was so still that I wondered if he had fallen asleep. But just then he stirred, and I took his head between my hands and, as he smiled at me, turned his face searchingly towards the light. It was calm as though washed by tidal waters. I knew that I could never ask my question.

At that moment the front door bell began to peal. We both jumped, and got to our feet.

'You go,' said Allan, disappearing into the back of the house.

The sharp-nosed young man in the dripping mackintosh

was aggrieved. 'Been sent to cut you off,' he said. 'Bill unpaid – nothing done – '

I turned back into the hall. About me, above me, the house lay quiet. Only against the window the boughs of the plane-tree clamoured in a sudden flurry of wind and rain. The question I could never ask – the answer never to be given – surely both were irrelevant? For all the tranquillity of the house, I felt my panic begin again to stir. There was only one thing that mattered to me – to us.

'Allan – ' I called – and I tried not to let my voice quaver – 'It's about the telephone. Do you – do you *want* it cut off?'

I held my breath. The reply came immediately.

'Why – darling – we're going back to Scotland tonight, out of this damnable climate. We don't want to pay for what we aren't going to need any more. Tell them they can disconnect it at once.'

J. SHERIDAN LE FANU

The Ghost of a Hand

Miss Rebecca Chattesworth, in a letter dated late in the autumn of 1753, gives a minute and curious relation of occurrences in the Tile House, which, it is plain, although at starting she protests against all such fooleries, she has heard with a peculiar sort of particularity.

I was for printing the entire letter, which is really very singular, as well as characteristic. But my publisher meets me with his veto; and I believe he is right. The worthy old lady's letter *is*, perhaps, too long; and I must rest content with a few hungry notes of its tenor.

That year, and somewhere about the 24th October, there broke out a strange dispute between Mr Alderman Harper, of High Street, Dublin, and my Lord Castlemallard, who, in virtue of his cousinship to the young heir's mother, had undertaken for him the management of the tiny estate on which the Tiled or Tyled House – for I find it spelt both ways – stood.

This Alderman Harper had agreed for a lease of the house for his daughter, who was married to a gentleman named Prosser. He furnished it and put up hangings, and otherwise went to considerable expense. Mr and Mrs Prosser came there some time in June, and after having parted with a good many servants in the interval, she made up her mind that she could not live in the house, and her father waited on Lord Castlemallard, and told him plainly that he would not take out the lease because the house was subjected to annoyances

which he could not explain. In plain terms, he said it was
haunted, and that no servants would live there more than a
few weeks, and that after what his son-in-law's family had
suffered there, not only should he be excused from taking a
lease of it, but that the house itself ought to be pulled down as
a nuisance and the habitual haunt of something worse than
human malefactors.

Lord Castlemallard filed a bill in the Equity side of the
Exchequer to compel Mr Alderman Harper to perform his
contract, by taking out the lease. But the Alderman drew an
answer, supported by no less than seven long affidavits,
copies of all which were furnished to his lordship, and with
the desired effect; for rather than compel him to place them
upon the file of the court, his lordship struck, and consented
to release him.

I am sorry the case did not proceed at least far enough to
place upon the files of the court the very authentic and
unaccountable story which Miss Rebecca relates.

The annoyances described did not begin till the end of
August, when, one evening, Mrs Prosser, quite alone, was
sitting in the twilight at the back parlour window, which was
open, looking out into the orchard, and plainly saw a hand
stealthily placed upon the stone window-sill outside, as if by
some one beneath the window, at her right side, intending to
climb up. There was nothing but the hand, which was rather
short, but handsomely formed, and white and plump, laid on
the edge of the window-sill; and it was not a very young
hand, but one aged, somewhere about forty, as she
conjectured. It was only a few weeks before that the horrible
robbery at Clondalkin had taken place, and the lady fancied
that the hand was that of one of the miscreants who was now
about to scale the windows of the Tiled House. She uttered a
loud scream and an ejaculation of terror, and at the same
moment the hand was quietly withdrawn.

Search was made in the orchard, but there were no
indications of any person's having been under the window,
beneath which, ranged along the wall, stood a great column
of flower-pots, which it seemed must have prevented
anyone's coming within reach of it.

The same night there came a hasty tapping, every now and

then, at the window of the kitchen. The women grew frightened, and the servant-man, taking fire-arms with him, opened the back door, but discovered nothing. As he shut it, however, he said, 'a thump came on it', and a pressure as of somebody striving to force his way in, which frightened *him*; and though the tapping went on upon the kitchen window panes, he made no further explorations.

About six o'clock on the Saturday evening following, the cook, 'an honest, sober woman, now aged nigh sixty years', being alone in the kitchen, saw, on looking up, it is supposed the same fat but aristocratic-looking hand, laid with its palm against the glass, as if feeling carefully for some inequality in its surface. She cried out, and said something like a prayer on seeing it. But it was not withdrawn for several seconds after.

After this, for a great many nights, there came at first a low, and afterwards an angry rapping, as it seemed with a set of clenched knuckles at the back-door. And the servant-man would not open it, but called to know who was there; and there came no answer, only a sound as if the palm of the hand was placed against it, and drawn slowly from side to side with a sort of soft, groping motion.

All this time, sitting in the back parlour, which, for the time, they used as a drawing-room, Mr and Mrs Prosser were disturbed by rappings at the window, sometimes very low and furtive, like a clandestine signal, and at others sudden, and so loud as to threaten the breaking of the pane.

This was all at the back of the house, which looked upon the orchard, as you know. But on a Tuesday night, at about half past nine, there came precisely the same rappings at the hall-door, and went on, to the great annoyance of the master and terror of his wife, at intervals, for nearly two hours.

After this, for several days and nights, they had no annoyance whatsoever, and began to think that the nuisance had expended itself. But on the night of the 13th September, Jane Easterbrook, an English maid, having gone into the pantry for the small silver bowl in which her mistress's posset was served, happening to look up at the little window of only four panes, observed, through an auger-hole which was drilled through the window frame, for the admission of a bolt to secure the shutter, a white pudgy finger – first the tip, and then the two first joints introduced, and turned about this way and that, crooked against the inside, as if in search of a fastening which its owner designed to push aside. When the maid got back into the kitchen, we are told 'she fell into "a swounde", and was all the next day very weak.'

Mr Prosser, being, I've heard, a hard-headed and conceited sort of fellow, scouted the ghost, and sneered at the fears of his family. He was privately of opinion that the whole affair was a practical joke or a fraud, and waited an opportunity of catching the rogue *flagrante delicto*. He did not long keep this theory to himself, but let it out by degrees with no stint of oaths, and threats, believing that some domestic traitor held the thread of the conspiracy.

Indeed it was time something were done; for not only his servants, but good Mrs Prosser herself, had grown to look unhappy and anxious. They kept at home from the hour of sunset, and would not venture about the house after nightfall, except in couples.

The knocking had ceased for about a week; when one night, Mrs Prosser being in the nursery, her husband, who was in the parlour, heard it begin very softly at the hall-door. The air was quite still, which favoured his hearing distinctly. This was the first time there had been any disturbance at that side of the house, and the character of the summons was changed.

Mr Prosser, leaving the parlour-door open, it seems, went quietly into the hall. The sound was that of beating on the outside of the stout door, softly and regularly, 'with the flat of the hand'. He was going to open it suddenly, but changed his mind; and went back very quietly, and on to the head of the kitchen stair, where was a 'strong closet' over the pantry, in which he kept his fire-arms, swords, and canes.

Here he called his manservant, whom he believed to be honest, and, with a pair of loaded pistols in his own coat-pockets, and giving another pair to him, he went as lightly as he could, followed by the man, and with a stout walking-cane in his hand, forward to the door.

Everything went as Mr Prosser wished. The besieger of his house, so far from taking fright at their approach, grew more impatient; and the sort of patting which had aroused his attention at first assumed the rhythm and emphasis of a series of double-knocks.

Mr Prosser, angry, opened the door with his right arm across, cane in hand. Looking, he saw nothing; but his arm was jerked up oddly, as it might be with the hollow of a hand, and something passed under it, with a kind of gentle squeeze. The servant neither saw nor felt anything, and did not know why his master looked back so hastily, cutting with his cane, and shutting the door with so sudden a slam.

From that time Mr Prosser discontinued his angry talk and swearing about it, and seemed nearly as averse from the subject as the rest of his family. He grew, in fact, very uncomfortable, feeling an inward persuasion that when, in answer to the summons, he had opened the hall-door, he had actually given admission to the besieger.

He said nothing to Mrs Prosser, but went up earlier to his bedroom, 'where he read a while in his Bible, and said his prayers'. I hope the particular relation of this circumstance does not indicate its singularity. He lay awake for a good while, it appears; and, as he supposed, about a quarter past twelve he heard the soft palm of a hand patting on the outside of the bedroom door, and then brushed slowly along it.

Up bounced Mr Prosser, very much frightened, and locked the door, crying, 'Who's there?' but receiving no answer, but the same brushing sound of a soft hand drawn over the panels, which he knew only too well.

In the morning the housemaid was terrified by the impression of a hand in the dust of the 'little parlour' table, where they had been unpacking delft and other things the day before. The print of the naked foot in the sea-sand did not frighten Robinson Crusoe half so much. They were by this time all nervous, and some of them half-crazed, about the hand.

Mr Prosser went to examine the mark, and made light of it, but, as he swore afterwards, rather to quiet his servants than from any comfortable feeling about it in his own mind; however, he had them all, one by one, into the room, and made each place his or her hand, palm downward, on the same table, thus taking a similar impression from every person in the house, including himself and his wife; and his 'affidavit' deposed that the formation of the hand so impressed differed altogether from those of the living inhabitants of the house, and corresponded with that of the hand seen by Mrs Prosser and by the cook.

Whoever or whatever the owner of that hand might be, they all felt this subtle demonstration to mean that it was declared he was no longer out of doors, but had established himself in the house.

And now Mrs Prosser began to be troubled with strange and horrible dreams, some of which as set out in detail, in Aunt Rebecca's long letter, are really very appalling nightmares. But one night, as Mr Prosser closed his bedchamber-door, he was struck somewhat by the utter silence of the room, there being no sound of breathing, which seemed unaccountable to him, as he knew his wife was in bed, and his ears were particularly sharp.

There was a candle burning on a small table at the foot of the bed, besides the one he held in one hand, a heavy ledger, connected with his father-in-law's business, being under his arm. He drew the curtain at the side of the bed, and saw Mrs Prosser lying, as for a few seconds he mortally feared, dead, her face being motionless, white, and covered with a cold dew; and on the pillow, close beside her head, and just within the curtains, was as he first thought, a toad – but really the same fattish hand, the wrist resting on the pillow, and the fingers extended towards her temple.

Mr Prosser, with a horrified jerk, pitched the ledger right at the curtains, behind which the owner of the hand might be supposed to stand. The hand was instantaneously and smoothly snatched away, the curtains made a great wave, and Mr Prosser got round the bed in time to see the closet-door, which was at the other side, pulled to by the same white, puffy hand, as he believed.

He drew the door open with a fling, and stared in: but the closet was empty, except for the clothes hanging from the pegs on the wall, and the dressing table and looking-glass facing the windows. He shut it sharply, and locked it, and felt for a minute, he says, 'as if he were like to lose his wits'; then, ringing at the bell, he brought the servants, and with much ado they recovered Mrs Prosser from a sort of 'trance', in which, he says, from her looks, she seemed to have suffered 'the pains of death'; and Aunt Rebecca adds, 'from what she told me of her visions, with her own lips, he might have added, "and of hell also".'

But the occurrence which seems to have determined the crisis was the strange sickness of their eldest child, a little boy aged between two and three years. He lay awake, seemingly in paroxysms of terror, and the doctors, who were called in, set down the symptoms to incipient water on the brain. Mrs Prosser used to sit up with the nurse, by the nursery fire, much troubled in mind about the condition of her child.

His bed was placed sideways along the wall, with its head against the door of a press or cupboard, which, however, did not shut quite close. There was a little valance, about a foot deep, round the top of the child's bed, and this descended within some ten or twelve inches of the pillow on which it lay.

They observed that the little creature was quieter whenever they took it up and held it on their laps. They had just replaced him, as he seemed to have grown quite sleepy and tranquil, but he was not five minutes in his bed when he began to scream in one of his frenzies of terror; at the same moment the nurse, for the first time, detected, and Mrs Prosser equally plainly saw, following the direction of *her* eyes, the real cause of the child's sufferings.

Protruding through the aperture of the press, and shrouded in the shade of the valance, they plainly saw the white fat hand, palm downwards, presented towards the head of the child. The mother uttered a scream, and snatched the child from its little bed, and she and the nurse ran down to the lady's sleeping-room, where Mr Prosser was in bed, shutting the door as they entered; and they had hardly done so, when a gentle tap came to it from the outside.

There is a great deal more, but this will suffice. The singularity of the narrative seems to me to be this, that it describes the ghost of a hand, and no more. The person to whom that hand belonged never once appeared; nor was it a hand separated from a body, but only a hand so manifested and introduced that its owner was always, by some crafty accident, hidden from view.

In the year 1819, at a college breakfast, I met a Mr

Prosser — a thin, grave, but rather chatty old gentleman, with very white hair drawn back into a pigtail — and he told us all, with a concise particularity, a story of his cousin, James Prosser, who, when an infant, had slept for some time in what his mother said was a haunted nursery in an old house near Chapelizod, and who, whenever he was ill, over-fatigued, or in any wise feverish, suffered all through his life as he had done from a time he could scarcely remember, from a vision of a certain gentleman, fat and pale, every curl of whose wig, every button and fold of whose laced clothes, and every feature and line of whose sensual, benignant, and unwholesome face, was as minutely engraven upon his memory as the dress and lineaments of his own grandfather's portrait, which hung before him every day at breakfast, dinner, and supper.

Mr Prosser mentioned this as an instance of a curiously monotonous, individualized, and persistent nightmare, and hinted the extreme horror and anxiety with which his cousin, of whom he spoke in the past tense as 'poor Jemmie', was at any time induced to mention it.

A. M. BURRAGE
(Ex-Private X)

The Sweeper

It seemed to Tessa Winyard that Miss Ludgate's strangest characteristic was her kindness to beggars. This was something more than a little peculiar in a nature which, to be sure, presented a surface like a mountain range of unexpected peaks and valleys; for there was a thin streak of meanness in her. One caught glimpses of it here and there, to be traced a little way and lost, like a thin elusive vein in a block of marble. One week she would pay the household bills without a murmur; the next she would simmer over them in a mild rage, questioning the smallest item, and suggesting the most absurd little economies which she would have been the first to condemn later if Mrs Finch the housekeeper had ever taken her at her word. She was rich enough to be indifferent, but old enough to be crotchety.

Miss Ludgate gave very sparsely to local charities, and those good busybodies who went forth at different times with subscription lists and tales of good causes often visited her and came empty away. She had plausible, transparent excuses for keeping her purse-strings tight. Hospitals should be State-aided; schemes for assisting the local poor destroyed thrift; we had heathen of our own to convert, and needed to send no missionaries abroad. Yet she was sometimes overwhelmingly generous in her spasmodic charities to individuals, and her kindness to itinerant beggars was proverbial among their fraternity. Her neighbours were not grateful to her for this, for it was said that she encouraged every doubtful character who came that way.

When she first agreed to come on a month's trial Tessa
Winyard had known that she would find Miss Ludgate
difficult, doubting whether she would be able to retain the
post of companion, and, still more, if she would want to
retain it. The thing was not arranged through the reading
and answering of an advertisement. Tessa knew a married
niece of the old lady who, while recommending the young
girl to her ancient kinswoman, was able to give Tessa hints as
to the nature and treatment of the old lady's crotchets. So she
came to the house well instructed and not quite as a stranger.

Tessa came under the spell of the house from the moment
when she entered it for the first time. She had an ingrained
romantic love of old country mansions, and Billingdon
Abbots, although nothing was left of the original priory after
which it was named, was old enough to be worshipped. It
was mainly Jacobean, but some eighteenth-century owner, a
devotee of the then fashionable cult of Italian architecture,
had covered the façade with stucco and added a pillared
portico. It was probably the same owner who had erected a
summer-house to the design of a Greek temple at the end of a
walk between nut bushes, and who was responsible for the
imitation ruin – to which Time had since added the
authentic touch – beside the reedy fishpond at the rear of the
house. Likely enough, thought Tessa, who knew the period,
that same romantic squire was wont to engage an imitation
'hermit' to meditate beside the spurious ruin on moonlight
nights.

The gardens around the house were well wooded, and thus
lent the house itself an air of melancholy and the inevitable
slight atmosphere of damp and darkness. And here and
there, in the most unexpected places, were garden gods,
mostly broken and all in need of scouring. Tessa soon
discovered these stone ghosts quite unexpectedly, and nearly
always with a leap and tingle of surprise. A noseless Hermes
confronted one at the turn of a shady walk; Demeter, minus a
hand, stood half hidden by laurels, still keeping vigil for
Persephone; a dancing faun stood poised and caught in a
frozen caper by the gate of the walled-in kitchen garden;
beside a small stone pond a satyr leered from his pedestal, as

if waiting for a naiad to break the surface.

The interior of the house was at first a little awe-inspiring to Tessa. She loved pretty things, but she was inclined to be afraid of furniture and pictures which seemed to her to be coldly beautiful and conscious of their own intrinsic values. Everything was highly polished, spotless and speckless, and the reception rooms had an air of state apartments thrown open for the inspection of the public.

The hall was square and galleried, and one could look straight up to the top storey and see the slanting balustrades of three staircases. Two suits of armour faced one across a parquet floor, and on the walls were three or four portraits by Lely and Kneller, those once fashionable painters of Court beauties whose works have lost favour with the collectors of today. The dining-room was long, rectangular, and severe, furnished only with a Cromwellian table and chairs and a great plain sideboard gleaming with silver candelabra. Two large seventeenth-century portraits by unknown members of the Dutch School were the only decorations bestowed on the panelled walls, and the window curtains were brown to match the one strip of carpet which the long table almost exactly covered.

Less monastic, but almost as severe and dignified, was the drawing-room in which Tessa spent most of her time with Miss Ludgate. The boudoir was a homelier room, containing such human things as photographs of living people, work-baskets, friendly arm-chairs, and a cosy, feminine atmosphere; but Miss Ludgate preferred more often to sit in state in her great drawing-room with the 'Portrait of Miss Olivia Ludgate', by Gainsborough, the Chippendale furniture, and the cabinet of priceless china. It was as if she realized that she was but the guardian of her treasures, and wanted to have them within sight now that her term of guardianship was drawing to a close.

She must have been well over eighty, Tessa thought; for she was very small and withered and frail, with that almost porcelain delicacy peculiar to certain very old ladies. Winter and summer, she wore a white woollen shawl inside the house, thick or thin according to the season, which matched in colour and to some extent in texture her soft and still plentiful hair. Her face and hands were yellow-brown with the veneer of old age, but her hands were blue-veined, light and delicate, so that her fingers seemed overweighted by the simplest rings. Her eyes were blue and still piercing, and her mouth, once beautiful, was caught up at the corners by puckerings of the upper lip, and looked grim in repose. Her voice had not shrilled and always she spoke very slowly with an unaffected precision, as one who knew that she had only to be understood to be obeyed and therefore took care always to be understood.

Tessa spent her first week with Miss Ludgate without knowing whether or no she liked the old lady, or whether or no she was afraid of her. Nor was she any wiser with regard to Miss Ludgate's sentiments towards herself. Their relations were much as they might have been had Tessa been a child and Miss Ludgate a new governess suspected of severity. Tessa was on her best behaviour, doing as she was told and thinking before she spoke, as children should and generally do not. At times it occurred to her to wonder that Miss Ludgate had not sought to engage an older woman, for in the cold formality of that first week's intercourse she wondered what gap in the household she was supposed to fill, and what return she was making for her wage and board.

Truth to tell, Miss Ludgate wanted to see somebody young about the house, even if she could share with her companion no more than the common factors of their sex and their humanity. The servants were all old retainers kept faithful to her by rumours of legacies. Her relatives were few and immersed in their own affairs. The house and the bulk of the property from which she derived her income were held in trust for an heir appointed by the same will which had given her a life interest in the estate. It saved her from the transparent attentions of any fortune-hunting nephew or niece, but it kept her lonely and starved for young companionship.

It happened that Tessa was able to play the piano quite reasonably well and that she had an educated taste in music. So had Miss Ludgate, who had been a performer of much the same quality until the time came when her rebel fingers stiffened with rheumatism. So the heavy grand piano, which had been scrupulously kept in tune, was silent no longer, and Miss Ludgate regained an old lost pleasure. It should be added that Tessa was twenty-two and, with no pretensions to technical beauty, was rich in commonplace good looks which were enhanced by perfect health and the freshness of her youth. She looked her best in candlelight, with her slim hands – they at least would have pleased an artist – hovering like white moths over the keyboard of the piano.

When she had been with Miss Ludgate a week, the old lady addressed her for the first time as 'Tessa'. She added: 'I hope you intend to stay with me, my dear. It will be dull for you, and I fear you will often find me a bother. But I shan't take up all your time, and I dare say you will be able to find friends and amusements.'

So Tessa stayed on, and beyond the probationary month. She was a soft-hearted girl who gave her friendship easily but always sincerely. She tried to like everybody who liked her, and generally succeeded. It would be hard to analyse the quality of the friendship between the two women, but certainly it existed and at times they were able to touch hands over the barrier between youth and age. Miss Ludgate inspired in Tessa a queer tenderness. With all her wealth and despite her domineering manner, she was a pathetic and lonely figure. She reminded Tessa of some poor actress playing the part of Queen, wearing the tawdry crown jewels, uttering commands which the other mummers obeyed like automata; while all the while there awaited her the realities of life at the fall of the curtain – the wet streets, the poor meal, and the cold and comfortless lodging.

It filled Tessa with pity to think that here, close beside her, was a living, breathing creature, still clinging to life, who must, in the course of nature, so soon let go her hold. Tessa could think: 'Fifty years hence I shall be seventy-two, and there's no reason why I shouldn't live till then.' She wondered painfully how it must feel to be unable to look a month hence with average confidence, and to regard every nightfall as the threshold of a precarious tomorrow.

Tessa would have found life very dull but for the complete change in her surroundings. She had been brought up in a country vicarage, one of seven brothers and sisters who had worn one another's clothes, tramped the carpets threadbare, mishandled the cheap furniture, broken everything frangible except their parents' hearts, and had somehow tumbled into adolescence. The unwonted 'grandeur' of living with Miss Ludgate flavoured the monotony.

We have her writing home to her 'Darling Mother' as follows:

I expect when I get back home again our dear old rooms will look absurdly small. I thought at first that the house was huge, and every room as big as a barrack-room – not that I've ever been in a barrack-room! But I'm getting used to it now, and really it isn't so enormous as I thought. Huge compared with ours, of course, but not so big as Lord Branbourne's house, or even Colonel Exted's.

Really, though, it's a darling old place and might have come out of one of those books in which there's a Mystery, and a Sliding Panel, and the heroine's a nursery governess who marries the Young Baronet. But there's no mystery that I've heard of, although I like to pretend there is, and even if I were the nursery governess there's no young baronet within a radius of miles. But at least it ought to have a traditional ghost, although, since I haven't heard of one, it's probably deficient even in that respect! I don't like to ask Miss Ludgate, because, although she's a dear, there are questions I couldn't ask her. She might believe in ghosts and it might scare her to talk about them; or she mightn't, and then she'd be furious with me for talking rubbish. Of course, I know it's all rubbish, but it would be very nice to know that we were supposed to be haunted by a nice Grey Lady – of, say, about the period of Queen Anne. But if we're haunted by nothing else, we're certainly haunted by tramps.

Her letter went on to describe the numerous daily visits of those nomads of the English countryside, who beg and steal on their way from workhouse to workhouse; those queer, illogical, feckless beings who prefer the most intense miseries and hardships to the comparative comforts attendant on honest work. Three or four was a day's average of such callers, and not one went empty away. Mrs Finch had very definite orders, and she carried them out with the impassive face of a perfect subject of discipline. When there was no spare food there was the pleasanter alternative of money which could be transformed into liquor at the nearest inn.

Tessa was for ever meeting these vagrants in the drive. Male and female, they differed in a hundred ways; some still trying to cling to the last rags of self-respect, others obscene, leering, furtive, potential criminals who lacked the courage to rise above petty theft. Most faces were either evil or carried the rolling eyes and lewd, loose mouth of the semi-idiot, but they were all alike in their personal uncleanliness and in the insolence of their bearing.

Tessa grew used to receiving from them direct and insolent challenges of the eyes, familiar nods, blatant grins. In their several ways they told her that she was nobody and that, if she hated to see them, so much the better. They knew she was an underling, subject to dismissal, whereas they, for some occult reason, were always the welcome guests. Tessa resented their presence and their dumb insolence, and secretly raged against Miss Ludgate for encouraging them. They were the sewer-rats of society, foul, predatory, and carrying disease from village to village and from town to town.

The girl knew something of the struggles of the decent poor. Her upbringing in a country vicarage had given her intimate knowledge of farm-hands and builders' labourers, the tragic poverty of their homes, their independence and their gallant struggles for existence. On Miss Ludgate's estate there was more than one family living on bread and potatoes and getting not too much of either. Yet the old lady had no sympathy for them, and gave unlimited largess to the undeserving. In the ditches outside the park it was always possible to find a loaf or two of bread flung there by some vagrant who had feasted more delicately on the proceeds of a visit to the tradesmen's door.

It was not for Tessa to speak to Miss Ludgate on the subject. Indeed, she knew that − in the phraseology of the servants' hall − it was as much as her place was worth. But she did mention it to Mrs Finch, whose duty was to provide food and drink, or, failing those, money.

Mrs Finch, taciturn through her environment but still with an undercurrent of warmth, replied at first with the one pregnant word, 'Orders!' After a moment she added: 'The mistress has her own good reasons for doing it – or thinks she has.'

It was late summer when Tessa first took up her abode at Billingdon Abbots, and sweet lavender, that first herald of the approach of autumn, was already blooming in the gardens. September came and the first warning gleams of yellow showed among the trees. Spiked chestnut husks opened and dropped their polished brown fruit. At evenings the ponds and the trout stream exhaled pale, low-hanging mists. There was a cold snap in the air.

By looking from her window every morning Tessa marked on the trees the inexorable progress of the year. Day by day the green tints lessened as the yellow increased. Then yellow began to give place to gold and brown and red. Only the hollies and the laurels stood fast against the advancing tide.

There came an evening when Miss Ludgate appeared for the first time in her winter shawl. She seemed depressed and said little during dinner, and afterwards in the drawing-room, when she had taken out and arranged a pack of patience cards preparatory to beginning her evening game, she suddenly leaned her elbows on the table and rested her face between her hands.

'Aren't you well, Miss Ludgate?' Tessa asked anxiously.

She removed her hands and showed her withered old face. Her eyes were piteous, fear-haunted, and full of shadows.

'I am very much as usual, my dear,' she said. 'You must bear with me. My bad time of the year is just approaching. If I can live until the end of November I shall last another year. But I don't know yet – I don't know.'

'Of course you're not going to die this year,' said Tessa, with a robust note of optimism which she had found useful in soothing frightened children.

'If I don't die this autumn it will be the next, or some other autumn,' quavered the old voice. 'It will be in the autumn that I shall die. I know that. I know that.'

'But how can you know?' Tessa asked, with just the right

note of gentle incredulity.

'I know it. What does it matter how I know? . . . Have many leaves fallen yet?'

'Hardly any as yet,' said Tessa. 'There has been very little wind.'

'They will fall presently,' said Miss Ludgate. 'Very soon now . . . '

Her voice trailed away, but presently she rallied, picked up the miniature playing cards, and began her game.

Two days later it rained heavily all the morning and throughout the earlier part of the afternoon. Just as the light was beginning to wane, half a gale of wind sprang up, and showers of yellow leaves, circling and eddying at the wind's will, began to find their way to earth through the level slant of the rain. Miss Ludgate sat watching them, her eyes dull with the suffering of despair, until the lights were turned on and the blinds were drawn.

During dinner the wind dropped again and the rain ceased. Tessa afterwards peeped between the blinds to see still silhouettes of trees against the sky, and a few stars sparkling palely. It promised after all to be a fine night.

As before, Miss Ludgate got out her patience cards, and Tessa picked up a book and waited to be bidden to go to the piano. There was silence in the room save for intermittent sounds of cards being laid with a snap upon the polished surface of the table, and occasional dry rustlings as Tessa turned the pages of her book.

. . . When she first heard it Tessa could not truthfully have said. It seemed to her that she had gradually become conscious of the sounds in the garden outside, and when at last they had so forced themselves upon her attention as to set her wondering what caused them it was impossible for her to guess how long they had actually been going on.

Tessa closed the book over her fingers and listened. The sounds were crisp, dry, long-drawn-out, and rhythmic. There was an equal pause after each one. It was rather like listening to the leisurely brushing of a woman's long hair. What was it? An uneven surface being scratched by something crisp and pliant? Then Tessa knew. On the long path behind the house which travelled the whole length of the building somebody was sweeping up the fallen leaves with a stable broom. But what a time to sweep up leaves!

She continued to listen. Now that she had identified the sounds they were quite unmistakable. She would not have had to guess twice had it not been dark outside, and the thought of a gardener showing such devotion to duty as to work at that hour had at first been rejected by her subconscious mind. She looked up, with the intention of making some remark to Miss Ludgate – and she said nothing.

Miss Ludgate sat listening intently, her face half turned towards the windows and slightly raised, her eyes upturned. Her whole attitude was one of strained rigidity, expressive of a tension rather dreadful to see in one so old. Tessa not only listened, she now watched.

There was a movement in the unnaturally silent room. Miss Ludgate had turned her head, and now showed her companion a white face of woe and doom-ridden eyes. Then, in a flash, her expression changed. Tessa knew that Miss Ludgate had caught her listening to the sounds from the path outside, and that for some reason the old lady was annoyed with her for having heard them. But why? And why that look of terror on the poor, white old face?

'Won't you play something, Tessa?'

Despite the note of interrogation, the words were an abrupt command, and Tessa knew it. She was to drown the noise of sweeping from outside, because, for some queer reason, Miss Ludgate did not want her to hear it. So, tactfully, she played pieces which allowed her to make liberal use of the loud pedal.

After half an hour Miss Ludgate rose, gathered her shawl tighter about her shoulders, and hobbled to the door, pausing on the way to say good night to Tessa.

Tessa lingered in the room alone and reseated herself before the piano. A minute or two elapsed before she began to strum softly and absent-mindedly. Why did Miss Ludgate object to her hearing that sound of sweeping from the path outside? It had ceased now, or she would have peeped out to see who actually was at work. Had Miss Ludgate some queer distaste for seeing fallen leaves lying about, and was she ashamed because she was keeping a gardener at work at that hour? But it was unlike Miss Ludgate to mind what people thought of her; besides, she rose late in the morning, and there would be plenty of time to brush away the leaves before the mistress of the house could set eyes on them. And then, why was Miss Ludgate so terrified? Had it anything to do with her queer belief that she would die in the autumn?

On her way to bed Tessa smiled gently to herself for having tried to penetrate to the secret places of a warped mind which was over eighty years old. She had just seen another queer phase of Miss Ludgate, and all of such seemed inexplicable.

The night was still calm and promised so to remain.

'There won't be many more leaves down tonight,' Tessa reflected as she undressed.

But when next morning she sauntered out into the garden before breakfast the long path which skirted the rear of the house was still thickly littered with them, and Toy, the second gardener, was busy among them with a barrow and one of those birch stable brooms which, in mediaeval imaginations, provided steeds for witches.

'Hullo!' exclaimed Tessa. 'What a lot of leaves must have come down last night!'

Toy ceased sweeping and shook his head.

'No, miss. This 'ere little lot come down with the wind early part o' the evenin'.'

'But surely they were all swept up. I heard somebody at work here after nine o'clock. Wasn't it you?'

The man grinned.

'You catch any of us at work arter nine o'clock, miss!' he said. 'No, miss, nobody's touched 'em till now. 'Tes thankless work, too. So soon as you've swept up one lot there's another waitin'. Not a hundred men could keep this 'ere garden tidy this time o' the year.'

Tessa said nothing more and went thoughtfully into the house. The sweeping was continued off and on all day, for more leaves descended, and a bonfire built up on the waste ground beyond the kitchen garden wafted its fragrance over to the house.

That evening Miss Ludgate had a fire made up in the

boudoir and announced to Tessa that they would sit there before and after dinner. But it happened that the chimney smoked, and after coughing and grumbling, and rating Mrs Finch on the dilatoriness and inefficiency of sweeps, the old lady went early to bed.

It was still too early for Tessa to retire. Having been left to herself she remembered a book which she had left in the drawing-room, and with which she purposed sitting over the dining-room fire. Hardly had she taken two steps past the threshold of the drawing-room when she came abruptly to a halt and stood listening. She could not doubt the evidence of her ears. In spite of what Toy had told her, and that it was now after half past nine, somebody was sweeping the path outside.

She tiptoed to the window and peeped out between the blinds. Bright moonlight silvered the garden, but she could see nothing. Now, however, that she was near the window, she could locate the sounds more accurately, and they seemed to proceed from a spot farther down the path which was hidden from her by the angle of the window setting. There was a door just outside the room giving access to the garden, but for no reason that she could name she felt strangely unwilling to go out and look at the mysterious worker. With the strangest little cold thrill she was aware of a distinct preference for seeing him – for the first time, at least – from a distance.

Then Tessa remembered a landing window, and after a little hesitation she went silently and on tiptoe upstairs to the first floor, and down a passage on the left of the stairhead. Here moonlight penetrated a window and threw a pale blue screen upon the opposite wall. Tessa fumbled with the window fastenings, raised the sash softly and silently, and leaned out.

On the path below her, but some yards to her left and close to the angle of the house, a man was slowly and rhythmically sweeping with a stable broom. The broom swung and struck the path time after time with a soft, crisp *swish*, and the strokes were as regular as those of the pendulum of some slow old clock.

From her angle of observation she was unable to see most

of the characteristics of the figure underneath. It was that of a working-man, for there was something in the silhouette subtly suggestive of old and baggy clothes. But apart from all else there was something queer, something odd and unnatural, in the scene on which she gazed. She knew that there was something lacking, something that she should have found missing at the first glance, yet for her life she could not have said what it was.

From below some gross omission blazed up at her, and though she was acutely aware that the scene lacked something which she had every right to expect to see, her senses groped for it in vain; although the lack of something which should have been there, and was not, was as obvious as a burning pyre at midnight. She knew that she was watching the gross defiance of some natural law, but what law she did not know. Suddenly sick and dizzy, she withdrew her head.

All the cowardice in Tessa's nature urged her to go to bed, to forget what she had seen and to refrain from trying to remember what she had *not* seen. But the other Tessa, the Tessa who despised cowards, and was herself capable under pressure of rising to great heights of courage, stayed and urged. Under her breath she talked to herself, as she always did when any crisis found her in a state of indecision.

'Tessa, you coward! How dare you be afraid! Go down at once and see who it is and what's queer about him. He can't eat you!'

So the two Tessas imprisoned in the one body stole downstairs again, and the braver Tessa was angry with their common heart for thumping so hard and trying to weaken her. But she unfastened the door and stepped out into the moonlight.

The Sweeper was still at work close to the angle of the house, near by where the path ended and a green door gave entrance to the stable yard. The path was thick with leaves, and the girl, advancing uncertainly with her hands to her breasts, saw that he was making little progress with his work. The broom rose and fell and audibly swept the path, but the dead leaves lay fast and still beneath it. Yet it was not this that she had noticed from above. There was still that unseizable Something missing.

Her footfalls made little noise on the leaf-strewn path, but they became audible to the Sweeper while she was still half a dozen yards from him. He paused in his work and turned and looked at her.

He was a tall, lean man with a white cadaverous face and eyes that bulged like huge rising bubbles as they regarded her. It was a foul, suffering face which he showed to Tessa, a face whose misery could – and did – inspire loathing and a hitherto unimagined horror, but never pity. He was clad in the meanest rags, which seemed to have been cast at random over his emaciated body. The hands grasping the broom seemed no more than bones and skin. He was so thin, thought Tessa, that he was almost – and here she paused in thought, because she found herself hating the word which tried to force itself into her mind. But it had its way, and blew in on a cold wind of terror. Yes, he was almost transparent, she thought, and sickened at the word, which had come to have a new and vile meaning for her.

They faced each other through a fraction of eternity not to be measured by seconds; and then Tessa heard herself scream. It flashed upon her now, the strange, abominable detail of the figure which confronted her – the Something missing which she had noticed, without actually seeing, from above. The path was flooded with moonlight, but the visitant had no shadow. And fast upon this vile discovery she saw dimly *through* it the ivy stirring upon the wall. Then, as unbidden thoughts rushed to tell her that the Thing was not of this world, and that it was not holy, and the sudden knowledge wrung that scream from her, so she was left suddenly and dreadfully alone. The spot where the Thing had stood was empty save for the moonlight and the shallow litter of leaves.

Tessa had no memory of returning to the house. Her next recollection was of finding herself in the hall, faint and gasping and sobbing. Even as she approached the stairs she saw a light dancing on the wall above and wondered what fresh horror was to confront her. But it was only Mrs Finch coming downstairs in a dressing-gown, candle in hand, an incongruous but a very comforting sight.

'Oh, it's you, Miss Tessa,' said Mrs Finch, reassured. She held the candle lower and peered down at the sobbing girl. 'Why, whatever is the matter? Oh, Miss Tessa, Miss Tessa! You haven't never been outside, have you?'

Tessa sobbed and choked and tried to speak.

'I've seen – I've seen . . . '

Mrs Finch swiftly descended the remaining stairs, and put an arm around the shuddering girl.

'Hush, my dear, my dear! I know what you've seen. You didn't ought never to have gone out. I've seen it too, once – but only once, thank God.'

'What is it?' Tessa faltered.

'Never you mind, my dear. Now don't be frightened. It's all over now. He doesn't come here for you. It's the mistress he wants. You've nothing to fear, Miss Tessa. Where was he when you saw him?'

'Close to the end of the path, near the stable gate.'

Mrs Finch threw up her hands.

'Oh, the poor mistress – the poor mistress! Her time's shortening! The end's nigh now!'

'I can't bear any more,' Tessa sobbed; and then she contradicted herself, clinging to Mrs Finch. 'I must know. I can't rest until I know. Tell me everything.'

'Come into my parlour, my dear, and I'll make a cup of tea. We can both do with it, I think. But you'd best not know. At least not tonight, Miss Tessa – not tonight.'

'I must,' whispered Tessa, 'if I'm ever to have any peace.'

The fire was still burning behind a guard in the housekeeper's parlour, for Mrs Finch had only gone up to bed a few minutes since. There was water still warm in the brass kettle, and in a few minutes the tea was ready. Tessa sipped and felt the first vibrations of her returning courage, and presently looked inquiringly at Mrs Finch.

'I'll tell you, Miss Tessa,' said the old housekeeper, 'if it'll make you any easier. But don't let the mistress know as I've ever told you.'

Tessa inclined her head and gave the required promise.

'You don't know why,' Mrs Finch began in a low voice, 'the mistress gives to every beggar, deserving or otherwise. The reason comes into what I'm going to tell you. Miss

Ludgate wasn't always like that – not until up to about fifteen years ago.

'She was old then, but active for her age, and very fond of gardenin'. Late one afternoon in the autumn, while she was cutting some late roses, a begger came to the tradesmen's door. Sick and ill and starved, he looked – but there, you've seen him. He was a bad lot, we found out afterwards, but I was sorry for him, and I was just going to risk givin' him some food without orders, when up comes Miss Ludgate. "What's this?" she says.

'He whined something about not being able to get work.

' "Work!" says the mistress. "You don't want work – you want charity. If you want to eat," she says, "you shall, but you shall work first. There's a broom," she says, "and there's a path littered with leaves. Start sweeping up at the top, and when you come to the end you can come and see me."

'Well, he took the broom, and a few minutes later I heard a shout from Miss Ludgate and come hurryin' out. There was the man lyin' at the top of the path where he'd commenced sweeping, and he'd collapsed and fallen down. I didn't know then as he was dying, but he did, and he gave Miss Ludgate a look as I shall never forget.

' "When I've swept to the end of the path," he says, "I'll come for you, my lady, and we'll feast together. Only see as you're ready to be fetched when I come." Those were his last words. He was buried by the parish, and it gave Miss Ludgate such a turn that she ordered something to be given to every beggar who came, and not one of 'em to be asked to do a stroke of work.

'But next autumn, when the leaves began to fall, he came back and started sweeping, right at the top of the path, round about where he died. We've all heard him and most of us have seen him. Year after year's he's come back and swept with his broom, which just makes a brushing noise and hardly stirs a leaf. But each year he's been getting nearer and nearer to the end of the path, and when he gets right to the end – well, I wouldn't like to be the mistress, with all her money.'

It was three evenings later, just before the hour fixed for dinner, that the Sweeper completed his task. That is to say, if one reposes literal belief in Mrs Finch's story.

The servants heard somebody burst open the tradesmen's door, and, having rushed out into the passage, two of them saw that the door was open but found no one there. Miss Ludgate was already in the drawing-room, but Tessa was still upstairs, dressing for dinner. Presently Mrs Finch had occasion to enter the drawing-room to speak to her mistress; and her screams warned the household of what had happened. Tessa heard them just as she was ready to go downstairs, and she rushed into the drawing-room a few moments later.

Miss Ludgate was sitting upright in her favourite chair. Her eyes were open, but she was quite dead; and in her eyes there was something that Tessa could not bear to see.

Withdrawing her own gaze from that fixed stare of terror and recognition she saw something on the carpet and presently stooped to pick it up.

It was a little yellow leaf, damp and pinched and frayed, and but for her own experience and Mrs Finch's tale she might have wondered how it had come to be there. She dropped it, shuddering, for it looked as if it had been picked up by, and had afterwards fallen from, the birch twigs of a stable broom.

EDITH WHARTON

Afterward

'Oh, there *is* one, of course, but you'll never know it.'

The assertion, laughingly flung out six months earlier in a bright June garden, came back to Mary Boyne with a new perception of its significance as she stood, in the December dusk, waiting for the lamps to be brought into the library.

The words had been spoken by their friend Alida Stair, as they sat at tea on her lawn at Pangbourne, in reference to the very house of which the library in question was the central, the pivotal, 'feature'. Mary Boyne and her husband, in quest of a country place in one of the southern or south-western counties, had, on their arrival in England, carried their problem straight to Alida Stair, who had successfully solved it in her own case; but it was not until they had rejected, almost capriciously, several practical and judicious suggestions, that she threw out: 'Well, there's Lyng, in Dorsetshire. It belongs to Hugo's cousins, and you can get it for a song.'

The reason she gave for its being obtainable on these terms — its remoteness from a station, its lack of electric light, hot-water pipes, and other vulgar necessities — were exactly those pleasing in its favour with two romantic Americans perversely in search of the economic drawbacks which were associated, in their tradition, with unusual architectural felicities.

'I should never believe I was living in an old house unless I was thoroughly uncomfortable,' Ned Boyne, the more extravagant of the two, had jocosely insisted; 'the least hint of "convenience" would make me think it had been bought out of an exhibition, with the pieces numbered, and set up again.' And they had proceeded to enumerate, with humorous precision, their various doubts and demands, refusing to believe that the house their cousin recommended was *really* Tudor till they learned it had no heating system, or that the village church was literally in the grounds, and till she assured them of the deplorable uncertainty of the water-supply.

'It's too uncomfortable to be true!' Edward Boyne had continued to exult as the avowal of each disadvantage was successively wrung from her; but he had cut short his rhapsody to ask, with a relapse to distrust: 'And the ghost? You've been concealing from us the fact that there is no ghost!'

Mary, at the moment, had laughed with him, yet almost with her laugh, being possessed of several sets of independent perceptions, had been struck by a note of flatness in Alida's answering hilarity.

'Oh, Dorsetshire's full of ghosts, you know.'

'Yes, yes; but that won't do. I don't want to have to drive ten miles to see somebody else's ghost. I want one of my own on the premises. *Is* there a ghost at Lyng?'

His rejoinder had made Alida laugh again, and it was then that she had flung back tantalizing: 'Oh, there *is* one, of course, but you'll never know it.'

'Never know it?' Boyne pulled her up. 'But what in the world constitutes a ghost except the fact of its being known for one?'

'I can't say. But that's the story.'

'That there's a ghost, but that nobody knows it's a ghost?'

'Well – not till afterward, at any rate.'

'Till afterward?'

'Not till long, long afterward.'

'But if it's once been identified as an unearthly visitant, why hasn't its *signalement* been handed down in the family? How has it managed to preserve its incognito?'

Alida could only shake her head. 'Don't ask me. But it has.'

'And then suddenly' – Mary spoke up as if from cavernous

depths of divination – 'suddenly, long afterward, one says to oneself, *"That was it!"* '

She was startled at the sepulchral sound with which her question fell on the banter of the other two, and she saw the shadow of the same surprise flit across Alida's pupils. 'I suppose so. One just has to wait.'

'Oh, hang waiting!' Ned broke in. 'Life's too short for a ghost who can only be enjoyed in retrospect. Can't we do better than that, Mary?'

But it turned out that in the event they were not destined to, for within three months of their conversation with Mrs Stair they were settled at Lyng, and the life they had yearned for, to the point of planning it in advance in all its daily details, had actually begun for them.

It was to sit, in the thick December dusk, by just such a wide-hooded fireplace, under just such black oak rafters, with the sense that beyond the mullioned panes the downs were darkened to a deeper solitude: it was for the ultimate indulgence of such sensations that Mary Boyne, abruptly exiled from New York by her husband's business, had endured for nearly fourteen years the soul-deadening ugliness of a Middle Western town, and that Boyne had ground on doggedly at his engineering till, with a suddenness that still made her blink, the prodigious windfall of the Blue Star Mine had put them at a stroke in possession of life and the leisure to taste it. They had never for a moment meant their new state to be one of idleness; but they meant to give themselves only to harmonious activities. She had her vision of painting and gardening (against a background of grey walls), he dreamed of the production of his long-planned book on the *Economic Basis of Culture*; and with such absorbing work ahead no existence could be too sequestered: they could not get far enough from the world, or plunge deep enough into the past.

Dorsetshire had attracted them from the first by an air of remoteness out of all proportion to its geographical position. But to the Boynes it was one of the ever-recurring wonders of the whole incredibly compressed island – a nest of counties, as they put it – that for the production of its effects so little of a given quality went so far: that so few miles made a distance, and so short a distance a difference.

'It's that,' Ned had once enthusiastically explained, 'that gives such depth to their efforts, such relief to their contrasts. They've been able to lay the butter so thick on every delicious mouthful.'

The butter had certainly been laid on thick at Lyng: the old house hidden under a shoulder of the downs had almost all the finer marks of commerce with a protracted past. The mere fact that it was neither large nor exceptional made it, to the Boynes, abound the more completely in its special charm – the charm of having been for centuries a deep, dim reservoir of life. The life had probably not been of the most vivid order: for long periods, no doubt, it had fallen as noiselessly into the past as the quiet drizzle of autumn fell, hour after hour, into the fish-pond between the yews; but these back-waters of existence sometimes breed, in their sluggish depths, strange acuities of emotion, and Mary Boyne had felt from the first the mysterious stir of intenser memories.

The feeling had never been stronger than on this particular afternoon when, waiting in the library for the lamps to come, she rose from her seat and stood among the shadows of the hearth. Her husband had gone off, after luncheon, for one of his long tramps on the downs. She had noticed of late that he preferred to go alone; and, in the tried security of their personal relations, had been driven to conclude that his book was bothering him, and that he needed the afternoons to turn over in solitude the problems left from the morning's work. Certainly the book was not going as smoothly as she had thought it would, and there were lines of perplexity between his eyes such as had never been there in his engineering days. He had often, then, looked fagged to the verge of illness, but the native demon of 'worry' had never branded his brow. Yet the few pages he had so far read to her – the introduction, and a summary of the opening chapter – showed a firm hold on his subject, and an increasing confidence in his powers.

The fact threw her into deeper perplexity, since, now that he had done with 'business' and its disturbing contingencies, the one other possible source of anxiety was eliminated.

Unless it were his health, then? But physically he had gained since they had come to Dorsetshire, grown robuster, ruddier and fresher-eyed. It was only within the last week that she had felt in him the undefinable change which made her restless in his absence, and as tongue-tied in his presence as though it were *she* who had a secret to keep from him!

The thought that there *was* a secret somewhere between them struck her with a sudden rap of wonder, and she looked about her down the long room.

'Can it be the house?' she mused.

The room itself might have been full of secrets. They seemed to be piling themselves up, as evening fell, like the layers and layers of velvet shadow dropping from the low ceiling, the row of books, the smoke-blurred sculpture of the hearth.

'Why, of course – the house is haunted!' she reflected.

The ghost – Alida's imperceptible ghost – after figuring largely in the banter of their first month or two at Lyng, had been gradually left aside as too ineffectual for imaginative use. Mary had, indeed, as became the tenant of a haunted house, made the customary inquiries among her rural neighbours, but, beyond a vague 'They du say so, ma'am,' the villagers had nothing to impart. The elusive spectre had apparently never had sufficient identity for a legend to crystallize about it, and after a time the Boynes had set the matter down to their profit-and-loss account, agreeing that Lyng was one of the few houses good enough in itself to dispense with supernatural enhancements.

'And I suppose, poor ineffectual demon, that's why it beats its beautiful wings in vain in the void,' Mary had laughingly concluded.

'Or, rather,' Ned answered in the same strain, 'why, amid so much that's ghostly, it can never affirm its separate existence as *the* ghost.' And thereupon their invisible housemate had finally dropped out of their references, which were numerous enough to make them soon unaware of the loss.

Now, as she stood on the hearth, the subject of their earlier curiosity revived in her with a new sense of its meaning – a sense gradually acquired through daily contact with the scene of the lurking mystery. It was the house itself, of course, that possessed the ghost-seeing faculty, that communed visually but secretly with its own past; if one could only get into close enough communion with the house one might surprise its secret, and acquire the ghost-sight on one's own account. Perhaps, in his long hours in this very room, where she never trespassed till the afternoon, her husband *had* acquired it already, and was silently carrying about the weight of whatever it had revealed to him. Mary was too well versed in the code of the spectral world not to know that one could not talk about the ghosts one saw: to do so was almost as great a breach of taste as to name a lady in a club. But this explanation did not really satisfy her. 'What, after all, except for the fun of the shudder,' she reflected, 'would he really care for any of their old ghosts?' And thence she was thrown back once more on the fundamental dilemma: the fact that one's greater or less susceptibility to spectral influences had no particular bearing on the case, since, when one *did* see a ghost at Lyng, one did not know it.

'Not till long afterward,' Alida Stair had said. Well, supposing Ned *had* seen one when they first came, and had known only within the last week what had happened to him? More and more under the spell of the hour, she threw back her thoughts to the early days of their tenancy, but at first only to recall a lively confusion of unpacking, settling, arranging of books, and calling to each other from remote corners of the house as, treasure after treasure, it revealed itself to them. It was in this particular connection that she presently recalled a certain soft afternoon of the previous October, when, passing from the first rapturous flurry of exploration to a detailed inspection of the old house, she had pressed (like a novel heroine) a panel that opened on a flight of corkscrew stairs leading to a flat ledge of the roof – the roof which, from below, seemed to slope away on all sides too abruptly for any but practised feet to scale.

The view from this hidden coign was enchanting, and she had flown down to snatch Ned from his papers and give him the freedom of her discovery. She remembered still how, standing at her side, he had passed his arm about her while their gaze flew to the long tossed horizon-line of the downs,

and then dropped contentedly back to trace the arabesque of
yew hedges about the fish-pond, and the shadow of the cedar
on the lawn.

'And now the other way,' he had said, turning her about
within his arm; and closely pressed to him, she had
absorbed, like some long satisfying draught, the picture of
the grey-walled court, the squat lions on the gates, and the
lime-avenue reaching up to the high-road under the downs.

It was just then, while they gazed and held each other, that
she had felt his arms relax, and heard a sharp 'Hullo!' that
made her turn to glance at him.

Distinctly, yes, she now recalled that she had seen, as she
glanced, a shadow of anxiety, of perplexity, rather, fall
across his face; and, following his eyes, had beheld the figure
of a man – a man in loose greyish clothes, as it appeared to
her – who was sauntering down the lime-avenue to the court
with the doubtful gait of a stranger who seeks his way. Her
short-sighted eyes had given her but a blurred impression of
slightness and greyishness, with something foreign, or at
least unlocal, in the cut of the figure or its dress; but her
husband had apparently seen more – seen enough to make
him push past her with a hasty 'Wait!' and dash down the
stairs without pausing to give her a hand.

A slight tendency to dizziness obliged her, after a
provisional clutch at the chimney against which they had
been leaning, to follow him first more cautiously; and when
she reached the landing she paused again, for a less definite
reason, leaning over the banister to strain her eyes through
the silence of the brown sun-flecked depths. She lingered
there until, somewhere in those depths she heard the closing
of a door; then, mechanically impelled, she went down the
shallow flight of steps till she reached the lower hall.

The front door stood open on the sunlight of the court,
and hall and court were empty. The library door was open,
too, and after listening in vain for any sound of voices within,
she crossed the threshold and found her husband alone,
vaguely fingering the papers on his desk.

He looked up, as if surprised at her entrance, but the
shadow of anxiety had passed from his face, leaving it even,
as she fancied, a little brighter and clearer than usual.

'What was it? Who was it?' she asked.

'Who?' he repeated, with the surprise still all on his side.

'The man we saw coming toward the house.'

He seemed to reflect. 'The man? Why, I thought I saw Peters; I dashed after him to say a word about the stable drains, but he had disappeared before I could get down.'

'Disappeared? But he seemed to be walking so slowly when we saw him.'

Boyne shrugged his shoulders. 'So I thought; but he must have got up steam in the interval. What do you say to our trying a scramble up Meldon Steep before sunset?'

That was all. At the time the occurrence had been less than nothing, had, indeed, been immediately obliterated by the magic of their first vision from Meldon Steep, a height which they had dreamed of climbing ever since they had first seen its bare spine rising above the roof of Lyng. Doubtless it was the mere fact of the other incident's having occurred on the very day of their ascent to Meldon that had kept it stored away in the fold of memory from which it now emerged; for in itself it had no mark of the portentous. At the moment there could have been nothing more natural than that Ned should dash down from the roof in pursuit of dilatory tradesmen. It was the period when they were always on the watch for one or the other of the specialists employed about the place; always lying in wait for them, and rushing out at them with questions, reproaches, or reminders. And certainly in the distance the grey figure had looked like Peters.

Yet now, as she reviewed the scene, she felt her husband's explanation of it to have been invalidated by the look of anxiety on his face. Why had the familiar appearance of Peters made him anxious? Why, above all, if it was of such prime necessity to confer with him on the subject of the stable drains, had the failure to find him produced such a look of relief? Mary could not say that any one of these questions had occurred to her at the time, yet, from the promptness with which they now marshalled themselves at her summons, she had a sense that they must all along have been there, waiting their hour.

Weary with her thoughts, she moved to the window. The library was now quite dark, and she was surprised to see how much faint light the outer world still held.

As she peered out into it across the court, a figure shaped itself far down the perspective of bare limes: it looked a mere blot of deeper grey in the greyness, and for an instant, as it moved toward her, her heart thumped to the thought, 'It's the ghost!'

She had time, in that long instant, to feel suddenly that the man of whom, two months earlier, she had had a distant vision from the roof, was now, at his predestined hour, about to reveal himself as *not* having been Peters; and her spirit sank under the impending fear of the disclosure. But almost with the next tick of the clock the figure, gaining substance and character, showed itself even to her weak sight as her husband's; and she turned to meet him, as he entered, with the confession of her folly.

'It's really too absurd,' she laughed out, 'but I never *can* remember!'

'Remember what?' Boyne questioned as they drew together.

'That when one sees the Lyng ghost one never knows it.'

Her hand was on his sleeve, and he kept it there, but with no response in his gesture or in the lines of his preoccupied face.

'Did you think you'd seen it?' he asked, after an appreciable interval.

'Why, I actually took *you* for it, my dear, in my mad determination to spot it!'

'Me – just now?' His arm dropped away, and he turned from her with a faint echo of her laugh. 'Really, dearest, you'd better give it up, if that's the best you can do.'

'Oh yes, I give it up. Have *you?*' she asked, turning round on him abruptly.

The parlour-maid had entered with letters and a lamp, and the light struck up into Boyne's face as he bent above the tray she presented.

'Have *you?*' Mary perversely insisted, when the servant had disappeared on her errand of illumination.

'Have I what?' he rejoined absently, the light bringing out

the sharp stamp of worry between his brows as he turned over the letters.

'Given up trying to see the ghost.' Her heart beat a little at the experiment she was making.

Her husband, laying his letters aside, moved away into the shadow of the hearth.

'I never tried,' he said, tearing open the wrapper of a newspaper.

'Well, of course,' Mary persisted, 'the exasperating thing is that there's no use trying, since one can't be sure until so long afterward.'

He was unfolding the paper as if he had hardly heard her; but after a pause, during which the sheets rustled spasmodically between his hands, he looked up to ask, 'Have you any idea *how long*?'

Mary had sunk into a low chair beside the fire-place. From her seat she glanced over, startled, at her husband's profile, which was projected against the circle of lamplight.

'No; none. Have *you*?' she retorted, repeating her former phrase with an added stress of intention.

Boyne crumpled the paper into a bunch, and then, inconsequently, turned back with it toward the lamp.

'Lord, no! I only meant,' he explained, with a faint tinge of impatience, 'is there any legend, any tradition as to that?'

'Not that I know of,' she answered; but the impulse to add, 'What makes you ask?' was checked by the reappearance of the parlour-maid, with tea and a second lamp.

With the dispersal of shadows, and the repetition of the daily domestic office, Mary Boyne felt herself less oppressed by that sense of something mutely imminent which had darkened her afternoon. For a few moments she gave herself to the details of her task, and when she looked up from it she was struck to the point of bewilderment by the change in her husband's face. He had seated himself near the farther lamp, and was absorbed in the perusal of his letters; but was it something he had found in them, or merely the shifting of her own point of view, that had restored his features to their normal aspect? The longer she looked the more definitely the change affirmed itself. The lines of tension had vanished, and such traces of fatigue as lingered were of the kind easily attributable to steady mental effort. He glanced up, as if drawn by her gaze, and met her eyes with a smile.

'I'm dying for my tea, you know; and here's a letter for you,' he said.

She took the letter he held out in exchange for the cup she proffered him, and, returning to her seat, broke the seal with the languid gesture of the reader whose interests are all enclosed in the circle of one cherished presence.

Her next conscious motion was that of starting to her feet, the letter falling to them as she rose, while she held out to her husband a newspaper clipping.

'Ned! What's this? What does it mean?'

He had risen at the same instant, almost as if hearing her cry before she uttered it; and for a perceptible space of time he and she studied each other, like adversaries watching for an advantage, across the space between her chair and his desk.

'What's what? You fairly made me jump!' Boyne said at length, moving toward her with a sudden half-exasperated laugh. The shadow of apprehension was on his face again, not now a look of fixed foreboding, but a shifting vigilance of lips and eyes that gave her the sense of feeling himself invisibly surrounded.

Her hand shook so that she could hardly give him the clipping.

'This article – from the *Waukesha Sentinel* – that a man named Elwell has brought suit against you – that there was something wrong about the Blue Star Mine. I can't understand more than half.'

They continued to face each other as she spoke, and to her astonishment she saw that her words had the almost immediate effect of dissipating the strained watchfulness of his look.

'Oh, *that*!' He glanced down the printed slip, and then folded it with the gesture of one who handles something harmless and familiar. 'What's the matter with you this afternoon, Mary? I thought you'd got bad news.'

She stood before him with her undefinable terror subsiding slowly under the reassurance of his tone.

'You knew about this, then – it's all right?'

'Certainly I knew about it; and it's all right.'

'But what *is* it? I don't understand. What does this man accuse you of?'

'Pretty nearly every crime in the calendar.' Boyne had tossed the clipping down and thrown himself into an armchair near the fire. 'Do you want to hear the story? It's not particularly interesting – just a squabble over interests in the Blue Star.'

'But who is this Elwell? I don't know the name.'

'Oh, he's a fellow I put into it – gave him a hand up. I told you all about him at the time.'

'I dare say. I must have forgotten.' Vainly she strained back among her memories. 'But if you helped him, why does he make this return?'

'Probably some shyster lawyer got hold of him and talked him over. It's all rather technical and complicated. I thought that kind of thing bored you.'

His wife felt a sting of compunction. Theoretically, she deprecated the American wife's detachment from her husband's professional interests, but in practice she had always found it difficult to fix her attention on Boyne's report of the transactions in which his varied interests involved him. Besides, she had felt during their years of exile, that, in a community where the amenities of living could be obtained only at the cost of efforts as arduous as her husband's professional labours, such brief leisure as he and she could command should be used as an escape from immediate preoccupations, a flight to the life they always dreamed of living. Once or twice, now that this new life had actually drawn its magic circle about them, she had asked herself if she had done right; but hitherto such conjectures had been no more than the retrospective excursions of an active fancy. Now, for the first time, it startled her a little to find how little she knew of the material foundation on which her happiness was built.

She glanced at her husband, and was again reassured by the composure of his face; yet she felt the need of more definite grounds for her reassurance.

'But doesn't this suit worry you? Why have you never spoken to me about it?'

He answered both questions at once. 'I didn't speak of it at first because it *did* worry me – annoyed me, rather. But it's all ancient history now. Your correspondent must have got hold of a back number of the *Sentinel*.'

She felt a quick thrill of relief. 'You mean it's over? He's lost his case?'

There was a just perceptible delay in Boyne's reply. 'The suit's been withdrawn – that's all.'

But she persisted, as if to exonerate herself from the inward charge of being too easily put off. 'Withdrawn it because he saw he had no chance?'

'Oh, he had no chance,' Boyne answered.

She was still struggling with a dimly felt perplexity at the back of her thoughts.

'How long ago was it withdrawn?'

He paused, as if with a slight return of his former uncertainty. 'I've just had the news now; but I've been expecting it.'

'Just now – in one of your letters?'

'Yes; in one of my letters.'

She made no answer, and was aware only, after a short interval of waiting, that he had risen and, strolling across the room, had placed himself on the sofa at her side. She felt him, as he did so, pass an arm about her, she felt his hand seek hers and clasp it, and turning slowly, drawn by the warmth of his cheek, she met his smiling eyes.

'It's all right – it's all right?' she questioned, through the flood of her dissolving doubts; and, 'I give you my word it was never righter!' he laughed back at her, holding her close.

One of the strangest things she was afterward to recall out of all the next day's strangeness was the sudden and complete recovery of her sense of security.

It was in the air when she awoke in her low-ceiled, dusky room; it went with her downstairs to the breakfast-table, flashed out at her from the fire, and reduplicated itself from the flanks of the urn and the sturdy flutings of the Georgian tea-pot. It was as if, in some roundabout way, all her diffused fears of the previous day, with their moment of sharp concentration about the newspaper article – as if this dim questioning of the future, and startled return upon the past, had between them liquidated the arrears of some haunting moral obligation. If she had indeed been careless of her husband's affairs, it was, her new state seemed to prove, because her faith in him instinctively justified such carelessness; and his right to her faith had now affirmed itself in the very face of menace and suspicion. She had never seen him more untroubled, more naturally and unconsciously himself, than after the cross-examination to which she had subjected him: it was almost as if he had been aware of her doubts, and had wanted the air cleared as much as she did.

It was as clear, thank heaven, as the bright outer light that surprised her almost with a touch of summer when she issued from the house for her daily round of the gardens. She had left Boyne at his desk, indulging herself, as she passed the library door, by a last peep at his quiet face, where he bent, pipe in mouth, above his papers; and now she had her own morning's task to perform. The task involved, on such charmed winter days, almost as much happy loitering about the different quarters of her demesne as if spring were already at work there. There were such endless possibilities still before her, such opportunities to bring out the latent graces of the old place, without a single irreverent touch of alteration, that the winter was all too short to plan what spring and autumn executed. And her recovered sense of safety gave, on this particular morning, a peculiar zest to her progress through the sweet, still place. She went first to the kitchen garden, where the espaliered pear trees drew complicated patterns on the walls, and pigeons were fluttering and preening about the silvery-slated roof of their cote.

There was something wrong about the piping of the hothouse and she was expecting an authority from Dorchester, who was to drive out between trains and make a diagnosis of the boiler. But when she dipped into the damp heat of the greenhouses, among the spiced scents and waxy pinks and reds of old-fashioned exotics – even the flora of Lyng was in the note! – she learned that the great man had not arrived, and, the day being too rare to waste in an artificial atmosphere, she came out again and paced along the springy turf of the bowling-green to the gardens behind the house. At their farther end rose a grass terrace, looking across the fish-pond and yew hedges to the long house-front with its twisted chimney-stacks and blue roof angels all drenched in the pale-gold moisture of the air.

Seen thus, across the level tracery of the gardens, it sent her, from open windows and hospitably smoking chimneys, the look of some warm human presence, of a mind slowly ripened on a sunny wall of experience. She had never before had such a sense of her intimacy with it, such a conviction that its secrets were all beneficent, kept, as they said to children, 'for one's own good', such a trust in its power to gather up her life and Ned's into the harmonious pattern of the long, long story it sat there weaving in the sun.

She heard steps behind her, and turned, expecting to see the gardener accompanied by the engineer from Dorchester. But only one figure was in sight, that of a youngish, slightly built man, who, for reasons she could not on the spot have given, did not remotely resemble her notion of an authority on hothouse boilers. The new-comer, on seeing her, lifted his hat, and paused with the air of a gentleman – perhaps a traveller – who wishes to make it known that his intrusion is involuntary. Lyng occasionally attracted the more cultivated traveller, and Mary half expected to see the stranger dissemble a camera, or justify his presence by producing it. But he made no gesture of any sort, and after a moment she asked, in a tone responding to the courteous hesitation of his attitude: 'Is there anyone you wish to see?'

'I came to see Mr Boyne,' he answered. His intonation, rather than his accent, was faintly American, and Mary, at the note, looked at him more closely. The brim of his soft felt hat cast a shade on his face, which, thus obscured, wore, to her short-sighted gaze, a look of seriousness, as of a person arriving 'on business', and civilly but firmly aware of his rights.

Past experience had made her equally sensible to such claims; but she was jealous of her husband's morning hours, and doubtful of his having given anyone the right to intrude on them.

'Have you an appointment with my husband?' she asked.

The visitor hesitated, as if unprepared for the question. 'I think he expects me,' he replied.

It was Mary's turn to hesitate. 'You see, this is his time for work: he never sees anyone in the morning.'

He looked at her a moment without answering; then, as if accepting her decision, he began to move away. As he turned, Mary saw him pause and glance up at the peaceful house-front. Something in his air suggested weariness and disappointment, the dejection of the traveller who has come from far off and whose hours are limited by the time-table. It occurred to her that if this were the case her refusal might have made his errand vain, and a sense of compunction caused her to hasten after him.

'May I ask if you have come a long way?'

He gave her the same grave look. 'Yes – I have come a long way.'

'Then, if you'll go to the house, no doubt my husband will see you now. You'll find him in the library.'

She did not know why she had added the last phrase, except from a vague impulse to atone for her previous inhospitality. The visitor seemed about to express his thanks, but her attention was distracted by the approach of the gardener with a companion who bore all the marks of being the expert from Dorchester.

'This way,' she said, waving the stranger to the house; and an instant later she had forgotten him in the absorption of her meeting with the boiler-maker.

The encounter led to such far-reaching results that the engineer ended by finding it expedient to ignore his train, and Mary was beguiled into spending the remainder of the morning in absorbed confabulation among the flower-pots. When the colloquy ended, she was surprised to find that it was nearly luncheon-time, and she half expected, as she hurried back to the house, to see her husband coming out to meet her. But she found no one in the court but an under-gardener raking the gravel, and the hall, when she entered it, was so silent that she guessed Boyne to be still at work.

Not wishing to disturb him, she turned into the drawing-room, and there, at her writing-table, lost herself in renewed calculations of the outlay to which the morning's conference had pledged her. The fact that she could permit herself such follies had not yet lost its novelty; and somehow, in contrast to the vague fears of the previous days, it now seemed an element of her recovered security, of the sense that, as Ned had said, things in general had never been 'righter'.

She was still luxuriating in a lavish play of figures when the parlour-maid, from the threshold, roused her with an inquiry as to the expediency of serving luncheon. It was one of their jokes that Trimmle announced luncheon as if she were divulging a State secret, and Mary, intent upon her papers, merely murmured an absent-minded assent.

She felt Trimmle wavering doubtfully on the threshold, as if in rebuke of such unconsidered assent; then her retreating steps sounded down the passage, and Mary, pushing away her papers, crossed the hall and went to the library door. It was still closed, and she wavered in her turn, disliking to disturb her husband, yet anxious that he should not exceed his usual measure of work. As she stood there, balancing her impulses, Trimmle returned with the announcement of luncheon, and Mary, thus impelled, opened the library door.

Boyne was not at his desk, and she peered about her, expecting to discover him before the book-shelves, somewhere down the length of the room; but her call brought no response, and gradually it became clear to her that he was not there.

She turned back to the parlour-maid.

'Mr Boyne must be upstairs. Please tell him that luncheon is ready.'

Trimmle appeared to hesitate between the obvious duty of obedience and an equally obvious conviction of the foolishness of the injunction laid on her. The struggle resulted in her saying: 'If you please, madam, Mr Boyne's not upstairs.'

'Not in his room? Are you sure?'

'I'm sure, madam.'

Mary consulted the clock. 'Where is he, then?'

'He's gone out,' Trimmle announced, with the superior air of one who has respectfully waited for the question that a well-ordered mind would have put first.

Mary's conjecture had been right, then; Boyne must have gone to the gardens to meet her, and since she had missed him, it was clear that he had taken the shorter way by the south door, instead of going round to the court. She crossed the hall to the french window opening directly on the yew garden, but the parlour-maid, after another moment of inner conflict, decided to bring out: 'Please, madam, Mr Boyne didn't go that way.'

Mary turned back. 'Where *did* he go? And when?'

'He went out of the front door, up the drive, madam.' It was a matter of principle with Trimmle never to answer more than one question at a time.

'Up the drive? At this hour?' Mary went to the door herself and glanced across the court through the tunnel of bare limes. But its perspective was as empty as when she had scanned it on entering.

'Did Mr Boyne leave no message?'

Trimmle seemed to surrender herself to a last struggle with the forces of chaos.

'No, madam. He just went out with the gentleman.'

'The gentleman? What gentleman?' Mary wheeled about, as if to front this new factor.

'The gentleman who called, madam,' said Trimmle resignedly.

'When did a gentleman call? Do explain yourself, Trimmle!'

Only the fact that Mary was very hungry, and that she wanted to consult her husband about the greenhouses, would have caused her to lay so unusual an injunction on her attendant; and even now she was detached enough to note in Trimmle's eyes the dawning defiance of the respectful subordinate who has been pressed too hard.

'I couldn't exactly say the hour, madam, because I didn't let the gentleman in,' she replied, with an air of discreetly ignoring the irregularity of her mistress's course.

'You didn't let him in?'

'No, madam. When the bell rang I was dressing, and Agnes – '

'Go and ask Agnes, then,' said Mary.

Trimmle still wore her look of patient magnanimity.

'Agnes would not know, madam, for she had unfortunately burnt her hand in trimming the wick of the new lamp from town' – Trimmle, as Mary was aware, had always been opposed to the new lamp – 'and so Mrs Dockett sent the kitchen-maid instead.'

Mary looked again at the clock. 'It's after two. Go and ask the kitchen-maid if Mr Boyne left any word.'

She went into luncheon without waiting, and Trimmle presently brought to her there the kitchen-maid's statement that the gentleman had called about eleven o'clock, and that Mr Boyne had gone out with him without leaving any message. The kitchen-maid did not even know the caller's name, for he had written it on a slip of paper, which he had folded and handed to her, with the injunction to deliver it at once to Mr Boyne.

Mary finished her luncheon, still wondering, and when it was over, and Trimmle had brought the coffee to the drawing-room, her wonder had deepened to a first faint tinge of disquietude. It was unlike Boyne to absent himself without explanation at so unwonted an hour, and the difficulty of identifying the visitor whose summons he had apparently obeyed made his disappearance the more unaccountable. Mary Boyne's experience as the wife of a busy engineer, subject to sudden calls and compelled to keep irregular hours, had trained her to the philosophic acceptance of surprises; but since Boyne's withdrawal from business he had adopted a Benedictine regularity of life. As if to make up for the dispersed and agitated years, with their 'stand-up' lunches and dinners rattled down to the joltings of the dining-cars, he cultivated the last refinements of punctuality and monotony, discouraging his wife's fancy for the unexpected, and declaring that to a delicate taste there were infinite gradations of pleasure in the recurrences of habit.

Still, since no life can completely defend itself from the unforeseen, it was evident that all Boyne's precautions would sooner or later prove unavailing, and Mary concluded that he had cut short a tiresome visit by walking with his caller to the station, or at least accompanying him for part of the way.

This conclusion relieved her from further preoccupation, and she went out herself to take up her conference with the gardener. Thence she walked to the village post office, a mile or so away; and when she turned toward home the early twilight was setting in.

She had taken a footpath across the downs, and as Boyne, meanwhile, had probably returned from the station by the high-road, there was little likelihood of their meeting. She felt sure, however, of his having reached the house before her; so sure that, when she entered it herself, without even pausing to inquire of Trimmle, she made directly for the library. But the library was still empty, and with an unwonted exactness of visual memory she observed that the papers on her husband's desk lay precisely as they had lain when she had gone in to call him to luncheon.

Then of a sudden she was seized by a vague dread of the unknown. She had closed the door behind her on entering, and as she stood alone in the long, silent room, her dread seemed to take shape and sound, to be there breathing and lurking among the shadows. Her short-sighted eyes strained through them, half discerning an actual presence, something aloof, that watched and knew; and in the recoil from that intangible presence she threw herself on the bell-rope and gave it a sharp pull.

The sharp summons brought Trimmle in precipitately with a lamp, and Mary breathed again at this sobering reappearance of the usual.

'You may bring tea if Mr Boyne is in,' she said, to justify her ring.

'Very well, madam. But Mr Boyne is not in,' said Trimmle, putting down the lamp.

'Not in? You mean he's come back and gone out again?'

'No, madam. He's never been back.'

The dread stirred again, and Mary knew that now it had her fast.

'Not since he went out with – the gentleman?'

'Not since he went out with the gentleman.'

'But who *was* the gentleman?' Mary insisted, with the shrill note of someone trying to be heard through a confusion of noises.

'That I couldn't say, madam.' Trimmle, standing there by the lamp, seemed suddenly to grow less round and rosy, as though eclipsed by the same creeping shade of apprehension.

'But the kitchen-maid knows – wasn't it the kitchen-maid who let him in?'

'She doesn't know either, madam, for he wrote his name on a folded paper.'

Mary, through her agitation, was aware that they were both designating the unknown visitor by a vague pronoun, instead of the conventional formula which, till then, had kept their allusions within the bounds of conformity. And at the same moment her mind caught at the suggestion of the folded paper.

'But he must have a name! Where's the paper?'

She moved to the desk and began to turn over the documents that littered it. The first that caught her eyes was an unfinished letter in her husband's hand, with his pen lying across it, as though dropped there at a sudden summons.

My dear Parvis – who was Parvis? – *I have just received your letter announcing Elwell's death, and while I suppose there is now no further risk of trouble, it might be safer –*

She tossed the sheet aside, and continued her search; but no folded paper was discoverable among the letters and pages of manuscript which had been swept together in a heap, as if by a hurried or a startled gesture.

'But the kitchen-maid *saw* him. Send her here,' she commanded, wondering at her dullness in not thinking sooner of so simple a solution.

Trimmle vanished in a flash, as if thankful to be out of the room, and when she reappeared, conducting the agitated underling, Mary had regained her self-possession and had her questions ready.

The gentleman was a stranger, yes – that she understood. But what had he said? And, above all, what had he looked like? The first question was easily enough answered, for the disconcerting reason that he had said so little – had merely asked for Mr Boyne, and, scribbling something on a bit of paper, had requested that it should at once be carried in to him.

'Then you don't know what he wrote? You're not sure it

was his name?'

The kitchen-maid was not sure, but supposed it was, since he had written it in answer to her inquiry as to whom she should announce.

'And when you carried the paper in to Mr Boyne, what did he say?'

The kitchen-maid did not think that Mr Boyne had said anything, but she could not be sure, for just as she had handed him the paper and he was opening it, she had become aware that the visitor had followed her into the library, and she had slipped out, leaving the two gentlemen together.

'But, then, if you left them in the library, how do you know that they went out of the house?'

This question plunged the witness into a momentary inarticulateness, from which she was rescued by Trimmle, who, by means of ingenious circumlocutions, elicited the statement that before she could cross the hall to the back passage she had heard the two gentlemen behind her, and had seen them go out of the front door together.

'Then, if you saw the strange gentleman twice, you must be able to tell me what he looked like.'

But with this final challenge to her powers of expression it became clear that the limit of the kitchen-maid's endurance had been reached. The obligation of going to the front door to 'show in' a visitor was in itself so subversive of the fundamental order of things that it had thrown her faculties into hopeless disarray, and she could only stammer out, after various panting efforts: 'His hat, mum, was different-like, as you might say – '

'Different? How different?' Mary flashed out, her own mind, in the same instant, leaping back to an image left on it that morning, and then lost under layers of subsequent impressions.

'His hat had a wide brim, you mean, and his face was pale – a youngish face?' Mary pressed her, with a white-lipped intensity of interrogation. But if the kitchen-maid found any adequate answer to this challenge, it was swept away for her listener down the rushing current of her own convictions. The stranger – the stranger in the garden! Why had not Mary thought of him before? She needed no one now to tell her that it was he who had called for her husband and gone away with him. But who was he, and why had Boyne obeyed him?

It leaped out at her suddenly, like a grin out of the dark, that they had often called England so little — 'such a confoundedly hard place to get lost in'.

A confoundedly hard place to get lost in! That had been her husband's phrase. And now, with the whole machinery of official investigation sweeping its flashlights from shore to shore, and across the dividing straits; now, with Boyne's name blazing from the walls of every town and village, his portrait (how that wrung her!) hawked up and down the country like the image of a hunted criminal; now the little, compact, populous island, so policed, surveyed and administered, revealed itself as a Sphinx-like guardian of abysmal mysteries, staring back into his wife's anguished eyes as if with the wicked joy of knowing something they would never know!

In the fortnight since Boyne's disappearance there had been no word of him, no trace of his movements. Even the usual misleading reports that raise expectancy in tortured bosoms had been few and fleeting. No one but the kitchen-maid had seen Boyne leave the house, and no one else had seen the 'gentleman' who accompanied him. All inquiries in the neighbourhood failed to elicit the memory of a stranger's presence that day in the neighbourhood of Lyng. And no one had met Edward Boyne, either alone or in company, in any of the neighbouring villages, or on the road across the downs, or at either of the local railway stations. The sunny English noon had swallowed him as completely as if he had gone out into Cimmerian night.

Mary, while every official means of investigation was working at its highest pressure, had ransacked her husband's papers for any trace of antecedent complications, of entanglements or obligations unknown to her, that might throw a ray into the darkness. But if any such had existed in the background of Boyne's life, they had vanished like the slip of paper on which the visitor had written his name. There remained no possible thread of guidance except — if it were indeed an exception – the letter which Boyne had apparently been in the act of writing when he received his mysterious summons. That letter, read and re-read by his wife, and submitted by her to the police, yielded little enough to feed conjecture.

'I have just heard of Elwell's death, and while I suppose there is now no further risk of trouble, it might be safer – ' That was all. The 'risk of trouble' was easily explained by the newspaper clipping which had apprised Mary of the suit brought against her husband by one of his associates in the Blue Star enterprise. The only new information conveyed by the letter was the fact of its showing Boyne, when he wrote it, to be still apprehensive of the results of the suit, though he had told his wife that it had been withdrawn, and though the letter itself proved that the plaintiff was dead. It took several days of cabling to fix the identity of the 'Parvis' to whom the fragment was addressed, but even after these inquiries had shown him to be a Waukesha lawyer, no new facts concerning the Elwell suit were elicited. He appeared to have had no direct concern in it, but to have been conversant with the facts merely as an acquaintance, and possible intermediary; and he declared himself unable to guess with what object Boyne intended to seek his assistance.

This negative information, sole fruit of the first fortnight's search, was not increased by a jot during the slow weeks that followed. Mary knew that the investigations were still being carried on, but she had a vague sense of their gradually slackening, as the actual march of time seemed to slacken. It was as though the days, flying horror-struck from the shrouded image of the one inscrutable day, gained assurance as the distance lengthened, till at last they fell back into their normal gait. And so with the human imaginations at work on the dark event. No doubt it occupied them still, but week by week and hour by hour it grew less absorbing, took up less space, was slowly but inevitably crowded out of the foreground of consciousness by the new problems perpetually bubbling up from the cloudy cauldron of human experience.

Even Mary Boyne's consciousness gradually felt the same lowering of velocity. It still swayed with the incessant oscillations of conjecture; but they were slower, more rhythmical in their beat. There were even moments of weariness when, like the victim of some poison which leaves the brain clear, but holds the body motionless, she saw herself domesticated with the Horror, accepting its perpetual presence as one of the fixed conditions of life.

These moments lengthened into hours and days, till she passed into a phase of stolid acquiescence. She watched the routine of daily life with the incurious eye of a savage on whom the meaningless processes of civilization make but the faintest impression. She had come to regard herself as part of the routine, a spoke of the wheel, revolving with its motion; she felt almost like the furniture of the room in which she sat, an insensate object to be dusted and pushed about with the chairs and tables. And this deepening apathy held her fast at Lyng, in spite of the entreaties of friends and the usual medical recommendation of 'change'. Her friends supposed that her refusal to move was inspired by the belief that her husband would one day return to the spot from which he had vanished, and a beautiful legend grew up about this imaginary state of waiting. But in reality she had no such belief: the depths of anguish enclosing her were no longer lighted by flashes of hope. She was sure that Boyne would never come back, that he had gone out of her sight as completely as if death itself had waited that day on the threshold. She had even renounced, one by one, the various theories as to his disappearance which had been advanced by the Press, the police, and her own agonized imagination. In sheer lassitude her mind turned from these alternatives of horror, and sank back into the blank fact that he was gone.

No, she would never know what had become of him – no one would ever know. But the house *knew*; the library in which she spent her long, lonely evenings knew. For it was here that the last scene had been enacted, here that the stranger had come and spoken the word which had caused Boyne to rise and follow him. The floor she trod had felt his tread; the books on the shelves had seen his face; and there were moments when the intense consciousness of the old dusky walls seemed about to break out into some audible revelation of their secret. But the revelation never came, and she knew it would never come. Lyng was not one of the garrulous old houses that betray the secrets entrusted to them. Its very legend proved that it had always been the mute accomplice, the incorruptible custodian, of the mysteries it had surprised. And Mary Boyne, sitting face to face with its silence, felt the futility of seeking to break it by any human means.

'I don't say it *wasn't* straight, and yet I don't say it *was* straight. It was business.'

Mary, at the words, lifted her head with a start and looked intently at the speaker.

When, half an hour before, a card with 'Mr Parvis' on it had been brought up to her, she had been immediately aware that the name had been a part of her consciousness ever since she had read it at the head of Boyne's unfinished letter. In the library she had found awaiting her a small, sallow man with a bald head and gold eye-glasses, and it sent a tremor through her to know that this was the person to whom her husband's last known thought had been directed.

Parvis, civilly, but without vain preamble – in the manner of a man who has his watch in his hand – had set forth the object of his visit. He had 'run over' to England on business, and finding himself in the neighbourhood of Dorchester, had not wished to leave it without paying his respects to Mrs Boyne; and without asking her, if the occasion offered, what she meant to do about Bob Elwell's family.

The words touched the spring of some obscure dread in Mary's bosom. Did her visitor, after all, know what Boyne had meant by his unfinished phrase? She asked for an elucidation of his question, and noticed at once that he seemed surprised at her continued ignorance of the subject. Was it possible that she really knew as little as she said?

'I know nothing – you just tell me,' she faltered out; and her visitor thereupon proceeded to unfold his story. It threw, even to her confused perceptions and imperfectly initiated vision, a lurid glare on the whole hazy episode of the Blue Star Mine. Her husband had made his money in that brilliant speculation at the cost of 'getting ahead' of someone less alert to seize the chance; and the victim of his ingenuity was young

Robert Elwell, who had 'put him on' to the Blue Star scheme.

Parvis, at Mary's first cry, had thrown her a sobering glance through his impartial glasses.

'Bob Elwell wasn't smart enough, that's all; if he had been, he might have turned round and served Boyne the same way. It's the kind of thing that happens every day in business. I guess it's what the scientists call the survival of the fittest – see?' said Mr Parvis, evidently pleased with the aptness of his analogy.

Mary felt a physical shrinking from the next question she tried to frame: it was as though the words on her lips had a taste that nauseated her.

'But then – you accuse my husband of doing something dishonourable?'

Mr Parvis surveyed the question dispassionately. 'Oh no, I don't. I don't even say it wasn't straight.' He glanced up and down the long lines of books, as if one of them might have supplied him with the definition he sought. 'I don't say it *wasn't* straight, and yet I don't say it *was* straight. It was business.' After all, no definition in his category could be more comprehensive than that.

Mary sat staring at him with a look of terror. He seemed to her like the indifferent emissary of some evil power.

'But Mr Elwell's lawyers apparently did not take your view, since I suppose the suit was withdrawn by their advice.'

'Oh yes; they knew he hadn't a leg to stand on, technically. It was when they advised him to withdraw the suit that he got desperate. You see, he'd borrowed most of the money he lost in the Blue Star, and he was up a tree. That's why he shot himself when they told him he had no show.'

The horror was sweeping over Mary in great deafening waves.

'He shot himself? He killed himself because of *that*?'

'Well, he didn't kill himself, exactly. He dragged on two months before he died.' Parvis emitted the statement as unemotionally as a gramophone grinding out its 'record'.

'You mean that he tried to kill himself, and failed? And tried again?'

'Oh, he didn't have to *try* again,' said Parvis grimly.

They sat opposite each other in silence, he swinging his eye-glasses thoughtfully about his finger, she motionless, her arms stretched along her knees in an attitude of rigid tension.

'But if you knew all this,' she began at length, hardly able to force her voice above a whisper, 'how is it that when I wrote you at the time of my husband's disappearance you said you didn't understand his letter?'

Parvis received this without perceptible embarrassment. 'Why, I didn't understand it – strictly speaking. And it wasn't the time to talk about it, if I had. The Elwell business was settled when the suit was withdrawn. Nothing I could have told you would have helped you to find your husband.'

Mary continued to scrutinize him. 'Then why are you telling me now?'

Still Parvis did not hesitate. 'Well, to begin with, I supposed you knew more than you appear to – I mean about the circumstances of Elwell's death. And then people are talking of it now; the whole matter's been raked up again. And I thought if you didn't know you ought to.'

She remained silent, and he continued: 'You see, it's only come out lately what a bad state Elwell's affairs were in. His wife's a proud woman, and she fought on as long as she could, going out to work, and taking sewing at home when she got too sick – something with the heart, I believe. But she had his mother to look after, and the children, and she broke down under it, and finally had to ask for help. That called attention to the case, and the papers took it up, and a subscription was started. Everybody out there liked Bob Elwell, and most of the prominent names in the place are down on the list, and people began to wonder why – '

Parvis broke off to fumble in an inner pocket. 'Here,' he continued, 'here's an account of the whole thing from the *Sentinel* – a little sensational, of course. But I guess you'd better look it over.'

He held out a newspaper to Mary, who unfolded it slowly, remembering, as she did so, the evening when, in that same room, the perusal of a clipping from the *Sentinel* had first shaken the depths of her security.

As she opened the paper her eyes, shrinking from the glaring headlines, 'Widow of Boyne's Victim Forced to

Appeal for Aid', ran down the column of text to two portraits inserted in it. The first was her husband's, taken from a photograph made the year they had come to England. It was the picture of him that she liked best, the one that stood on the writing-table upstairs in her bedroom. As the eyes in the photograph met hers, she felt it would be impossible to read what was said of him, and closed her lids with the sharpness of the pain.

'I thought if you felt disposed to put your name down – ' she heard Parvis continue.

She opened her eyes with an effort, and they fell on the other portrait. It was that of a youngish man, slightly built, with features somewhat blurred by the shadow of a projecting hat-brim. Where had she seen that outline before? She stared at it confusedly, her heart hammering in her ears. Then she gave a cry.

'This is the man – the man who came for my husband!'

She heard Parvis start to his feet, and was dimly aware that she had slipped backward into the corner of the sofa, and that he was bending above her in alarm. She straightened herself and reached out for the paper, which she had dropped.

'It's the man! I should know him anywhere!' she persisted in a voice that sounded to her own ears like a scream.

Parvis's answer seemed to come to her from far off, down endless fog-muffled windings.

'Mrs Boyne, you're not very well. Shall I call someone? Shall I get a glass of water?'

'No, no, no!' She threw herself toward him, her hand frantically clutching the newspaper. 'I tell you, it's the man! I *know* him! He spoke to me in the garden!'

Parvis took the journal from her, directing his glasses to the portrait. 'It can't be, Mrs Boyne. It's Robert Elwell.'

'Robert Elwell?' Her white stare seemed to travel into space. 'Then it was Robert Elwell who came for him.'

'Came for Boyne? The day he went away from here?' Parvis's voice dropped as hers rose. He bent over, laying a fraternal hand on her, as if to coax her gently back into her seat. 'Why, Elwell was dead! Don't you remember?'

Mary sat with her eyes fixed on the picture, unconscious of what he was saying.

'Don't you remember Boyne's unfinished letter to me – the one you found on his desk that day? It was written just after he'd heard of Elwell's death.' She noticed an odd shake in Parvis's unemotional voice. 'Surely you remember!' he urged her.

Yes, she remembered: that was the profoundest horror of it. Elwell had died the day before her husband's disappearance; and this was Elwell's portrait; and it was the portrait of the man who had spoken to her in the garden. She lifted her head and looked slowly about the library. The library could have borne witness that it was also the portrait of the man who had come in that day to call Boyne from his unfinished letter. Through the misty surgings of her brain she heard the faint boom of half-forgotten words – words spoken by Alida Stair on the lawn at Pangbourne before Boyne and his wife had ever seen the house at Lyng, or had imagined that they might one day live there.

'This was the man who spoke to me,' she repeated.

She looked again at Parvis. He was trying to conceal his disturbance under what he probably imagined to be an expression of indulgent commiseration; but the edges of his lips were blue. 'He thinks me mad, but I'm not mad,' she reflected; and suddenly there flashed upon her a way of justifying her strange affirmation.

She sat quiet, controlling the quiver of her lips, and waiting till she could trust her voice; then she said, looking straight at Parvis: 'Will you answer me one question, please? When was it that Robert Elwell tried to kill himself?'

'When – when?' Parvis stammered.

'Yes; the date. Please try to remember.'

She saw that he was growing still more afraid of her. 'I have a reason,' she insisted.

'Yes, yes. Only I can't remember. About two months before, I should say.'

'I want the date,' she repeated.

Parvis picked up the newspaper. 'We might see here,' he said, still humouring her. He ran his eyes down the page. 'Here it is. Last October – the – '

She caught the words from him. 'The 20th, wasn't it?' With a sharp look at her, he verified. 'Yes, the 20th. Then you *did* know?'

'I know now.' Her gaze continued to travel past him. 'Sunday, the 20th – that was the day he came first.'

Parvis's voice was almost inaudible. 'Came *here* first?'

'Yes.'

'You saw him twice, then?'

'Yes, twice.' She just breathed it at him. 'He came first on the 20th of October. I remember the date because it was the day we went up Meldon Steep for the first time.' She felt a faint gasp of inward laughter at the thought that but for that she might have forgotten.

Parvis continued to scrutinize her, as if trying to intercept her gaze.

'We saw him from the roof,' she went on. 'He came down the lime-avenue toward the house. He was dressed just as he is in that picture. My husband saw him first. He was frightened, and ran down ahead of me; but there was no one there. He had vanished.'

'Elwell had vanished?' Parvis faltered.

'Yes.' Their two whispers seemed to grope for each other. 'I couldn't think what had happened. I see now. He *tried* to come then; but he wasn't dead enough – he couldn't reach us. He had to wait for two months to die; and then he came back again – and Ned went with him.'

She nodded at Parvis with the look of triumph of a child who has worked out a difficult puzzle. But suddenly she lifted her hands with a desperate gesture, pressing them to her temples.

'Oh, my God! I sent him to Ned – I told him where to go! I sent him to this room!' she screamed.

She felt the walls of books rush toward her, like inward falling ruins; and she heard Parvis, a long way off, through the ruins, crying to her and struggling to get at her. But she was numb to his touch, she did not know what he was saying. Through the tumult she heard but one clear note, the voice of Alida Stair speaking on the lawn at Pangbourne:

'You won't know till afterward,' it said. 'You won't know till long, long afterward.'

RICHARD MIDDLETON

On the Brighton Road

Slowly the sun had climbed up the hard white downs, till it broke with little of the mysterious ritual of dawn upon a sparkling world of snow. There had been a hard frost during the night, and the birds, who hopped about here and there with scant tolerance of life, left no trace of their passage on the silver pavements. In places the sheltered caverns of the hedges broke the monotony of the whiteness that had fallen upon the coloured earth, and overhead the sky melted from orange to deep blue, from deep blue to a blue so pale that it suggested a thin paper screen rather than illimitable space. Across the level fields there came a cold, silent wind which blew fine dust of snow from the trees, but hardly stirred the crested hedges. Once above the sky-line, the sun seemed to climb more quickly, and as it rose higher it began to give out a heat that blended with the keenness of the wind.

It may have been this strange alternation of heat and cold that disturbed the tramp in his dreams, for he struggled for a moment with the snow that covered him, like a man who finds himself twisted uncomfortably in the bed-clothes, and then sat up with staring, questioning eyes. 'Lord! I thought I was in bed,' he said to himself as he took in the vacant landscape, 'and all the while I was out here.' He stretched his limbs, and rising carefully to his feet, shook the snow off his body. As he did so the wind set him shivering, and he knew that his bed had been warm.

'Come, I feel pretty fit,' he thought. 'I suppose I am lucky to wake at all in this. Or unlucky – it isn't much of a business to come back to.' He looked up and saw the downs shining against the blue like the Alps on a picture-postcard. 'That means another forty miles or so, I suppose,' he continued grimly. 'Lord knows what I did yesterday. Walked till I was done, and now I'm only about twelve miles from Brighton. Damn the snow, damn Brighton, damn everything!' The sun crept up higher and higher, and he started walking patiently along the road with his back turned to the hills.

'Am I glad or sorry that it was only sleep that took me, glad or sorry, glad or sorry?' His thoughts seemed to arrange themselves in a metrical accompaniment to the steady thud of his footsteps, and he hardly sought an answer to his question. It was good enough to walk to.

Presently, when three milestones had loitered past, he overtook a boy who was stooping to light a cigarette. He wore no overcoat, and looked unspeakably fragile against the snow. 'Are you on the road, guv'nor?' asked the boy huskily as he passed.

'I think I am,' the tramp said.

'Oh! then I'll come a bit of the way with you if you don't walk too fast. It's a bit lonesome walking this time of day.' The tramp nodded his head, and the boy started limping along by his side.

'I'm eighteen,' he said casually. 'I bet you thought I was younger.'

'Fifteen, I'd have said.'

'You'd have backed a loser. Eighteen last August, and I've been on the road six years. I ran away from home five times when I was a little 'un, and the police took me back each time. Very good to me, the police was. Now I haven't got a home to run away from.'

'Nor have I,' the tramp said calmly.

'Oh, I can see what you are,' the boy panted; 'you're a gentleman come down. It's harder for you than for me.' The tramp glanced at the limping, feeble figure and lessened his pace.

'I haven't been at it as long as you have,' he admitted.

'No, I could tell that by the way you walk. You haven't got tired yet. Perhaps you expect something the other end?'

The tramp reflected for a moment. 'I don't know,' he said bitterly, 'I'm always expecting things.'

'You'll grow out of that,' the boy commented. 'It's warmer in London, but it's harder to come by grub. There isn't much in it really.'

'Still, there's the chance of meeting somebody there who will understand – '

'Country people are better,' the boy interrupted. 'Last night I took a lease of a barn for nothing and slept with the cows, and this morning the farmer routed me out and gave me tea and toke because I was little. Of course, I score there; but in London, soup on the Embankment at night, and all the rest of the time coppers moving you on.'

'I dropped by the roadside last night and slept where I fell. It's a wonder I didn't die,' the tramp said. The boy looked at him sharply.

'How do you know you didn't?' he said.

'I don't see it,' the tramp said, after a pause.

'I tell you,' the boy said hoarsely, 'people like us can't get away from this sort of thing if we want to. Always hungry and thirsty and dog-tired and walking all the time. And yet if anyone offers me a nice home and work my stomach feels sick. Do I look strong? I know I'm little for my age, but I've been knocking about like this for six years, and do you think I'm not dead? I was drowned bathing at Margate, and I was killed by a gipsy with a spike; he knocked my head right in, and twice I was froze like you last night, and a motor cut me down on this very road, and yet I'm walking along here now, walking to London to walk away from it again, because I can't help it. Dead! I tell you we can't get away if we want to.'

The boy broke off in a fit of coughing, and the tramp paused while he recovered.

'You'd better borrow my coat for a bit, Tommy,' he said, 'your cough's pretty bad.'

'You go to hell!' the boy said fiercely, puffing at his cigarette; 'I'm all right. I was telling you about the road. You haven't got down to it yet, but you'll find out presently. We're all dead, all of us who're on it, and we're all tired, yet somehow we can't leave it. There's nice smells in the summer, dust and hay and the wind smack in your face on a hot day; and it's nice waking up in the wet grass on a fine morning. I don't know, I don't know – ' he lurched forward suddenly, and the tramp caught him in his arms.

'I'm sick,' the boy whispered – 'sick.'

The tramp looked up and down the road, but he could see no houses or any sign of help. Yet even as he supported the boy doubtfully in the middle of the road a motor-car suddenly flashed in the middle distance, and came smoothly through the snow.

'What's the trouble?' said the driver quietly as he pulled up. 'I'm a doctor.' He looked at the boy keenly and listened to his strained breathing.

'Pneumonia,' he commented. 'I'll give him a lift to the infirmary, and you, too, if you like.'

The tramp thought of the workhouse and shook his head. 'I'd rather walk,' he said.

The boy winked faintly as they lifted him into the car.

'I'll meet you beyond Reigate,' he murmured to the tramp. 'You'll see.' And the car vanished along the white road.

All the morning the tramp splashed through the thawing snow, but at midday he begged some bread at a cottage door and crept into a lonely barn to eat it. It was warm in there, and after his meal he fell asleep among the hay. It was dark when he woke, and started trudging once more through the slushy roads.

Two miles beyond Reigate a figure, a fragile figure, slipped out of the darkness to meet him.

'On the road, guv'nor?' said a husky voice. 'Then I'll come a bit of the way with you if you don't walk too fast. It's a bit lonesome walking this time of day.'

'But the pneumonia!' cried the tramp aghast.

'I died at Crawley this morning,' said the boy.

F. MARION CRAWFORD

The Upper Berth

Somebody asked for the cigars. We had talked long, and the conversation was beginning to languish; the tobacco smoke had got into the heavy curtains, the wine had got into those brains which were liable to become heavy, and it was already perfectly evident that, unless somebody did something to rouse our oppressed spirits, the meeting would soon come to its natural conclusion, and we, the guests, would speedily go home to bed, and most certainly to sleep. No one had said anything very remarkable; it may be that no one had anything very remarkable to say. Jones had given us every particular of his last hunting adventure in Yorkshire. Mr Tompkins, of Boston, had explained at elaborate length those working principles, by the due and careful mainten-ance of which the Atchison, Topeka, and Santa Fé Railroad not only extended its territory, increased its departmental influence, and transported livestock without starving them to death before the day of actual delivery, but, also, had for years succeeded in deceiving those passengers who bought its tickets into the fallacious belief that the corporation aforesaid was really able to transport human life without destroying it. Signor Tombola had endeavoured to persuade us, by arguments which we took no trouble to oppose, that the unity of his country in no way resembled the average modern torpedo, carefully planned, constructed with all the skill of the greatest European arsenals, but, when con-structed, destined to be directed by feeble hands into a region where it must undoubtedly explode, unseen, un-feared, and unheard, into the illimitable wastes of political chaos.

It is unnecessary to go into further details. The conversation had assumed proportions which would have bored Prometheus on his rock, which would have driven Tantalus to distraction, and which would have impelled Ixion to seek relaxation in the simple but instructive dialogues of Herr Ollendorff, rather than submit to the greater evil of listening to our talk. We had sat at table for hours; we were bored, we were tired, and nobody showed signs of moving.

Somebody called for cigars. We all instinctively looked towards the speaker. Brisbane was a man of five-and-thirty years of age, and remarkable for those gifts which chiefly attract the attention of men. He was a strong man. The external proportions of his figure presented nothing extra-ordinary to the common eye, though his size was above the average. He was a little over six feet in height, and moderately broad in the shoulder; he did not appear to be stout, but, on the other hand, he was certainly not thin; his small head was supported by a strong and sinewy neck; his broad, muscular hands appeared to possess a peculiar skill in breaking walnuts without the assistance of the ordinary cracker, and, seeing him in profile, one could not help remarking the extraordinary breadth of his sleeves, and the unusual thickness of his chest. He was one of those men who are commonly spoken of among men as deceptive; that is to say, that though he looked exceedingly strong he was in reality very much stronger than he looked. Of his features I need say little. His head is small, his hair is thin, his eyes are blue, his nose is large, he has a small moustache, and a square jaw. Everybody knows Brisbane, and when he asked for a cigar everybody looked at him.

'It is a very singular thing,' said Brisbane.

Everybody stopped talking. Brisbane's voice was not loud, but possessed a peculiar quality of penetrating general conversation, and cutting it like a knife. Everybody listened. Brisbane, perceiving that he had attracted their general attention, lit his cigar with great equanimity.

'It is very singular,' he continued, 'that thing about ghosts. People are always asking whether anybody has seen a ghost. I have.'

'Bosh! What, you? You don't mean to say so, Brisbane? Well, for a man of his intelligence!'

A chorus of exclamations greeted Brisbane's remarkable statement. Everybody called for cigars, and Stubbs, the butler, suddenly appeared from the depths of nowhere with a fresh bottle of dry champagne. The situation was saved; Brisbane was going to tell a story.

I am an old sailor, said Brisbane, and as I have to cross the Atlantic pretty often, I have my favourites. Most men have their favourites. I have seen a man wait in a Broadway bar for three-quarters of an hour for a particular car which he liked. I believe the bar-keeper made at least one-third of his living by that man's preference. I have a habit of waiting for certain ships when I am obliged to cross that duck-pond. It may be a prejudice, but I was never cheated out of a good passage but once in my life. I remember it very well; it was a warm morning in June, and the Custom House officials, who were hanging about waiting for a steamer already on her way up from the Quarantine, presented a peculiarly hazy and thoughtful appearance. I had not much luggage – I never have. I mingled with the crowd of passengers, porters, and officious individuals in blue coats and brass buttons, who seemed to spring up like mushrooms from the deck of a moored steamer to obtrude their unnecessary services upon the independent passenger. I have often noticed with a certain interest the spontaneous evolution of these fellows. They are not there when you arrive; five minutes after the pilot has called 'Go ahead!' they, or at least their blue coats and brass buttons, have disappeared from deck and gangway as completely as though they had been consigned to that locker which tradition unanimously ascribes to Davy Jones. But, at the moment of starting, they are there, clean shaved, blue coated, and ravenous for fees. I hastened on board. The *Kamtschatka* was one of my favourite ships. I say was, because she emphatically no longer is. I cannot conceive of any inducement which could entice me to make another voyage in her. Yes, I know what you are going to say. She is uncommonly clean in the run aft, she has enough bluffing off in the bows to keep her dry, and the lower berths are most of them double. She has a lot of advantages, but I won't cross in her again. Excuse the digression. I got on board. I hailed a steward, whose red nose and redder whiskers were equally familiar to me.

'One hundred and five, lower berth,' said I, in the business-like tone peculiar to men who think no more of crossing the Atlantic than taking a whisky cocktail at down-town Delmonico's.

The steward took my portmanteau, great-coat, and rug. I shall never forget the expression of his face. Not that he turned pale. It is maintained by the most eminent divines that even miracles cannot change the course of nature. I have no hesitation in saying that he did not turn pale; but, from his expression, I judged that he was either about to shed tears, to sneeze, or to drop my portmanteau. As the latter contained two bottles of particularly fine old sherry presented to me for my voyage by my old friend Snigginson van Pickyns, I felt extremely nervous. But the steward did none of these things.

'Well, I'm d——d!' said he in a low voice, and led the way.

I suppose my Hermes, as he led me to the lower regions, had had a little grog, but I said nothing, and followed him. 105 was on the port side, well aft. There was nothing remarkable about the state-room. The lower berth, like most of those upon the *Kamtschatka*, was double. There was plenty of room; there was the usual washing apparatus, calculated to convey an idea of luxury to the mind of a North American Indian; there were the usual inefficient racks of brown wood, in which it is more easy to hang a large-sized umbrella than the common tooth-brush of commerce. Upon the uninviting mattresses were carefully folded together those blankets which a great modern humorist has aptly compared to cold buckwheat cakes. The question of towels was left entirely to the imagination. The glass decanters were filled with a transparent liquid faintly tinged with brown, but from which an odour less faint, but not more pleasing, ascended to the nostrils, like a far-off sea-sick reminiscence of oily machinery. Sad-coloured curtains half-closed the upper berth. The hazy June daylight shed a faint illumination upon the desolate little scene. Ugh! how I hate that state-room!

The steward deposited my traps and looked at me, as though he wanted to get away – probably in search of more passengers and more fees. It is always a good plan to start in favour with those functionaries, and I accordingly gave him certain coins there and then.

'I'll try and make yer comfortable all I can,' he remarked, as he put the coins in his pocket. Nevertheless, there was a doubtful intonation in his voice which surprised me. Possibly his scale of fees had gone up, and he was not satisfied; but on the whole I was inclined to think that, as he himself would have expressed it, he was 'the better for a glass'. I was wrong, however, and did the man injustice.

Nothing especially worthy of mention occurred during that day. We left the pier punctually, and it was very pleasant to be fairly under way, for the weather was warm and sultry, and the motion of the steamer produced a refreshing breeze. Everybody knows what the first day at sea is like. People pace the decks and stare at each other, and occasionally meet acquaintances whom they did not know to be on board. There is the usual uncertainty as to whether the food will be good, bad, or indifferent, until the first two meals have put the matter beyond a doubt; there is the usual uncertainty about the weather, until the ship is fairly off Fire Island. The tables are crowded at first, and then suddenly thinned. Pale-faced people spring from their seats and precipitate themselves towards the door, and each old sailor breathes more freely as his sea-sick neighbour rushes from his side, leaving him plenty of elbow-room and an unlimited command over the mustard.

One passage across the Atlantic is very much like another, and we who cross very often do not make the voyage for the sake of novelty. Whales and icebergs are indeed always objects of interest, but, after all, one whale is very much like another whale, and one rarely sees an iceberg at close quarters. To the majority of us the most delightful moment of the day on board an ocean steamer is when we have taken our last turn on deck, have smoked our last cigar, and having succeeded in tiring ourselves, feel at liberty to turn in with a clear conscience. On that first night of the voyage I felt particularly lazy, and went to bed in 105 rather earlier than I usually do. As I turned in, I was amazed to see that I was to have a companion. A portmanteau, very like my own, lay in the opposite corner, and in the upper berth had been deposited a neatly-folded rug, with a stick and umbrella. I had hoped to be alone, and I was disappointed; but I wondered who my room-mate was to be, and I determined to have a look at him.

Before I had been long in bed he entered. He was, as far as I could see, a very tall man, very thin, very pale, with sandy hair and whiskers and colourless grey eyes. He had about him, I thought, an air of rather dubious fashion; the sort of man you might see in Wall Street, without being able precisely to say what he was doing there – the sort of man who frequents the Café Anglais, who always seems to be alone and who drinks champagne; you might meet him on a racecourse, but he would never appear to be doing anything there either. A little over-dressed – a little odd. There are three or four of his kind on every ocean steamer. I made up my mind that I did not care to make his acquaintance, and I went to sleep saying to myself that I would study his habits in order to avoid him. If he rose early, I would rise late; if he went to bed late, I would go to bed early. I did not care to know him. If you once know people of that kind they are always turning up. Poor fellow! I need not have taken the trouble to come to so many decisions about him, for I never saw him again after that first night in 105.

I was sleeping soundly when I was suddenly waked by a loud noise. To judge from the sound, my room-mate must have sprung with a single leap from the upper berth to the floor. I heard him fumbling with the latch and bolt of the door, which opened almost immediately, and then I heard his footsteps as he ran at full speed down the passage, leaving the door open behind him. The ship was rolling a little, and I expected to hear him stumble or fall, but he ran as though he were running for his life. The door swung on its hinges with the motion of the vessel, and the sound annoyed me. I got up and shut it, and groped my way back to my berth in the darkness. I went to sleep again; but I have no idea how long I slept.

When I awoke it was still quite dark, but I felt a disagreeable sensation of cold, and it seemed to me that the air was damp. You know the peculiar smell of a cabin which has been wet with sea-water. I covered myself up as well as I could and dozed off again, framing complaints to be made the next day, and selecting the most powerful epithets in the language. I could hear my room-mate turn over in the upper berth. He had probably returned while I was asleep. Once I thought I heard him groan, and I argued that he was sea-sick. That is particularly unpleasant when one is below. Nevertheless I dozed off and slept till early daylight.

The ship was rolling heavily, much more than on the previous evening, and the grey light which came in through the porthole changed in tint with every movement according as the angle of the vessel's side turned the glass seawards or skywards. It was very cold – unaccountably so for the month of June. I turned my head and looked at the porthole, and I saw to my surprise that it was wide open and hooked back. I believe I swore audibly. Then I got up and shut it. As I turned back I glanced at the upper berth. The curtains were drawn close together; my companion had probably felt cold as well as I. It struck me that I had slept enough. The state-room was uncomfortable, though, strange to say, I could not smell the dampness which had annoyed me in the night. My room-mate was still asleep – excellent opportunity for avoiding him, so I dressed at once and went on deck. The day was warm and cloudy, with an oily smell on the water. It was seven o'clock as I came out – much later than I had imagined. I came across the doctor, who was taking his first sniff of the morning air. He was a young man from the West of Ireland – a tremendous fellow, with black hair and blue eyes, already inclined to be stout; he had a happy-go-lucky, healthy look about him which was rather attractive.

'Fine morning,' I remarked, by way of introduction.

'Well,' said he, eyeing me with an air of ready interest, 'it's a fine morning and it's not a fine morning. I don't think it's much of a morning.'

'Well, no – it is not so very fine,' said I.

'It's just what I call fuggly weather,' replied the doctor.

'It was very cold last night, I thought,' I remarked. 'However, when I looked about, I found that the porthole was wide open. I had not noticed it when I went to bed. And the state-room was damp, too.'

'Damp!' said he. 'Whereabouts are you?'

'One hundred and five – '

To my surprise the doctor started visibly, and stared at me.

'What is the matter?' I asked.

'Oh – nothing,' he answered; 'only everybody has complained of that state-room for the last three trips.'

'I shall complain too,' I said. 'It has certainly not been properly aired. It is a shame!'

'I don't believe it can be helped,' answered the doctor. 'I believe there is something – well, it is not my business to frighten passengers.'

'You need not be afraid of frightening me,' I replied. 'I can stand any amount of damp. If I should get a bad cold I will come to you.'

I offered the doctor a cigar, which he took and examined very critically.

'It is not so much the damp,' he remarked. 'However, I dare say you will get on very well. Have you a room-mate?'

'Yes; a deuce of a fellow, who bolts out in the middle of the night, and leaves the door open.'

Again the doctor glanced curiously at me. Then he lit the cigar and looked grave.

'Did he come back?' he asked presently.

'Yes. I was asleep, but I waked up, and heard him moving. Then I felt cold and went to sleep again. This morning I found the porthole open.'

'Look here,' said the doctor quietly , 'I don't care much for this ship. I don't care a rap for her reputation. I tell you what I will do. I have a good-sized place up here. I will share it with you, though I don't know you from Adam.'

I was very much surprised at the proposition. I could not imagine why he should take such a sudden interest in my welfare. However, his manner as he spoke of the ship, was peculiar.

'You are very good, doctor,' I said. 'But, really, I believe even now the cabin could be aired, or cleaned out, or something. Why do you not care for the ship?'

'We are not superstitious in our profession, sir,' replied the doctor, 'but the sea makes people so. I don't want to prejudice you, and I don't want to frighten you, but if you will take my advice you will move in here. I would as soon see you overboard,' he added earnestly, 'as know that you or any other man was to sleep in 105.'

'Good gracious! Why?' I asked.

'Just because on the last three trips the people who have slept there actually have gone overboard,' he answered gravely.

The intelligence was startling and exceedingly unpleasant, I confess. I looked hard at the doctor to see whether he was making game of me, but he looked perfectly serious. I thanked him warmly for his offer, but told him I intended to be the exception to the rule by which every one who slept in that particular state-room went overboard. He did not say much, but looked grave as ever, and hinted that, before we got across, I should probably reconsider his proposal. In the course of time we went to breakfast, at which only an inconsiderable number of passengers assembled. I noticed that one or two of the officers who breakfasted with us looked grave. After breakfast I went into my state-room in order to get a book. The curtains of the upper berth were still closely drawn. Not a word was to be heard. My room-mate was probably still asleep.

As I came out I met the steward whose business it was to look after me. He whispered that the captain wanted to see me, and then scuttled away down the passage as if very anxious to avoid any questions. I went toward the captain's cabin, and found him waiting for me.

'Sir,' said he, 'I want to ask a favour of you.'

I answered that I would do anything to oblige him.

'Your room-mate has disappeared,' he said. 'He is known to have turned in early last night. Did you notice anything extraordinary in his manner?'

The question coming, as it did, in exact confirmation of

the fears the doctor had expressed half an hour earlier, staggered me.

'You don't mean to say he has gone overboard?' I asked.

'I fear he has,' answered the captain.

'This is the most extraordinary thing – ' I began.

'Why?' he asked.

'He is the fourth, then?' I explained. In answer to another question from the captain, I explained without mentioning the doctor, that I had heard the story concerning 105. He seemed very much annoyed at hearing that I knew of it. I told him what had occurred in the night.

'What you say,' he replied, 'coincides almost exactly with what was told me by the room-mates of two of the other three. They bolt out of bed and run down the passage. Two of them were seen to go overboard by the watch; we stopped and lowered boats, but they were not found. Nobody, however, saw or heard the man who was lost last night – if he is really lost. The steward, who is a superstitious fellow, perhaps, and expected something to go wrong, went to look for him this morning, and found his berth empty, but his clothes lying about, just as he had left them. The steward was the only man on board who knew him by sight, and he has been searching everywhere for him. He has disappeared! Now, sir, I want to beg you not to mention the circumstance to any of the passengers; I don't want the ship to get a bad name, and nothing hangs about an ocean-goer like stories of suicides. You shall have your choice of any one of the officers' cabins you like, including my own, for the rest of the passage. Is that a fair bargain?'

'Very,' said I; 'and I am much obliged to you. But since I am alone, and have the state-room to myself, I would rather not move. If the steward will take out that unfortunate man's things, I would as lief stay where I am. I will not say anything about the matter, and I think I can promise you that I will not follow my room-mate.'

The captain tried to dissuade me from my intention, but I preferred having a state-room alone to being the chum of any officer on board. I do not know whether I acted foolishly, but if I had taken his advice I should have had nothing more to tell. There would have remained the disagreeable coincidence of several suicides occurring among men who had slept in the same cabin, but that would have been all.

That was not the end of the matter, however, by any means. I obstinately made up my mind that I would not be disturbed by such tales, and I even went so far as to argue the question with the captain. There was something wrong about the state-room, I said. It was rather damp. The porthole had been left open last night. My room-mate might have been ill when he came on board, and he might have become delirious after he went to bed. He might even now be hiding somewhere on board, and might be found later. The place ought to be aired and the fastening of the port looked to. If the captain would give me leave, I would see that what I thought necessary was done immediately.

'Of course you have a right to stay where you are if you please,' he replied, rather petulantly; 'but I wish you would turn out and let me lock the place up, and be done with it.'

I did not see it in the same light, and left the captain, after promising to be silent concerning the disappearance of my companion. The latter had had no acquaintances on board, and was not missed in the course of the day. Towards evening I met the doctor again, and he asked me whether I had changed my mind. I told him I had not.

'Then you will before long,' he said, very gravely.

We played whist in the evening, and I went to bed late. I will confess now that I felt a disagreeable sensation when I entered my state-room. I could not help thinking of the tall man I had seen on the previous night, who was now dead, drowned, tossing about in the long swell, two or three hundred miles astern. His face rose very distinctly before me as I undressed, and I even went so far as to draw back the curtains of the upper berth, as though to persuade myself that he was actually gone. I also bolted the door of the state-room. Suddenly I became aware that the porthole was open, and fastened back. This was more than I could stand. I hastily threw on my dressing-gown and went in search of Robert, the steward of my passage. I was very angry, I remember, and when I found him I dragged him roughly to the door of 105, and pushed him towards the open porthole.

'What the deuce do you mean, you scoundrel, by leaving that port open every night? Don't you know it is against the regulations? Don't you know that if the ship heeled and the water began to come in, ten men could not shut it? I will report you to the captain, you blackguard, for endangering the ship!'

I was exceedingly wroth. The man trembled and turned pale, and then began to shut the round glass plate with the heavy brass fittings.

'Why don't you answer me?' I said roughly.

'If you please, sir,' faltered Robert, 'there's nobody on board as can keep this 'ere port shut at night. You can try it yourself, sir. I ain't a-going to stop hany longer on board o' this vessel, sir; I ain't, indeed. But if I was you, sir, I'd just clear out and go and sleep with the surgeon, or something, I would. Look 'ere, sir, is that fastened what you may call securely, or not, sir? Try it, sir, see if it will move a hinch.'

I tried the port, and found it perfectly tight.

'Well, sir,' continued Robert triumphantly, 'I wager my reputation as a A1 steward that in 'arf an hour it will be open again; fastened back, too, sir, that's the horful thing – fastened back!'

I examined the great screw and the looped nut that ran on it.

'If I find it open in the night, Robert, I will give you a sovereign. It is not possible. You may go.'

'Soverin did you say, sir? Very good, sir. Thank ye, sir. Good night, sir. Pleasant reepose, sir, and all manner of hinchantin' dreams, sir.'

Robert scuttled away, delighted at being released. Of course, I thought he was trying to account for his negligence by a silly story, intended to frighten me, and I disbelieved him. The consequence was that he got his sovereign, and I spent a very peculiarly unpleasant night.

I went to bed, and five minutes after I had rolled myself up in my blankets the inexorable Robert extinguished the light that burned steadily behind the ground-glass pane near the door. I lay quite still in the dark trying to go to sleep, but I soon found that impossible. It had been some satisfaction to be angry with the steward, and the diversion had banished that unpleasant sensation I had at first experienced when I thought of the drowned man who had been my chum; but I was no longer sleepy, and I lay awake for some time, occasionally glancing at the porthole, which I could just see from where I lay, and which, in the darkness, looked like a faintly-luminous soup-plate suspended in blackness. I believe I must have lain there for an hour, and, as I remember, I was just dozing into sleep when I was roused by a draught of cold air, and by distinctly feeling the spray of the sea blown upon my face. I started to my feet, and not having allowed in the dark for the motion of the ship, I was instantly thrown violently across the state-room upon the couch which was placed beneath the porthole. I recovered myself immediately, however, and climbed upon my knees. The porthole was again wide open and fastened back!

Now these things are facts. I was wide awake when I got up, and I should certainly have been waked by the fall had I still been dozing. Moreover, I bruised my elbows and knees badly, and the bruises were there on the following morning to testify to the fact, if I myself had doubted it. The porthole was wide open and fastened back – a thing so unaccountable that I remember very well feeling astonishment rather than fear when I discovered it. I at once closed the plate again, and screwed down the loop nut with all my strength. It was very dark in the state-room. I reflected that the port had certainly been opened within an hour after Robert had at first shut it in my presence, and I determined to watch it, and see whether it would open again. Those brass fittings are very heavy and by no means easy to move. I could not believe that the clump had been turned by the shaking of the screw. I stood peering out through the thick glass at the alternate white and grey streaks of the sea that foamed beneath the ship's side. I must have remained there a quarter of an hour.

Suddenly, as I stood, I distinctly heard something moving behind me in one of the berths, and a moment afterwards, just as I turned instinctively to look – though I could, of course, see nothing in the darkness – I heard a very faint groan. I sprang across the state-room, and tore the curtains of the upper berth aside, thrusting in my hands to discover if there were any one there. There was some one.

I remember that the sensation as I put my hands forward was as though I were plunging them into the air of a damp cellar, and from behind the curtains came a gust of wind that smelled horribly of stagnant sea-water. I laid hold of something that had the shape of a man's arm, but was smooth, and wet, and icy cold. But suddenly, as I pulled, the creature sprang violently forward against me, a clammy, oozy mass, as it seemed to me, heavy and wet, yet endowed with a sort of supernatural strength. I reeled across the state-room, and in an instant the door opened and the thing rushed out. I had not had time to be frightened, and quickly recovering myself, I sprang through the door and gave chase at the top of my speed, but I was too late. Ten yards before me I could see − I am sure I saw it − a dark shadow moving in the dimly lighted passage, quickly as the shadow of a fast horse thrown before a dog-cart by the lamp on a dark night. But in a moment it had disappeared, and I found myself holding on to the polished rail that ran along the bulkhead where the passage turned towards the companion. My hair stood on end, and the cold perspiration rolled down my face. I am not ashamed of it in the least: I was very badly frightened.

Still I doubted my senses, and pulled myself together. It was absurd, I thought. The Welsh rarebit I had eaten had disagreed with me. I had been in a nightmare. I made my way back to my state-room, and entered it with an effort. The whole place smelled of stagnant sea-water, as it had when I had waked on the previous evening. It required my utmost strength to go in, and grope among my things for a box of wax lights. As I lighted a railway reading lantern which I always carry in case I want to read after the lamps are out, I perceived that the porthole was again open, and a sort of creeping horror began to take possession of me which I never felt before, nor wish to feel again. But I got a light and proceeded to examine the upper berth, expecting to find it drenched with sea-water.

But I was disappointed. The bed had been slept in, and the smell of the sea was strong; but the bedding was as dry as a bone. I fancied that Robert had not had the courage to make the bed after the accident of the previous night − it had all been a hideous dream. I drew the curtains back as far as I could and examined the place very carefully. It was perfectly dry. But the porthole was open again. With a sort of dull bewilderment of horror I closed it and screwed it down, and thrusting my heavy stick through the brass loop, wrenched it with all my might, till the thick metal began to bend under the pressure. Then I hooked my reading lantern into the red velvet at the head of the couch, and sat down to recover my senses if I could. I sat there all night, unable to think of rest – hardly able to think at all. But the porthole remained closed, and I did not believe it would now open again without the application of a considerable force.

The morning dawned at last, and I dressed myself slowly, thinking over all that had happened in the night. It was a beautiful day and I went on deck, glad to get out into the early, pure sunshine, and to smell the breeze from the blue water, so different from the noisome, stagnant odour of my state-room. Instinctively I turned aft, towards the surgeon's cabin. There he stood, with a pipe in his mouth, taking his morning airing precisely as on the preceding day.

'Good morning,' said he quietly, but looking at me with evident curiosity.

'Doctor, you were quite right,' said I. 'There is something wrong about that place.'

'I thought you would change your mind,' he answered, rather triumphantly. 'You have had a bad night, eh? Shall I make you a pick-me-up? I have a capital recipe.'

'No, thanks,' I cried. 'But I would like to tell you what happened.'

I then tried to explain as clearly as possible precisely what had occurred, not omitting to state that I had been scared as I had never been scared in my whole life before. I dwelt particularly on the phenomenon of the porthole, which was a fact to which I could testify, even if the rest had been an illusion. I had closed it twice in the night, and the second time I had actually bent the brass in wrenching it with my stick. I believe I insisted a good deal on this point.

'You seem to think I am likely to doubt the story,' said the doctor, smiling at the detailed account of the state of the porthole. 'I do not doubt it in the least. I renew my invitation to you. Bring your traps here, and take half my cabin.'

'Come and take half of mine for one night,' I said. 'Help me to get at the bottom of this thing.'

'You will get to the bottom of something else if you try,' answered the doctor.

'What?' I asked.

'The bottom of the sea. I am going to leave this ship. It is not canny.'

'Then you will not help me to find out – '

'Not I,' said the doctor quickly. 'It is my business to keep my wits about me – not to go fiddling about with ghosts and things.'

'Do you really believe it is a ghost? I inquired, rather contemptuously. But as I spoke I remembered very well the horrible sensation of the supernatural which had got possession of me during the night. The doctor turned sharply on me.

'Have you any reasonable explanation of these things to offer?' he asked. 'No; you have not. Well, you say you will find an explanation. I say that you won't, sir, simply because there is not any.'

'But, my dear sir,' I retorted, 'do you, a man of science, mean to tell me that such things cannot be explained?'

'I do,' he answered stoutly. 'And, if they could, I would not be concerned in the explanation.'

I did not care to spend another night alone in the state-room, and yet I was obstinately determined to get at the root of the disturbances. I do not believe there are many men who would have slept there alone, after passing two such nights. But I made up my mind to try it, if I could not get any one to share a watch with me. The doctor was evidently not inclined for such an experiment. He said he was a surgeon, and that in case any accident occurred on board he must always be in readiness. He could not afford to have his nerves unsettled. Perhaps he was quite right, but I am inclined to think that his precaution was prompted by his inclination. On inquiry, he informed me that there was no one on board who would be likely to join me in my investigations, and after a little more conversation I left him. A little later I met the captain, and told him my story. I said that, if no one would spend the night with me, I would ask leave to have the light burning all night, and would try it alone.

'Look here,' said he, 'I will tell you what I will do. I will share your watch myself, and we will see what happens. It is my belief that we can find out between us. There may be some fellow skulking on board, who steals a passage by frightening the passengers. It is just possible that there may be something queer in the carpentering of that berth.'

I suggested taking the ship's carpenter below and examining the place; but I was overjoyed at the captain's offer to spend the night with me. He accordingly sent for the workman and ordered him to do anything I required. We went below at once. I had all the bedding cleared out of the upper berth, and we examined the place thoroughly to see if there was a board loose anywhere, or a panel which could be opened or pushed aside. We tried the planks everywhere, tapped the flooring, unscrewed the fittings of the lower berth and took it to pieces – in short, there was not a square inch of the state-room which was not searched and tested. Everything was in perfect order, and we put everything back in its place. As we were finishing our work, Robert came to the door and looked in.

'Well, sir – find anything, sir?' he asked, with a ghastly grin.

'You were right about the porthole, Robert,' I said, and I gave him the promised sovereign. The carpenter did his work silently and skilfully, following my directions. When he had done he spoke.

'I'm a plain man, sir,' he said. 'But it's my belief you had better just turn out your things, and let me run half a dozen four-inch screws through the door of this cabin. There's no good never came o' this cabin yet, sir, and that's all about it. There's been four lives lost out o' here to my own remembrance, and that in four trips. Better give it up, sir – better give it up!'

'I will try it for one night more,' I said.

'Better give it up, sir – better give it up! It's a precious bad job,' repeated the workman, putting his tools in his bag and leaving the cabin.

But my spirits had risen considerably at the prospect of

having the captain's company, and I made up my mind not to be prevented from going to the end of the strange business. I abstained from Welsh rarebits and grog that evening, and did not even join in the customary game of whist. I wanted to be quite sure of my nerves, and my vanity made me anxious to make a good figure in the captain's eyes.

The captain was one of those splendidly tough and cheerful specimens of seafaring humanity whose combined courage, hardihood, and calmness in difficulty leads them naturally into high positions of trust. He was not the man to be led away by an idle tale, and the mere fact that he was willing to join me in the investigation was proof that he thought there was something seriously wrong, which could not be accounted for on ordinary theories, nor laughed down as a common superstition. To some extent, too, his reputation was at stake, as well as the reputation of the ship. It is no light thing to lose passengers overboard, and he knew it.

About ten o'clock that evening, as I was smoking a last cigar, he came up to me, and drew me aside from the beat of the other passengers who were patrolling the deck in the warm darkness.

'This is a serious matter, Mr Brisbane,' he said. 'We must make up our minds either way – to be disappointed or to have a pretty rough time of it. You see I cannot afford to laugh at the affair, and I will ask you to sign your name to a statement of whatever occurs. If nothing happens tonight we will try it again tomorrow and the next day. Are you ready?'

So we went below, and entered the state-room. As we went in I could see Robert the steward, who stood a little further down the passage, watching us, with his usual grin, as though certain that something dreadful was about to happen. The captain closed the door behind us and bolted it.

'Supposing we put your portmanteau before the door,' he suggested. 'One of us can sit on it. Nothing can get out then. Is the port screwed down?'

I found it as I had left it in the morning. Indeed, without using a lever, as I had done, no one could have opened it. I drew back the curtains of the upper berth so that I could see well into it. By the captain's advice I lighted my reading lantern, and placed it so that it shone upon the white sheets above. He insisted upon sitting on the portmanteau, declaring that he wished to be able to swear that he had sat before the door.

Then he requested me to search the state-room thoroughly, an operation very soon accomplished, as it consisted merely in looking beneath the lower berth and under the couch below the porthole. The spaces were quite empty.

'It is impossible for any human being to get in,' I said, 'or for any human being to open the port.'

'Very good,' said the captain calmly. 'If we see anything now, it must be either imagination or something supernatural.'

I sat down on the edge of the lower berth.

'The first time it happened,' said the captain, crossing his legs and leaning back against the door, 'was in March. The passenger who slept here, in the upper berth, turned out to have been a lunatic – at all events, he was known to have been a little touched, and he had taken his passage without the knowledge of his friends. He rushed out in the middle of the night, and threw himself overboard, before the officer who had the watch could stop him. We stopped and lowered a boat; it was a quiet night, just before that heavy weather came on; but could not find him. Of course his suicide was afterwards accounted for on the ground of his insanity.'

'I suppose that often happens?' I remarked, rather absently.

'Not often – no,' said the captain; 'never before in my experience, though I have heard of it happening on board of other ships. Well, as I was saying, that occurred in March. On the very next trip – What are you looking at?' he asked, stopping suddenly in his narration.

I believe I gave no answer. My eyes were riveted upon the porthole. It seemed to me that the brass loop-nut was beginning to turn very slowly upon the screw – so slowly, however, that I was not sure it moved at all. I watched it intently, fixing its position in my mind, and trying to ascertain whether it changed. Seeing where I was looking, the captain looked, too.

'It moves!' he exclaimed, in a tone of conviction. 'No, it

does not,' he added, after a minute.

'If it were the jarring of the screw,' said I, 'it would have opened during the day; but I found it this evening jammed tight as I left it this morning.'

I rose and tried the nut. It was certainly loosened, for by an effort I could move it with my hands.

'The queer thing,' said the captain, 'is that the second man who was lost is supposed to have got through that very port. We had a terrible time over it. It was in the middle of the night, and the weather was very heavy; there was an alarm that one of the ports was open and the sea running in. I came below and found everything flooded, the water pouring in every time she rolled, and the whole port swinging from the top bolts – not the porthole in the middle. Well, we managed to shut it, but the water did some damage. Ever since that the place smells of sea-water from time to time. We supposed the passenger had thrown himself out, though the Lord only knows how he did it. The steward kept telling me that he cannot keep anything shut here. Upon my word – I can smell it now, cannot you?' he inquired, sniffing the air suspiciously.

'Yes – distinctly,' I said, and I shuddered as that same odour of stagnant sea-water grew stronger in the cabin. 'Now, to smell like this, the place must be damp,' I continued, 'and yet when I examined it with the carpenter this morning everything was perfectly dry. It is most extraordinary – hallo!'

My reading lantern, which had been placed in the upper berth, was suddenly extinguished. There was still a good deal of light from the pane of ground glass near the door, behind which loomed the regulation lamp. The ship rolled heavily, and the curtain of the upper berth swung far out into the state-room and back again. I rose quickly from my seat on the edge of the bed; and the captain at the same moment started to his feet with a loud cry of surprise. I had turned with the intention of taking down the lantern to examine it, when I heard his exclamation, and immediately afterwards his call for help. I sprang towards him. He was wrestling with all his might with the brass loop of the port. It seemed to turn against his hands in spite of all his efforts. I caught up my cane, a heavy oak stick I always used to carry, and thrust it through the ring and bore on it with all my strength. But the strong wood snapped suddenly and I fell upon the couch. When I rose again the port was wide open, and the captain was standing with his back against the door, pale to the lips.

'There is something in that berth!' he cried, in a strange voice, his eyes almost starting from his head. 'Hold the door, while I look – it shall not escape us, whatever it is!'

But instead of taking his place, I sprang upon the lower bed, and seized something which lay in the upper berth.

It was something ghostly, horrible beyond words, and it moved in my grip. It was like the body of a man long drowned, and yet it moved, and had the strength of ten men living; but I gripped it with all my might – the slippery, oozy, horrible thing – the dead white eyes seemed to stare at me out of the dusk; the putrid odour of rank sea-water was about it, and its shiny hair hung in foul wet curls over its dead face. I wrestled with the dead thing; it thrust itself upon me and forced me back and nearly broke my arms; it wound its corpse's arms about my neck, the living death, and overpowered me, so that I, at last, cried aloud and fell, and left my hold.

As I fell the thing sprang across me, and seemed to throw itself upon the captain. When I last saw him on his feet his face was white and his lips set. It seemed to me that he struck a violent blow at the dead being, and then he, too, fell forward upon his face, with an inarticulate cry of horror.

The thing paused an instant, seeming to hover over his prostrate body, and I could have screamed again for very fright, but I had no voice left. The thing vanished suddenly, and it seemed to my disturbed senses that it made its exit through the open port, though how that was possible, considering the smallness of the aperture, is more than any one can tell. I lay a long time upon the floor, and the captain lay beside me. At last I partially recovered my senses and moved, and instantly I knew that my arm was broken – the small bone of the left forearm near the wrist.

I got upon my feet somehow, and with my remaining hand I tried to raise the captain. He groaned and moved, and at last came to himself. He was not hurt, but he seemed badly stunned.

Well, do you want to hear any more? There is nothing more. That is the end of my story. The carpenter carried out his scheme of running half a dozen four-inch screws through the door of 105; and if ever you take a passage in the *Kamtschatka*, you may ask for a berth in that state-room. You will be told that it is engaged – yes – it is engaged by that dead thing.

I finished the trip in the surgeon's cabin. He doctored my broken arm, and advised me not to 'fiddle about with ghosts and things' any more. The captain was very silent, and never sailed again in that ship, though it is still running. And I will not sail in her either. It was a very disagreeable experience, and I was very badly frightened, which is a thing I do not like. That is all. That is how I saw a ghost – if it was a ghost. It was dead, anyhow.